Passages

A SERENITY PRESS ANTHOLOGY

Serenity Press

First published by Serenity Press Pty Ltd, 2018
Copyright © 2018 Serenity Press
Cover design by Monique Mulligan
Edited by Juanita Pirozzi
Proofread and typeset by Lisa A. Wolstenholme

This is a work of fiction. Names, characters, businesses, places, events and incidents are either the products of the author/s' imagination or used in a fictitious manner. Any resemblance to actual persons, living or dead, or actual events is purely coincidental.

Because of the dynamic nature of the Internet, any web addresses or links contained in this book may have changed since publication and may no longer be valid. The views expressed in this work are solely those of the authors and do not necessarily reflect the views of the publisher and the publisher hereby disclaims any responsibility for them.

National Library of Australia
Cataloguing-in-Publication data:
Passages/Serenity Press
ISBN: (sc) 978-0-6484525-0-8
ISBN: (e) 978-0-6484525-1-5
general – fiction

Serenity Press books may be ordered through online booksellers or by contacting:
SERENITYPRESS.ORG
publisher@serenitypress.org

Contents

Introduction

The idea for Passages is rooted in a small short story writing group that I ran through Rockingham Writers Centre. I really wanted to publish the authors there as they were fabulous writers and storytellers. After moving on from the group, we set up a Facebook group called The Synonyms where we kept in touch.

A few months passed and I posted an opportunity for the members of the group to write a short, fictional piece based on a life adventure. It was well received. I also knew the benefits of having other more well-known authors in a short story collection and how it raises the vibration of the group, so I opened it up to my network and had ten signups within twelve hours. The submission doors were closed, the stories were written and now the book is being published.

Passages may not have come into being the conventional way, but Serenity Press is proud to publish this collection of diverse life adventure stories and we hope that you enjoy each of the authors.

I would like to give special thanks to Lisa Wolstenholme who jumped in to help get the book ready for print through proofreading, typesetting and much more. Also thank you to Juanita Pirozzi for editing.

It is when amazing people come together, that magic happens. I believe that this is a magical collection.

Happy reading,

Karen x

Hiraeth

MONIQUE MULLIGAN

"You will never be completely at home again, because part of your heart always will be elsewhere. That is the price you pay for the richness of loving and knowing people in more than one place."
—Miriam Adeney

'Think of it as an adventure,' he said.

She tried.

'You have no choice,' they said.

She complied.

'It's only for two years …'

Her mum cried.

She played her part: the good wife; the supportive mother; cheerleader; dream-weaver; adventurer.

But no-one told her how hard it would be.

'Go along with it,' they said.

'Put on your happy face.'

'Look for the positives in a haystack of negatives.'

What they were really saying was, 'Suck it up. That's life.'

And so she did.

They buy a better car and drive four thousand kilometres cross-country, listening to The War of the Worlds on cassette as dry wheat paddocks and distant dome-like hills give way to endless plains of mulga scrub and bluebush. Stretch their legs on cracked salt lakes and fossick for space junk and fossils on the desert floor. Wave to semi-trailers and road-train drivers and follow caravan convoys down long dirt tracks to look-outs over crumbling limestone clifftops. Stare down the long line of ancient sea cliffs and play 'spot the whale' while waves smash-crash against rock. Watch the sun set over an ocean of shifting sand dunes and stare open-mouthed into a cavernous open-cut gold mine where ant-like trucks scurry around spiralling roads. The Goldfields and Wheatbelt blur as their destination beckons and finally, after days of driving, they crest a hill and glimpse their new city, and beyond that, the deep blue haze of a new ocean.

The moving trucks are delayed, so they play tourist: ride bikes and swim in The Basin on Rottnest; eat fish and chips under towering Norfolk Pines at Fremantle's Esplanade; zip up and down the coastal highway, pinching themselves that this beach life will soon be for real. It's an adventure, just like everyone said it would be.

A week later, they're unpacking box after box like robots; the boys are whining because they can't find their stuff and there's nothing to eat. After pizza, they follow a path down the hill and across a sports oval to the Indian Ocean. The kids snigger at one sign saying, 'Clothing Optional Beach' and gawk at the next, which warns of 'snakes', 'live firing' from the rifle range, and 'dumping surf'. They turn left down the dual-use path, keeping left as bell-ringing cyclists whizz past, stopping to pat pedigree dogs with double-barrelled names they've never heard of. Finally, they drop their towels on Cottesloe Beach and leap towards the waves.

We live here now, she thinks. We can come here whenever we like. Two years of this will be easy.

The enormity of what they have done hits when he starts work the next day, leaving her home with the boys, a near-empty fridge, ants in the kitchen, and more boxes to unpack. She brings it up when he comes home, tempering her fears with philosophical statements about being here for a reason and, 'a greater plan,' for she believes in a higher power, always has.

He brushes her off. 'This is your home now,' he says.

She zips her lips. They're here because they have to be here and that's that.

Home is a beige 1980s-style brick block in a military village—simple and boring on the inside and out. She makes it homely, as much as she can. Hangs pictures on the hooks left in by the last tenants because she's not allowed to add holes to the walls. Collects shells from the beach and adds them to a jar in the bathroom. Doesn't bother with the garden because it's all sand and dry couch grass, with a couple of she-oaks bordering the back fence. Barely more than a sandpit, really. Front yard's not much better, but at least there's a park across the road where, if she stands on tiptoes, she can see the ocean and that's more of a view than she's ever had before.

Before she knows it, the school holidays are over, and her sons start at the local primary school. The different school system, which determines that her youngest can start school now instead of staying home another year as she'd expected, catches her off guard. She's not prepared for the loneliness she feels when she walks home alone and enters her empty, too-quiet house. As she brings in the washing—it's stiff on the line because the water's harder here and she forgot to get softener—it occurs to her that she's the only one in the family who doesn't yet belong in this new life. The boys have school and her husband has work. Right now, her only connection to this community is what her husband does.

And that's how it will stay, because these places thrive on gossip and bitching, so she's already decided to keep the other wives at arm's length. Besides, she's only here for two years and there's no point putting down deep roots (she's been uprooted before and even shallow roots hurt when they're ripped from the earth). She'll find friends for this season outside the village. Won't she?

At the end of that long, lonely day, she waits at the gate and scans the yummy mummies, military mums, rich stay-at-home mums, career women, earth mothers and rainbow mothers for a friendly face. And then she remembers that she's the new mum, her boys are the new kids, and they're on an adventure that's meant leaving everyone they know behind.

Beyond the village, she's no less an outsider. Reminders of her other-ness are everywhere. At the supermarket with its unfamiliar products and early closing times; at an unmanned train station without the correct change to buy a ticket; at a deserted shopping centre carpark on a Sunday. The culture shock is unexpected and real even though it's the same country.

'I'm sorry, I'm from Sydney.'

The excuse pops out every time she encounters something new, something different, something that feels ten years behind the times. She wants people to know that she did belong somewhere once, but no one really cares. The rude people roll their eyes or look bored because Sydney means zilch over here on the west coast. The nice ones offer a sympathetic look–'poor thing, so confused'–but still leave her to wallow like a fish dropped in the wrong fishpond.

Eventually, she meets someone who's also from Sydney; excitement ripples in her chest when they exclaim, 'OMG, me too!' Back home, the answer to the next question–'Which part of Sydney?'–would have determined the outcome of any further interaction: Westies don't mix with the Northern Beaches or North Shore tribes, for example. But over here, the answer is a mere detail, glossed over in the thrill of bumping into someone from 'home,' someone who doesn't look confused when she says things like devon ('polony'), peanut butter ('peanut paste'), milk bar ('deli'), and soft drink ('cool drink').

Adventure. It's an adventure.

The mantra keeps her going when the going gets tough, even though she really dreamt of adventures in far-off places, like London and New York, not in Perth or Dullsville, as some call it (and she privately agrees).

Determined to look on the bright side of this adventure she didn't want, she challenges herself to make the most of things. To get to know the place–to find a special café, a park to take the kids, a shortcut to the beach. She lists places to visit and ticks them off one by one: weekend trips to Albany and Lancelin and Margaret River and The Hills; wineries and parks and bushwalking and beachcombing.

And then one day–perhaps while she was waiting at the school gate or teaching the boys to ride their bikes in the cul-de-sac, or maybe at the deli–she starts to recognise people, to nod hello. To belong, just a little.

Six weeks after the move, she's back in Sydney for her mother's birthday, courtesy of a never-to-be-repeated airfare bargain. Her heart thumps–'I'm home, I'm home, I'm home'–as the plane touches down with a hoppity-skip. She falls into her mother's arms, teary with relief and exhaustion and pent-up anticipation. From the back seat of the car, bookended by her sleeping sons, she soaks in the deliciously familiar soup of sounds and smells, the snaking traffic, the recognisable roads.

She's home.

They catch a ferry to the zoo and drive up the mountains. Visit the rellies and friends in the outer suburbs. At first it feels like she's simply been on an extended holiday, but then the question comes from every direction: 'When are you coming back?' Two years, she says with confidence before distracting them with stories about shops that close at 6 pm and don't open on Sundays, the nudist beach down the road, snakes in sand dunes and the deadly shark attack that happened at the next beach down. She feels oddly gratified by their barely concealed envy that the beach is now her backyard. But right here, right now, the Indian Ocean's a continent away, and she belongs without even trying.

But one morning, she notices a feeling of irritation. Like a switch has flicked inside her. She's tired of being dependent on others. Of worrying that the boys will knock over something in her mother's just-so home. Of eating out and living out of a suitcase. Of being a guest— no, a tourist—in the city she grew up in. She longs for habit, for bedtimes and mealtimes, for walking to school time and after-school sport.

It's time to leave this home-not-home.

She fidgets in the back seat all the way to the airport, anxious to feel 'home' again, driven by a deep need she can't explain to her mother, who's wiping tears from her eyes when she thinks no one is looking. She's agitated when they're held up in the meandering check-out line, certainly too preoccupied to feel anything but stressed. But as the plane lifts off, this is followed by a welling up of sadness; she nurses the fresh understanding that, for the next two years, her heart will remain stuck in this in-between.

She arrives home, quiet with melancholy. The first thing she does when she gets to her own house is unpack the bags and wash the dirty clothes. She cooks dinner for the kids, readjusts her body clock, and re-establishes their normal.

School. Play. Dinner. Bath. Bed. Repeat.

Months later, she's back in Sydney for a quick work trip. Just enough time to see her mum and some of the rellies. A lump forms in her throat at the familiar smiles and voices—not on the phone but here, in the same room. She revels in the jokes, the shared memories, the honeymoon feel of it. No time to catch up with friends, but there's always next time, she tells herself. Nostalgia runs through her veins; she's high on it and doesn't want to come down.

But if anyone looked close enough, if they looked beyond the smiles and laughter (which are genuine), beyond their own pleasure, they would also see a woman yearning. While she's been gone, this place has changed—her mother's changed the furniture, for a start—and she's stuck in memories of what used to be. Likewise, she misses her family. Her bed. Her cooking. Her stuff. The relaxed pace of life she now favours.

If they could read her mind, they would see how she habitually marks time: This is the last time I'll see this person, do that thing. Until next time, whenever that is. My last day. My last night. One more day till I see the kids. One more sleep.

She doesn't want to leave and she doesn't want to stay.

That first year, Christmas passes like any old day, albeit one with presents and pancakes with ice-cream for breakfast. The neighbourhood is quiet because most people in the military village have gone back to their own 'back home.' She wanted to do the same but they couldn't afford the plane fares.

She feigns Christmas cheer for the kids but cries in the bathroom, imagining how Christmas Eve at her mum's panned out, what her dad's side is doing right now, and wishing they'd just hopped on a plane anyway. That night they take a picnic to the beach and watch the sunset. And then it's over for another year and she packs the tree away the next day so she doesn't have to dwell on what she's missing.

One more year to go.

In that second year, they buy a house an hour or so down the coast. Not a forever house, because they're going back home in twelve months, she reminds him. Of course not, he tells her, it's just an investment property that they'll live in until it's time to leave. This is just another part of the adventure.

'We're not staying,' she assures relatives who express concern at this unexpected development.

But then the kids start a new school and make new friends, and she makes friends with some of the mums, and suddenly she has a full life: last-minute play dates for the boys, and friends who pop in for a cuppa and stay for dinner. Barbecues and impromptu picnics at the beach. Soccer games and netball comps. Camping trips and holidays down south. She puts down roots without even meaning to.

She's always wanted a garden, so she plants roses down one side of the driveway and veggies out the back. Hangs pictures wherever she wants. Paints walls—first a feature wall, then the boys' bedrooms in their favourite (not neutral) colours. Talks about upgrading to her dream kitchen, even though this house on a hill, ten minutes' walk to the beach, was never meant to be her long-term home.

In time, she comes to understand that she doesn't want to give up the beach, the friends, the life they've made. They would never have anything like this back in Sydney—they'd be lucky to afford a box out in the sticks. She's prepared to sacrifice the distance from her extended family to give her kids this life.

And that's when she learns he doesn't feel the same way. He's tired of the routine, the bills, the house that shackles him to weekend cleaning, gardening and maintenance. He never wanted to settle down like this, he admits one evening.

She's shocked, of course, but deep down, she's always known that what scares him most is stillness and stagnation and responsibility. She knows this and he knows this, but she ignores it and so does he, and life goes on.

And so, the two years go by in a wink and a smile (mostly) and they don't move back. They surprise everyone, even themselves, by deciding to stay. Suddenly, home is here, and they come from 'over there'.

One year she goes home for a funeral. The next year it's a wedding. Then there's another wedding and another funeral. By now she knows that this is how it will be. Going back for weddings and funerals, rarely 'just because.' She's used to the question her rellies ask without fail: 'When are you coming back?' To them, it's always when, not if. It annoys her sometimes, this expectation—don't they know it's hard enough being so far away without them putting pressure on her? Bit rich coming from a family of immigrants who left family in another country for a better life in Australia.

When she offers a vague 'Don't know' or the unthinkable 'Maybe never,' she's met with disbelief: 'Why would you want to bring the kids up all the way over there? So far from family. I thought you were only going for two years.' Sometimes they say nothing but still she wears their disappointment and disapproval like a scarf on a hot day.

Eventually, they stop asking.

What none of them know is that the way things are now, she'd move back 'over east'—not to Sydney, somewhere smaller—in a heartbeat. She just hasn't told them because it's hard enough coming and going, saying hello and waving goodbye, as it is.

They have no idea how much she longs for the place—no, not the place, the people—that shaped her and wishes she'd never left them behind, because she feels so alone. But she puts on a front and tells them she's happy with the way things have turned out; she makes them believe it and herself believe it, because there's no room for home-sickness in her fragile heart.

Three years after they buy the house, she sets him free. As her life detonates around her, and loneliness creeps back in, she thinks seriously about taking the boys back to the other home. Stoic as ever, she focuses on practicality: house prices and jobs. Tells no one—what if she can't afford it after all's said and done? No point getting anyone's hopes up too high. Facts and figures and 'what ifs' get her through the next year, but by the end of it, she's no closer to packing up the house. Even less close to believing in a hope and a future. For now, she's faking it till she makes it.

That Christmas is the hardest of all.

One day, a new love appears, reviving her faith in a greater plan. The idea of moving back east fades like a morning star. Going back would mean losing love, and more than anything, she wants a future with love in it. For her and her sons. But as soon as she decides, homesickness sneaks up on her like a thief in the night and hits her with a gut-punch of fear and doubt. It catches her off guard as she moves in with a man who craves stability and breathes responsibility, a man who's lived all his life within a twenty-five-kilometre radius.

I'm not going back.

And so, she marries him, eyes wide open, and a couple of weeks later, when they go back east so he can meet her family, no one asks when she's coming back. Because they already know the answer. She had her chance and she has a new family to belong to now.

In their new home for six, she signs up to Facebook and opens up a world of connection with once-upon-a-time friends, old schoolmates, and faraway family. Loves keeping up-to-date with family news about new babies and travels. Loathes the 'Grrr. I just banged my toe' updates from people she barely remembers but clings to because they are connections to that other place. Social media, she realises, is a blessing and a curse—in turn, it lifts her spirits and brings them down. When she sees photos of family events after the fact—her cousin's 30th, her aunt's 60th—and realises she wasn't invited, she cries. Feels silly because logically, she knows there's no point, she wouldn't have been able to go; feels sad because they don't realise that she still needs to belong to them too.

She spends precious time looking backwards, reminiscing through nostalgic glasses, comparing old and new. Sometimes she barely notices the feeling as it flits in and out of her mind; other times she is flooded with memory and loneliness and confusion.

'I'm homesick,' she says to her husband. She can't hide it—it knocks her for six every Christmas and Easter, and on birthdays, reducing her to tears and a period of withdrawal that he can't break through.

'But this is your home,' he says, bewildered. He waves his hand around the room, the room he's painted the colour she wanted and she's decorated with things that are him and her and the kids all at once.

She tries to explain that no matter how much she loves him and the life they're making, she's split between two worlds—the old, the place of history, and the new, the place of new memories. This is her home. But so is the other place. This, here, is where she lives. There, that's where she once lived. So, it's part of her. But, she's quick to assure him, that when she's there, she craves here.

He tries so hard to understand. But his parents live ten minutes away. He sees his sisters and their families on birthdays, Christmas, Easter, Mother's Day, Father's Day, and sometimes, 'just because.' He's never gone on a gap year, never left them behind, never felt that ache of homesickness deep inside. Never felt the sting of tears she feels each time she leaves one home and arrives at the other. They fall at the exact moment the wheels lift and she's no longer on home ground.

Some get it. People who, like her, have their hearts tied by an invisible string to two places. People who know that it's hardest at special times, like Christmas and Easter and birthdays. People who know that memories of the other are triggered so easily … by a bird call, the smell of a flower, photos in someone's Facebook update …

But not everyone feels the same. Some say they never want to go back. They're hardened by whatever shaped them and they'll spend the rest of their lives shaking that part of them away, pretending it didn't exist, or it was a means to an end. They point to the negatives of that place, and there's no affection in their voices. It's them she doesn't understand.

She meets a woman one day, a woman whose tentative smile is eclipsed by her boisterous young daughter's energy. But the woman's eyes brim with tears and memories and doubts. She looks at her and sees a woman who's heartsick and won't stay. Not everyone does.

Another Christmas passes. She calls her extended family; enjoys a precious hour of being passed from one relative to the next, grabbing five minutes from each of them before they go back to their festivities. She hears the chatter in the background and imagines what they are eating. Oma's potato salad, without a doubt. She closes her eyes, and she's there with them, sitting on a chair next to one of her aunties, smiling at her uncle, marvelling at how her cousins have changed, how much older they all look. But then something–a cupboard door slamming?–draws her back, and she's sitting on her lounge, clutching the phone as if it were a lifeline, and the house is quiet because the kids are watching the new DVD they got and everyone else on the street is off visiting rellies.

One year, she waits for someone at the family gathering to phone her–she's always the one who rings, because she can't wait any longer–and no one does. She has to go out, and so she masks her disappointment when her husband's family ask if she's heard from home. Can they possibly understand how important it is to her that she's part of that other celebration, even if only in the smallest of ways?

Not even her sons get it any more. They've been here too long, almost their whole lives.

As she gets older, the split within herself widens and deepens, narrows and shallows, changing by the day, hour, week. It's better and harder at the same time. It's hard to explain, so she rarely bothers trying. Most of the time she accepts that she is where she's meant to be. That part of her remains in the place she came from, like a spiritual shadow. She knows that even though it wasn't entirely her choice to leave, it was her choice to stay. This place has become part of her and it too has shaped her. She learns to live in the present, fighting the urge to look backward and forward.

But whenever she goes back to visit or talks to her parents on the phone, guilt and loss weigh in with their two cents. Each time she sees her parents they look older, tired, worn down by life. It's worse when she visits, because she knows that in a matter of days, hours, minutes, she'll be leaving and doesn't know when she'll be back. Will this be the last time?

What will I do if they get sick and can't look after themselves, she wonders, then pushes the thought far down. But she can't squash it completely and she knows that this ever-present heart-pain is the price she pays to know and love people in two places. It is a splitting and an expansion at once, like motherhood, when love for one becomes love for many.

They start talking about moving away from the suburbs. About finding the place that makes their spirits soar with knowing this is it. They'll wait until the kids are all settled in their own lives, of course. It seems so far off, but the next thing they know, they've gone from six to four in the house, and increasingly, it's just the two of them. Suddenly, it's not a one-day, but a when. They travel south for weekends, here and there, checking out small towns, asking, 'Could we live here?' They travel to Tasmania for a holiday and fall in love with the climate and landscape, so now they're split between moving a few hours 'down south' or even further south on the other side of the country.

And as they look at real estate and narrow down their options, at the back of her mind, she wonders: Is this another adventure? Will it be exciting in its new-ness? Or will it make them both heartsick, because this time, the kids won't be coming. They'll be staying behind, doing their own thing. Are they okay with that? With leaving a big piece of them behind? With moving away from the state he's spent almost half a century in?

She asks him this and after some thought, he nods: 'Yes. Yes, I think so.' Part of him is here, but it's not the place that sings to his being.

She thinks so too but she wants him to understand that while the head might know what to expect, the heart takes a while to catch up.

'We'll have to start again,' she tells him. 'New routines, new people, new everything.

'An adventure,' he says.

'Yes,' she agrees. 'And sometimes it'll be scary and uncertain, like venturing into a fairy tale forest against all warnings. But still,' she adds, 'it is an adventure. I just prefer to call it life.'

New York, New York

MEAGAN DUX

I've sat behind my computer screen, glaring at it for two hours now. In which time I have gone online shopping, checked my feed on Facebook, looked at what's new on Netflix and Googled how people willingly sit at a keyboard and type up something interesting enough for just one person to want to read. I've done everything I shouldn't be doing. But the clock is ticking, and I now have no choice but to sit here and write and hope something interesting comes out.

I've been asked to contribute to the magazine my mum is an editor at. Writing is not something I've ever enjoyed, but I guess my mum feels I have an important story to share. Although, when I called her and asked what that story was, she said, 'Ariel, it's not your story if I have to tell you.' I rolled my eyes at her—several times—even though she couldn't see me. I then proceeded to walk around the house I've been living in ever since I was seven. I walked in and out of every single room until something stopped me dead in my tracks. On our entrance hall table, there are six photos and two candles. The six pictures are of my dog and me. *My dog.* I can still hear her running down the stairs to go for a walk. I close my eyes and feel the tears well in my eyes before they drop onto my cheeks.

And that's when it hit me. My story, the one I need to tell, is about the unbreakable bond that I had with my dog, Frankie. You see I live in New York, but I'm not American. My mum split up from my dad when

I was five, and she decided to change her entire life. Since she had sole custody of me, I went where she went, and after one of her university friends convinced her to move to New York with her for her dream job, we packed up our lives into two suitcases and we headed to the big apple.

I don't know how she did it, but my mum somehow managed to find a house in the heart of the city. It was squished in between two houses that were double the size of ours, but it was close to Central Park, and that's all she wanted. While I've always had a fascination with dogs, my mum has always had a fascination with New York City. I remember the way she used to read stories to me about how grand it was, how people never sleep in New York, how the lights never go off and the city is always buzzing, and how everyone in New York just lives a different life to the rest of the world. I never picked up on how much she loved this place until I was old enough to understand. When you're six and you've lived with your mum and her parents for the last year it confuses you to be told you have to pack up your life into one suitcase and get on a plane to move to the other side of the world.

Living in Australia was all I had ever known, and suddenly that was all changing. The way I spoke, the way I spelt, the way I even saw cars drive changed entirely. It was like learning to be human all over again. I had to make all new friends, and I had to go to a new school, with people who laughed at my accent and couldn't understand everything I was saying. At first it used to bother me. I got sick of trying to explain why I spoke differently and how I pronounced words like 'mum' and 'tomato' differently, why I said Autumn and not Fall, and how I didn't realise how important it was to celebrate the 4th of July, since I was used to Australia Day.

And I didn't understand why people laughed at my name. I was never self-conscious about my name until I went to school and I'd always have to try to explain why my mum called me Ariel–yes, as in Ariel from *The Little Mermaid*. Ever since my mum saw that movie she's loved that name, so when she had me she knew Ariel was the perfect name. I'm an only child so my mum has always made a big fuss over every milestone moment in my life. And my name was just the beginning. It only got more intense when we moved to New York. I think she felt like she had to make a bigger deal out of things like my birthday since it was always just the two of us for so long. I think she also wanted to make things more enjoyable for me too since I had to leave the only life I had ever known behind when we moved. I went from seeing my family all the time to having to talk to them through a computer screen.

My mum adjusted ridiculously well–and quickly–while it took me longer than she had hoped to adapt to our new life. She loved being in the place she'd always dreamed of being, while I used to beg her to take me home. She would always tell me that this was our home, but it never felt that way. To me, home was the house we used to live in. Home was Australia, and I wanted more than anything to be back there. But no matter how much I rebelled or how much I would refuse to talk, my mum told me I had to learn to love New York since we weren't going anywhere.

It probably didn't help that the more I went to school the more I thought people would get used to me and stop making fun of my accent. I even went as far as trying to sound American instead of Australian, but it didn't help one bit. Although over time I embraced my accent and I refused to let anyone tell me differently, when I did that, things started to change. I finally began to settle in and I even made friends, but nothing prepared me for the happiness I'd experience on my tenth birthday, when my life changed. I didn't even realise the impact that this particular birthday would have on my life until long after I was no longer a child.

When I was ten, my mum gave me the one present I had begged her for all my life–she gave me a dog. She'd always hesitated to give into my persistence, and when I was young I didn't understand why my mum was being mean and saying no to me, but now I know. She was trying to protect me, to spare me, to save me from the pain and grief one feels when they lose their four-legged friend. I didn't think pain from losing a pet could ever hurt so badly, but Frankie was different. She was unlike any dog I had ever encountered, and I have yet to come across another dog even remotely like her. It's pretty easy for any dog owner to say that they have the world's best dog. I think we're pretty lucky to even find a dog that special, but sometimes there are dogs like Frankie who come along and change everything. They turn your life upside down in the best possible way, and it's not until you can fully grasp the power of human emotions that you realise just how much a spotted dog and a pair of brown eyes can change your life forever.

It probably sounds ridiculous to say, but my dog saved my life. Crazy, right? How could a dog–who can't even talk–possibly save a human life? I wouldn't have believed it if it hadn't happened to me, but it did, and I quickly realised just how powerful the bond between a dog and human can be. It's no lie when people say that dogs are man's best friend and it's no lie that the love of a dog can become the best part of your life.

Whenever I would have a bad day, or I'd get homesick, I'd spend time with Frankie. We would go out and explore, and we would spend hours upon hours walking through Central Park, especially in winter. While most people tried their hardest to avoid the snow and the cold weather that came along with it, I embraced it wholeheartedly. I guess when you come from a place where it never snows you learn to love the things that many people become used to. It was just a bonus that Frankie loved the cold weather as much as I did. We could easily spend hours walking through parks, although we'd often have to sprint home when a snowstorm would come out of nowhere. On the days when a snowstorm would hit we would snuggle up on the couch in my mum's office, where the wooden fireplace sat, and I'd read book after book while Frankie would sleep by my side. When the storm passed through, Frankie and I would go back out and continue to explore our new home. Even my mum couldn't understand the love we had for the cold, but there's something so magical about winter time, especially if you get to experience winter in a place like New York.

I used to watch New Yorkers run from one place to the other, not slowing down for anything, and I used to think how lucky I was that I didn't have to rush from place to place. I could simply go get a coffee and take my best friend for a walk through our favourite park while watching how the delicate snow would fall from the sky and blanket everything around us.

When I went to high school, everything just clicked for me. I had finally fallen into a better place, and I had fully transitioned to my life in

America. I felt much more comfortable, and I was able to accept every aspect of who I was, even if things weren't always sunshine and rainbows. Although I don't think anything really prepared me to grow up on the Upper East Side.

I was pretty oblivious to the world around me since I liked to spend most of my time reading or walking through the bustling streets with Frankie, whilst my mum's career continued to boom and she continued to become increasingly sort after. She ended up taking a job at one of the biggest magazine companies in the world. She was suddenly travelling more and going to the fanciest of fancy parties, and it was almost always guaranteed that I'd be dragged along to them with her. Since she was too busy to date, I was regularly her plus one, which would have been fine if we had lived anywhere other than the Upper East Side.

I remember the first 'elite' party I had gone to with my mum. There were cameras everywhere, with people fighting to get photos of anyone and everyone who entered the building where said party was, and there were people who were wearing clothes that cost enough to pay for rent for at least a year. I hated those kinds of events. I had nothing to talk about to the people there. My mum had banned me from taking a book with me after I snuck into the cloakroom and read my book all night when she took me to a smaller event a few months back. Anyway, at this party, I remember standing with my mum while she talked to another magazine editor. I began to scan the room and I felt like I was in a scene straight out of Gossip Girl. I had loved that show until that very moment. I didn't think that show was accurate, but boy was I wrong. It was scary how accurate that show was in its portrayal of the elitists that you find here. In fact, I felt like I was a real-life Jenny Humphry–minus all the drama. I was introduced to more people that night than I had ever met in my entire life, and I felt underdressed whenever I met other girls my age, despite wearing more makeup than I'd ever worn before and being in the most uncomfortable pair of Louboutin's that ever existed. My mum worked hard so she enjoyed the luxuries that came with her job. I, however, did not. I wasn't into $1,000 dinners and $4,000 dresses. I was into being with my dog, exploring the city and loaning as many paperback novels from the library as I was allowed.

Two months into my Freshman year (aka my first year in high school) I made my first best friend. Emily was pretty much my twin; the only real difference was the fact that she had a thick New York accent and my Aussie accent was as strong as ever. We had the same sense of humour, our personalities were similar, and we both loved reading. Emily ran her own book blog, and after we became close she asked me to blog with her, but my distaste for writing let me down, and I decided not to do it. I loved reading, but sharing my opinions with others wasn't something I enjoyed so I left that to Emily. She had a dog too, so we'd often take them for walks together, and she lived a few blocks away, so we would walk to each other's places before finding ways to have sleepovers that always entailed way too much sugar and not enough sleep.

Emily's parents were divorced too, and while she saw her mum in the last week of every month, she lived with her dad for the other three weeks. So in that three weeks we tried to do as much together as we possibly could. Then one day we had a brilliant–well, we thought it would be brilliant–idea. Her dad was the sports teacher at our high school, and he coached the baseball team, so he, like my mum, was often always busy. That's when Emily and I decided to play matchmakers. We thought what could be better than our single parents dating so we could be sisters? We didn't think it would work, but to our surprise, they clicked, and within months they were officially a couple.

Emily and I continued to grow closer, and our parents kept falling further in love. Life was pretty good until my mum decided I needed to spend more time with my new potential step-dad. Emily was away with her mum, so after much protesting from me, I somehow managed to end up at baseball practice with Larry. I wouldn't have minded if it was just the two of us, but since he was the baseball coach, his time was limited. So any bonding time was either at practice or during the limited time Emily and I actually wanted to talk to our parents when we had sleepovers. I can still remember the conversation I had with my mum about not wanting to go to baseball practice.

'Mum, seriously. I'm already uncool. I'm one of the only girls who wears glasses, and while Emily is fine with everyone at school, I'm not. Everyone calls me a book nerd, which I mean, I am, but still! I'm sure the last thing that'll help is going to training with my sports teacher, who's dating my mum, while he coaches the most popular boys in school.'

She would merely giggle at me. 'Maybe they will be your friends.'

I laughed at her comment before noticing she was serious. 'Good joke. I'd rather go to Barnes and Nobel and get a new book.'

She sighed and put down the pieces of paper she had in her hands. 'Honey, I love that you're so passionate about reading, but it would be good for you to get out of the house. Larry always says he needs help at training. Why don't you take Frankie with you?'

I sighed. Usually I'd continue to protest, but I liked Larry, and since Emily wasn't around to help, it was the least I could do.

And that's where I met Carter Prescott. We were in the same year at school, but we ran with different crowds and I liked to avoid his group at all costs. Although, Carter was unlike anyone I'd ever seen before. He had the greenest eyes I'd ever seen, he was built like a tank, and his smile could melt snow. No, seriously, he was handsome beyond belief. I guess that helped with every aspect of his life. Not only was he the most popular guy in our school, but he was also the captain of the baseball team. Even at training, he'd have a fan club of a least ten girls screaming his name. I used to laugh while texting Emily about it, and then I'd laugh even more when Carter would wave at me, and the groupies would get jealous. I remember a few of them coming up to me and asking how I knew him and I'd always wear a big smile as I answered that question. 'Oh, we're the best of friends!' I'd say before walking off. I always tried my best to avoid Carter, but that all changed two and a half years later.

In my Senior year, I was in the best place I'd ever been in, although I'd dealt with Carter trying to get me to date him for two-and-a-half years. I was pretty impressed that he hadn't had a girlfriend by that point, although I didn't know if I believed how true that was. One night I walked Emily to a party, she had begged me to go with her, but I wasn't feeling the greatest, so I decided to walk her to the party and then take Frankie for a quick walk before retreating to the comforts of my room. Just after I waved goodbye to Emily, Carter came running up to me.

'Hey, stranger! I thought this wasn't your kinda scene,' he said before stopping in front of me.

'And I thought you were a star athlete, why are you out of breath?' I asked sarcastically as I watched him take a deep breath.

'Ha ha, very funny. Seriously, why are you here, though?'

I looked at him, curiously.

'I walked Emily here. Now I'm going home.'

I started to walk back the way I came, and to my surprise, Carter kept following me. 'You know, people come to a place like New York when they're trying to run away,' he suddenly said to me matter-of-factly.

I raised my eyebrows at him before answering. 'You do know I've been here for well over ten years now? And I'm not running away—I had to move here when my mum did.'

He just laughed at me, like he was trying to get a reaction out of me. I defensively tightened my grip on Frankie's lead as we walked in silence.

'I'm glad I left that party when I did, though. It was lame. Too many people, and way too many girls!'

I laughed at his statement before my sarcasm got the better of me, again. 'Yeah it must be tough to have every girl want to be with you,' I said as I rolled my eyes again.

He stopped dead in his tracks, and when I looked at him, he simply said, 'Not every girl,' followed by a smirk.

'Are you always this up yourself?'

He just continued to smirk. 'I'm the baseball captain, and I'm the most popular guy at our school, of course, I am.'

I started to pick my pace up as I weaved my way through the odd amount of people on the sidewalk. 'I forgot popularity is more important than being a decent person,' I called over my shoulder.

'Hey, I'm a decent person. I can't help it that everyone likes me, sometimes I wish they didn't.'

His reply had caught me off guard, and there was something different in his tone, it was almost a sad tone, so I dropped my shoulders and asked if he wanted to go get ice cream with me, which he excitedly said yes to.

As we began to walk towards the ice cream shop he asked to take Frankie's lead, and I reluctantly let him. Frankie seemed to like him, so I convinced myself to give him a chance too. So that's what I did. I let

Carter in, and before I knew it, I had developed strong feelings for him and we became more than friends. My mum was beside herself; she was ecstatic that not only did I have a best friend, but I now had a boyfriend. Although she always said I spent too much time on my own for someone who had two close relationships. She always used to encourage me to go to parties with Carter, which was the last thing I ever wanted to do.

'Mum, do you even know what the kids around here get up to? Those parties are next level, they're not like any normal party,' I tried to tell her.

She'd always say, 'You might have fun.'

I'd try not to laugh, but I could never resist, 'Mum, you shouldn't be encouraging me to go.' And she'd always have a response to anything I'd say back to her.

'You spend too much time with your head in books and with the dog. I know you love that, but you need to go out and live.'

I guess being around Carter and Emily helped with that. I went from always wanting to stay home reading with Frankie to going to parties, Carter's baseball games, and events that our school had. Like prom, which was way out of my comfort zone too, but I slowly began to love the social life I now had for myself.

As I continued to bloom in life, I continued to be more social, and before I knew it, I was only home here and there. I didn't take Frankie for as many walks as I used to, and I eventually stopped reading books every Friday and Saturday night.

It wasn't until my mum, Larry and Emily took a trip to Texas to visit Larry's family that I realised just how much Frankie meant to me, and it was in that moment that I realised losing her was the worst thing I'd ever faced in my 18 years of living.

It was a typical winter night, a snowstorm had hit, and Carter was staying with me at my mum's house. We were one movie into our Batman marathon when I heard Frankie make a strange noise. I got up and walked to the back door where she was waiting. I figured she just wanted to go the toilet so I let her out. I went and grabbed my thick coat before telling Carter I was going outside with her. As I closed the door behind me, I couldn't spot Frankie. I called her name a few times, but she didn't come back. I started to panic when Carter joined me. He got his phone light up, and we walked through the backyard as we frantically searched for her. I finally found her lying in a pile of snow. There was blood next to her, and all I could do was drop to my knees and hold her frail head in my hands. I knew something was wrong; I just didn't realise that moment was going to change my life forever.

We rushed her to the vets, and after tests, the vet told me that Frankie was riddled with cancer and that despite how healthy she was, there was nothing we could do. It had spread to her lungs, and it was now a matter of how much time she had left. The vet told me how quickly she had deteriorated. She was struggling to stand and she couldn't stomach water or food. When I asked her if Frankie was in pain, the vet quietly said yes, and my whole world collapsed around me. I called my mum, and she tried to comfort me, but she said the decision was mine.

I knew it was selfish to want Frankie to come home with me when she was so sick. I mean I was considering it, but when I went in and saw her, I knew what I had to do. Frankie wasn't the dog she used to be. She was weak and she had lost her spark. I didn't want her to suffer any more than she already was, so I knew it was time to let her go, even though it was the hardest decision I've ever had to make. Thankfully, Carter was there for me every step of the way. Having him there for me made the world of difference and made the whole process somewhat bearable.

But saying goodbye to Frankie was nothing short of heartbreaking. I sat on the floor with her and she rested her head on my lap. I continued to pat her head as I remembered all the times she was there for me. I remembered all the sandwiches we had shared, all the late nights we had sat up in my bed reading, every birthday cake I had secretly shared with her while my mum wasn't looking, every cuddle we shared, and every walk we had taken in the snow through Central Park played out in my mind. She was there when I was sad, when I was happy and when I just needed a friend. She helped me in so many ways, and in her time of need, I couldn't do anything. I was powerless, and that was the worst feeling. It took all my strength to smile and not cry in front of her. I didn't want my best friend to leave this world behind seeing me hysterical when she needed me the most.

So I got up, and the vet and Carter gently lifted her onto the table. I said my final goodbyes to her, where I told her how thankful I was to have had her in my life and how she was my best friend and that I loved her more than anything. I told her she was the best dog and I thanked her for picking me from the very start. I kissed her nose the same way I did when I first picked her, and I continued to pat her head gently as I continued to smile at her as she left this world behind. Within minutes, she was gone.

I didn't think losing a dog would hurt the way it did when I lost Frankie, but it's clear to see just how much of an impact our dogs can have on our lives. I've always had a love for dogs. There's something about them—they're more than just animals, they're more than just fur, they're more than four legs, two ears and a tail. They're more than a beating heart and a pair of eyes that look at you every day; they save us when we didn't even realise we need to be saved.

Dogs are more than just the names we give them—they are members of the family, and if you're ever lucky enough to be blessed by a dog that is loyal to you, then you can learn just how far a bond can go. If we open ourselves up to the possibility of things we didn't think would work out, then we can unlock a whole new world that is worth sharing with our furry friends.

It's not the happiest of endings in the fact that I lost my best friend and I've had to learn to live without her, but despite how much I wish I could have her back, I've learnt more from her death than I ever thought possible and now. For the first time, I'm excited to embrace my future and explore the places that terrify and excite me.

To quote my favourite movie, *Marley and Me*, John Grogan said, 'A dog has no use for fancy cars or big houses or designer clothes. A waterlogged stick will do just fine. A dog doesn't care if you're rich or poor, clever or dull, smart or dumb. Give him your heart, and he'll give you his. How many people can make you feel rare and pure and special? How many people can make you feel extraordinary?'

You did, Frankie girl. You did all of that, and I am a much better person because I was able to love, laugh and cry with you. You made me feel extraordinary.

Ariel.

Freedom

VERONICA GYPSY

"Better to die fighting for freedom than be
a prisoner all the days of your life."
—Bob Marley

I couldn't handle it anymore. I found myself leaving earlier and earlier every morning, coming up with a new excuse whenever needed. Although, to be honest, I felt my father was beginning to switch off from me more and more that I don't think it even mattered what I shared with him.

Most mornings I was allowed to enter the factory early and begin my shift. They didn't care as long as I filled my production quota for the day. If I exceeded my quota I was sometimes rewarded, but it generally went unnoticed. Too much happening and too many serious war threats were all much more important than why I chose to arrive early or finish late.

However, this particular morning I wasn't permitted to enter early. In fact, I was encouraged to leave the area completely until 6 am. This didn't faze me. I decided to take my usual walk along the Docklands. This was another one of my methods to avoid returning home. Although I had never explored the area at this early time of morning before, so I was more than happy to wander.

I watched the floating barges. I listened to the early call of gulls and took in the slow, gentle magic of the sun's arrival for the day. All of a sudden, the sound of stern, male voices caught my attention. Questions were asked, muffled answers shared. I stopped and found myself trying to hide, yet I couldn't bring myself to leave. I strained my ears to take in every detail that was said. As I listened, as every description and element were spoken, my body began to buzz; a combination of nerves, excitement, and disbelief, with one continuous thought occurring in my head over and over. *Could this be the answer? Could this be it?*

My mind raced and my heart beat wildly. At that moment I decided that this was it! I needed to find out more no matter what and the urgency to make it happen washed over me with such intensity it took my breath away.

Within minutes the older man ran off. As the other two men placed their caps on their heads, trying to disguise themselves while pocketing their secret, I approached. They were reluctant to answer my questions at first. However, once they could see that I was serious, they gave me all the detail I needed, repeating the importance of secrecy and emphasising how dangerous it was for a 'woman.' I heard them loud and clear, but they underestimated my intense desire to escape. I let out a deep breath, not realising how long I had been holding it, and slowly blew away all of my fears. I knew it was dangerous, but I had no choice. They handed me a way out, and I was going to take it. It wasn't going to be easy or cheap, and the risk was immense, but I knew deep in my core that if I did not take this chance, I would die while living in this trapped existence, and that was not an option. My life had to have more value and meaning to it. I knew it deep within my soul.

It was 3.30 am in Oleander State. My father was snoring while in a state of exhausted sleep. A sleep that was aided by the bottle in an effort to forget his lost love, my existence, and his altered life since the beginning of the war. This was the way he chose to cope with his despair, with few sober moments in between. Tonight his presence went unnoticed as I was too focused on preparing for the journey ahead.

I was instructed to pack lightly with minimal food and basic living necessities only. I was told to dress inconspicuously in warm clothing and sturdy shoes. Most important of all, I had to securely fasten my personal belongings to my body. I assumed they meant my new ID papers, money, and any valuables such as jewellery. Lastly, they shared the unknowns. However, they stressed that the length of the journey, the specific destination and my safety were only guesses and once my journey began, everything going forward was out of their hands. I accepted these terms, which was crazy, but my intense need to survive made my decision crystal clear. I simply had no other choice.

Everything was organised, the money was exchanged, the new papers were assigned, the time, dock and boat details delivered. All that was left was down to me. When and how to sneak out early enough, before James Brown Senior noticed.

My father was a successful man until all he lived for was gone. Firstly, my sweet angel mamma becoming ill and then passing away, and soon after his posting was declined. We could blame his age, his depressive state or my uncanny resemblance to my mother, including her defined birthmark, that drove him to drink. But it didn't matter, he took it all out on me. The harshness of his ways, his demands, his bitterness and his continuing growing distance was becoming too hard to bare. I knew leaving would not help the situation for him, but being here slaving at home in this numb state wasn't helping me either.

I had decided at the last minute that I would leave a short note. Nothing deep, just a few words letting him know that I was safe.

Dear Father,
I'm off to lessen your burden. I have decided to explore possibilities, where I can be of more assistance. I miss Mum too. I still love you, but I can't live and survive as we are anymore.
Love Claudette.

I placed the note in a well-hidden spot so he would not find it for weeks, allowing me time to reach my destination and to begin my new life.

I arrived at the dock as the sun began to rise. Before I knew it, I was being roughly shoved onboard and told that I needed to hide and stay hidden until I reached my destination. They explained that the departure had been pushed forward and that I would be departing immediately.

From what I could see, the hull was filled with crates and containers but no specific vessel name or any other details or clues to where we were going. I was guided into an enclosed storage section that seemed to be hidden under a small wooden landing craft. I was told to hide and to get as comfortable as I could, as this would be my spot for the duration of the journey.

I was cramped with what seemed to be damaged goods, from torn life-jackets, cracked containers to random tools. I needed to keep a low profile and had decided to get myself as set up as possible for whatever this journey would throw my way. All of a sudden it dawned on me that I hadn't stopped to think about what I was expecting of this voyage and yet here I was, on my way to the unknown. Did I think I would have a cabin? Have access to the decks? Would there be others like me? None of this had crossed my mind.

Time went by slowly on the boat. I slept, I ate, and I tried to move around as much as I could to avoid cramps setting in. Sometimes I heard voices, but always at a safe distance. All of a sudden, I sensed an intense weather change. Was it a storm? What did that mean? What would happen to the ship? To me? I felt splashes of water flush down the decking holes. I was rolled, thrown, and then I heard it. More scampering, running and shouting, along with swift dragging and shifting realizing that this was all getting more intense, therefore closer and right above me! I panicked and tried to hide, but with minimum lighting and room, I knew this was a going to be a long shot when all of a sudden, my mind recalled a torn tarp of army greens squashed in a corner under a rummaged pile. I grabbed, spread and rolled myself and all my belongings into it, trying furiously to hide my very existence. Then I froze, holding my breath as the lid was lifted. More scurrying, desperate discussions, wind blowing and sounds intense but undistinguishable had occurred. Then metal tools clanging and a distinct shift, drag and BANG!

Oh, it was like heaven, that bang, the lid slamming down again. I was safe. I let out a deep sigh of relief. I hadn't realised the angst, fear and loneliness I was holding inside of me until that very moment, and it all came flooding out in an avalanche of tears. It washed over me like the intense storm washed over the crew above, without warning and with great effect. I was crying so much, my mind was reeling like a movie, but stuck, a glitch in my life, caught in the unknown. What was I thinking leaving like this? My life was hanging in the balance out in the open sea, with no direction, no idea of where or what I was doing? I took another deep breath in an attempt to settle my fraying nerves. There was no way to back out now, my course was set, my journey had already begun. I braced myself tightly and somehow drifted off into a deep sleep.

I woke sometime later to the gentle rocking of the boat and the peaceful sounds of nothingness. The storm had passed. A small, gold lining of light was glowing through the deck and I smiled for the first time in what felt like a lifetime. I was alive. A wave of love, a sense of something wonderful, someone wonderful filled my soul. I realised who immediately. Her presence overtook me, her hold, her protection, her pride, and that's when I realised it was her that had helped me get this far. Her and her forever binding love and belief in me ... my sweet mamma.

I knew we had arrived but where I didn't know. My new future destination was waiting for me. I took in the sounds of my surroundings trying to decipher what was happening. There was movement, perhaps items carried and removed from the boat. It felt like hours and finally, after feeling like I had waited forever, there was silence. I collected myself and my belongings and decided it was time to begin this new adventure.

There was hardly anyone around except what looked like locals. But where was I? It didn't look familiar. Then like an advertisement just released, headings, signs, directions, everything seemed to leap out wildly in front of me. My heart was beating uncontrollably, I couldn't believe it. I had literally been shoved to the most unexpected place in the world, Rubia.

I looked around for answers while trying to look like part of the scenery. But to be honest, how could I not stand out? I was in a panic, but again with perfect timing, a small old lady appeared from nowhere and approached me with a sign:

PENSIONE, ROOM TO LET!

I nearly grabbed her in a relieved embrace, but instead, she grabbed my hand in haste, encouraging me to keep quiet as she pulled me along. It was like she had been waiting for me. We walked and walked, finally arriving at a small, bright coloured street. We walked up to a house with the reddest front door and a planter box filled with geraniums.

Geraniums! My mum's favourite.

I found myself in the sweetest of rooms, a view of the small, vibrant street, a blessed old lady and contacts for a job. I could feel that my new life was about to begin.

I had no knowledge of the Rubian way, the people, or even its direct connection to America or its role in the war. But I could feel deep down that I was not to rock anymore boats, and I needed to accept my destination and all the unknown, as this was now my path.

The culture was unique, the language was animated and the people so warm. As the days passed I realised I was now known as 'Claudia' with the most divine of accents. I even began to pick up small words. I don't know how, and it's hard to believe, but I felt welcomed wholeheartedly by these people. I felt such a sense of belonging, that a comfort began to set in. I felt a true sense of freedom for the first time in so long.

I took in my days watching how my world and its development unfolded. A job had even come my way, with no expectations just feelings of gratitude passed through me. It was a basic job, an apprentice-type position as a seamstress at a small shop called *Casita de Camisa*. I was the runaround, stitch and unpick girl. But I knew it was only the beginning of my venture here. It was allowing me to earn enough money for my basic needs. But with time, individuals started to take me under their wing, guiding me and trusting me more and more. I knew in the deepest part of my soul that my mamma had laid her hands all over this.

The shopfront was small with a simple layout, but hidden at the back was a sewing factory. Behind the façade of the street were sewing jobs assisting the war, small adjustments and repairs of uniforms, bandages, and even the occasional parachutes, but all of this was kept low key and very discreet.

My days were pretty routine from work to home. Some might not have seen my little room as a home, but to me it was mine and it was perfect. My landlord, Senora Rosita, was very sweet and always helpful. She often fed me, and over time introduced me to this new world. I made a few friends over the months. Valentina, in particular, decided I was so special that she showed me off so proudly like she owned me, sharing me where she saw fit. She loved dressing up and traipsing through the local markets. The markets were always filled with treasures from new to old, fresh homegrown produce, home-cooked delicacies and local crafts all made from expertise hands.

Valentina was wild and carefree and truly stunning. Long black shiny feathered hair that fell down her back like a tasselled shawl. Mine, on the other hand, had flicks and kicks like a wild dance, but with some curling and rolling efforts, held a form I was used to. The most exciting thing about our friendship was the huge influence she had on my surroundings, my home space. We created a place that was me; feminine, bright, filled with finds of floral beauty which I would never have considered before. She also helped me find a new dress style that I loved, which inspired me to begin sketching designs again. My old passion was slowly finding it's way back into my life again. I realised that it's strength and desire never left my essence, but instead sat patiently beneath my skin awaiting my interest to peak again, and with Valentina's guidance it found its way back to the surface. The ideas had begun to dance in my mind with small thoughts overflowing with flourishing lines of skirt hems and scooped necks caressing the decolletage. I was dreaming designs which awakened living cells within me. It was crazy.

Another beautiful aspect I had been introduced to was the backstreet dancing fiestas. I had been dragged there by my friends, but what continued to draw me there was the flooding river of colourful corners and all of Rubia's thoroughfares. These festivals of life were an abundance of divine flowing textures wrapped around women of all shapes and sizes, heights and characters, then combined with music tones and beats that until recently I had only heard from a distance, all of which would make anybody's vitals spring to life.

A few times I had been encouraged by some older gentlemen to try using my American feet with Salsa-like steps. To be honest, though, I was a klutz and every attempt at dancing ended in an entaglement of hands and feet.

By the third dance night, I was coming to terms with the idea that this was not what my body was made for. Again I found myself in someones uncle's embrace, between translations and patience I was guided, but I could feel they were getting over their efforts to help me dance. But all of a sudden in the blurry mess of feet and hands and a change of Latin tune, we were interrupted, so politely and subtly that I was almost unaware a partner change had occurred. Especially as my embarrassment was continuously growing, I began finding myself trying to avoid too much eye contact.

But this time my body felt held in an embrace of strength, my posture seemed altered, even heightened, so I couldn't help but look up and there stood the most exquisite man I had ever imagined. Was it his demeanour of safety compared to the previous calamities of movement I experienced? Or was it his physique of God-like presence? Could it have been his eyes of deep molasses brown? I could sense his intenseness like salted caramel with an underlying sweet, honeyed gentleness, and the care he expressed along with a stiffened mouth, yet playful smile.

All of my senses were heightened in his presence of total control. My whole body lengthened from my limbs to my shoulders. We began to flow, move and sway to the actual rhythmed beat rather than the erraticness I was beginning to think I was hearing. It was shortlived, though. He allowed this magic to happen through two dances and then he excused himself and left. No name, no details. Unfortunately, no one knew of him, where he was from or why he was there.

I went to as many dances as possible hoping to see him again. Then one night my universe changed and the gift of this human being appeared again, lifting me to highest of heights, my soul rising in energy. We danced, and over the next few weeks we talked, shared and enjoyed each others company. Looking back, it was funny but we never really shared too many details of our personal lives, but we grew intimate, we grew closer, we grew together. I was being raised and enlightened with feelings of love direct to my soul.

His name was Sebastian, he was approximately ten years older than me. He worked in some local offices and was born and bred in Rubia, but he didn't really venture out much until that first night. He was asked to search out someone in the area when he heard the music and had recalled the dances from his younger years. As much as he tried to get away, he was drawn to stay.

I was so happy for the first time in so long, and I could sense how serious we were becoming. I think because he was quite private himself, he never demanded a lot of information from me, so all felt right.

I was so absorbed in my new life. My work was fulfilling, my drawings were coming freely, and my confidence was building in all aspects that I felt a shift in my role at work. I was no longer the bits and bobs girl, I was given large jobs and I even got to play with some design finishes that some wealthier customers were asking for. My life was more exciting than ever.

Sebastian and I saw each other a few times a week. We would go dancing, go out for dinners and sometimes we would just take long, slow walks through the streets while talking. One afternoon, he had decided to surprise me by taking me to explore some of the island's natural beauty.

After walking for a while we reached a set of steep, overgrown steps. As we began the incline Sebastian became quiet. All of a sudden, I felt his warm hand caress my back. I should have assumed it was for support but my body sensed it was something different. We reached the top where the view seemed to expand to the ends of the earth, with colours of luscious greens to the depths of sea blues. It was truly majestic. As I went to comment, Sebastian turned towards me cupping my face. I felt his smooth skin as he began to brush my lips with his fingertips while he looked straight into my eyes. His lips paused over my mouth and then it happened—the kind of kiss that I did not even know existed. Nothing else crossed my mind other than his moist lips as his tongue played so tenderly in my mouth. He nibbled and nudged my inner lip with slow persistence. It wasn't sexual, but it was an intimacy of a different kind, like he was kissing the centre of my soul. I was entranced by his love. It was magic and this was just from a kiss. I felt like I had found my true love.

After that first kiss, we spent as many hours as we could together. One night after walking me home, our goodnight embrace seemed to linger a little longer then usual. Sebastian began to stroke my arm, taking hold of my wrist and bringing it to his soft lips creating a shiver through my body. He kissed my palm, brushing his lips down my fingers, then he pulled me closer, biting my lip, nibbling along my jawline and down my throat. Then he turned me around slowly. His gentle kisses travelled down the nape of my neck which sent direct messages to my womanhood. My breasts tingled, my centre core moistened and my legs literally gave way. We soon found ourselves at the base of my bed. He laid me down so gently, as if part of a dance, and then stopped to take me all in. As I stared back into his eyes, all I could see was love looking back at me. *'Te adoro con todo mi corazón.'* He whispered (I adore you with all my heart).

Before I could process what was happening, our naked bodies were entwined. Our breathing grew rapid with desire as his hands stroked and fondled my breasts, slightly pinching the flesh of my nipples. This caused me to behave like I never knew I could. All of a sudden I started to devour him with my tongue, my hands frantically exploring his body. I found myself reaching for his firm, hard manhood. I followed his strokes of my torso along his shaft. I could feel his body tense with desire. And then he began the journey up my inner thighs gently teasing, my body arched. I was too absorbed in our togetherness to stop him. All I wanted was more. His fingers were deliberate as they moved across my inner folds. He then found the sweetest of spots that took my breath with every pinch and tweak. He wrapped my legs around him and he slid into me. I felt engulfed with every move. It felt like nothing else existed other than the two of us at that moment.

A unique rhythm began between us. It was like a new dance, again he lead but we flowed together. A dance that I never wanted to end. There were more sliding motions and thrusts until our heartbeats increased. We moved until a shower of sensation overtook us both. He held me so close with a tight embrace. A love was felt though unspoken, so overpowering and yet so nurturing.

I was so grateful for so many things that I realised I was listing them throughout the day. And I was sure from how he left in the early hours that he felt the same way. I was excited and so looking forward to our next wonderful time together.

Then something changed. Saturday morning I awoke with a heavy feeling. My father's presence entered my soul, like a winter chill. He hadn't crossed my mind for a while, not like this anyway. Occasionally I wondered how he was, and whether he just accepted my disappearance, but this heavy feeling was so different. I tried to just brush it away and concentrate on my new life and beau.

There were only a few hours left of work, the following Friday, then I would meet my Sebastian at the dance gathering. I dressed in his favourite rose patterned A-line dress, that gave me the perfect shape. My hair was flicked and Valentina had lent me a ruby coloured hair pin, large enough to cover half my head. I was ready, I was so thrilled and so excited, but … he didn't show.

One hour, two hours, then the third hour arrived and just as the crowd started to disperse I sensed his heavy presence. He came from nowhere, and before I knew it he was pulling me off into the night. He was rough as he dragged me down the street away from the crowds. What had happened? Why was he acting this way? Then I realised he was holding a Via Air Envelope and just as we passed a streetlight I caught a glimpse of the writing:

To: Detective Sebastian Perez

Sender: James Brown Senior

I stopped and snatched the letter from him. He stared at me with a harsh look on his face.

'What is this Claudia?' He said through clenched teeth. He was trying hard not to explode, but anger was radiating off of him.

I opened it and there was a sketch, a letter, and a description, all describing a missing daughter and a demand for an immediate return to Oleander State, with a reward offered. The sketch was uncannily accurate, everything from my beauty spot on my lip, which at that moment felt like a witches mole. I was shaking so hard that I found myself collapsing onto a nearby bench. My breathing became short and quick as tears began to well in my eyes. Could this really be happening? Could my father's ugly piercing ways have caught up with me and robbed me of my happiness again?

All of a sudden I looked up and met Sebastian's inquisitive stare. I began to share my story with him and the reason for all of my secrets. I shared every detail without thinking, unsure whether it was the safest thing to do, but I felt I had no choice. I decided if he was a detective and he had strict orders to take me back then I wanted to share my story.

I began to slow down, both with my speech and my sobbing. I could tell he was torn between wanting to console and hold me and wanting to question and arrest me for being in a foreign country illegally.

I suddenly realised we had been sitting there for hours with nothing more said. Just our legs and shoulders lightly touching. I began to shiver with the drop in temperature. He draped his coat over my shoulders and then as if someone else was guiding, we were in an embrace. I felt a sense of understanding and sadness from him. We pulled apart and decided that it was time to head home. That night we held each other tight, neither of us wanting to let go.

The next day I felt exhausted, drained and physically spent like I had been belted. We decided a slow walk and a lot of communication were necessary on both our parts. This allowed secrets to be shared and a deeper openness that we hadn't ever really had in our relationship.

Before I knew it, Monday morning came and I was back at work. There was no resolution between us. In the end, he had two choices: either he decided to fulfil his role as a detective and send me back to my father, or he went against all he thought he stood for and followed his heart.

Days came and went with no word from my Sebastian. I struggled to find all that I had once been grateful for. When would he decide? What would happen to me? Would I cope if he sent me back? Did I not mean something to him? Oh, sweet Mamma, give me strength, send me some faith. Could this really be where my freedom ends?

This continued for weeks. I felt like I was grieving all over again. Valentina was there, but to be honest, I didn't take much notice. The waiting was like death. It was getting harder and harder and nothing could distract me. I struggled to work, struggled to eat, struggled to sleep.

It was Sunday morning, and as usual, I was exhausted from another sleepless night. Most mornings I could hear Rosita leaving treats, flowers and tokens of love at my door, and Valentina coming and going trying to get a response from me. But I had nothing left for anyone, not even for myself.

The morning dragged into the afternoon when suddenly there was an abrupt knock on the door. My heart sank as I knew this was it. Was it him or did he send someone else? I just wanted to disappear. More knocks came and suddenly, I found myself going into some sort of trance. I couldn't react. The fear intensified taking over my mind. The thought of being sucked of all my happiness again by my father was unbearable. I couldn't, wouldn't go back. I began to sink deeper into nothingness.

Then I felt I was being shaken. My name called, my face touched, a cool sensation on my forehead and the strongest smell. I had blacked out and then awoke to see my beau, my sweet Sebastian. He was holding me like he would never let me go. I felt tears on my cheeks, and then I realised they were not mine but my soulful man's. I began to cry happy, relieved tears. I knew in my core that he had made his choice and that he would forever keep me safe and secure. That this vivid, magical existence, on this unique island with its passionate ways would be a part of our lives forever.

The Power of Ten

SONIA BELLHOUSE

Somewhere in Britain in the 1970s

'Cara, Wake up!'

There was no movement from the figure in the bed. Rick shook her harder as she burrowed deeper under the bed clothes.

'Go away!' A groan emitted from the lump of blankets.

'Cara, Cara. WAKE UP!'

She pushed the bedclothes off her face and looked groggily around for the source of the voice realising that it was Rick.

She sat up in bed. 'Rick?'

What was he doing in her room? What did he want?

Her eyes were gritty and why could she smell smoke? Cara scrubbed at her stinging eyes.

Rick shook her again. 'Come on—we haven't much time.'

She stared at him dully, still half asleep.

'FIRE! We need to get out,' he tugged her arm hard.

'Huh?'

'There's no time to argue, COME ON!'

'How did you get in?'

Rick groaned, she still wasn't moving.

'I kicked the front door in,' he said, casually.

'You kicked the front door in?' she moaned. 'I'm going to be in so much trouble!'

Cara couldn't see him, but then she felt the touch of his hand on her arm.

'We'll both be in trouble if we don't get out of here.'

She heard a different tone in his voice. Was it fear? It jolted her awake.

'Roll out of bed onto the floor and crawl out with me. We need to stay low under the smoke and heat.' Rick's tone was authoritative.

'Now?' She scrambled round the bed and grabbed a blanket.

'COME ON!'

This time the urgency in his voice made her act. They crawled towards the door with the blanket wrapped over them. Rick held a small flashlight, which shone a sliver of light just a short way ahead through the dense smoke. Slowly they made it to the top of the stairs.

Cara shivered, hearing popping and the sharp splinter of breaking glass. Rick half-dragged, half-pushed her down the stairs and out of the broken front door. The cold night air hit them as they collapsed onto the coolness of the tiny front lawn, coughing and spluttering.

It felt as if time slowed down as Cara struggled to make sense of what had happened. Across the street a couple of neighbours were outside to see what was going on.

'Are you alright?' one called, her voice tiny in the chill night air.

Cara shook her head, the question made her realise it wasn't a dream, this was real. She shivered gulping in the air. When she could breathe more clearly, she said, 'What about the others?'

'Others?' Rick groaned and wiped his hand across his grimy face.

'Mrs M the landlady, she's on the ground floor and Tom, next door to me.'

Rick's shoulders slumped as he dragged his hand through his hair. He said wearily, 'I'll have to go back for them.'

Her heart pounding, Cara clutched his arm. 'Are you sure that you're okay?'

Rick rolled onto his knees still gasping. 'The fire brigade will be on its way. I radioed it in.'

Cara saw Rick's white taxi was parked in the street. In the distance they heard the clang of the fire engine's bell. As Rick struggled to his feet, still breathless, the fire engine had arrived and screamed to a halt. A small crowd of onlookers cheered as the crew of burly firemen leapt off the engine and began unrolling hoses and moving equipment in a well-rehearsed routine. A broad-shouldered fireman dashed across to them.

'Is there anyone else inside?'

Rick answered, his breath coming in short gasps. 'Two we think: a woman on the ground floor and Tom upstairs.' He nodded to Cara. 'I managed to get her out.'

Cara started to splutter as the smoke got thicker. The fireman patted Rick on the shoulder.

'OK,' he said, nodding to Cara. 'Good job. Now leave it to us.'

The fireman left them and raced back to the crew. A quick conversation went on. Moments later a group of firemen began entering the two-storey house. Others sprayed the adjoining buildings with water. They could catch fire too, as they were so close, and the fire could easily spread. The onlookers murmured amongst themselves as a ladder was put to the first-floor window and the broken glass smashed out. Cara was trembling, and Rick put his arms around her.

'Hey, hey … it's okay. I've got you, we're safe.' He hugged her close. 'Lucky that I was passing.'

They'd met at Seasons Nightclub a little over a week ago. Since then they'd met each other at some time each day. Even just for a quick coffee.

The firemen swarmed over the building. There were loud bangs and crackles. Mrs M was escorted out and sat on the kerb sobbing quietly, head in her hands, as the fire bit into the house. One of her neighbours came across to comfort her. The two-way radio crackled into life as a fireman said, 'We're going to need an ambulance.'

A police car arrived, its two-tone klaxon blaring, and screamed to a stop as two officers jumped out. They nodded to the fire crew and moved the small crowd of onlookers back. Cara drew in some shaky breaths, and started hacking again. Rick rocked her gently. As his arms tightened around her, she leaned back against him, drawing strength from his warmth.

'How did you find me?' Cara swivelled to look at Rick, he'd never been inside the house.

'When I dropped you off I used to wait to see you go safely inside and your light to go on.'

'Lucky for me that you did,' she pulled closer to him, shivering. She was in her nightclothes, with a blanket wrapped around her.

An ambulance arrived all flashing lights and sirens and screeched to a halt. The crew raced out and unloaded a stretcher. Dark shapes moved as the flames crackled and the hoses hissed water causing torrents of steam to rise from the house. Someone was howling with pain. A medic bent over a shadowy figure and moments later, the screaming stopped.

'Was that Tom?' Cara said with a catch in her voice, thinking it could so easily have been her.

'Want me to check?' Rick tilted his head to look at her as she nodded, tears trickling down her face. She put her head in her hands and sobbed. He cradled her gently in his arms and rocked her. 'Ssh, Ssh … I've got you.'

'I'm not usually such a wimp,' her voice wobbled a bit as she continued. 'It's just everything I have was in that flat. I haven't even got any clothes!'

Rick took his jacket off, draped it around her shoulders and pulled it tightly around her. Cara trembled as he drew her close. Cara clung to Rick, her rescuer.

'I'll ask about Tom and see if we can leave.' Rick gently prised her fingers from his arm, commenting on how pale she looked. A few moments later he returned.

'They've stabilised Tom–he'll be treated in hospital. If they know where you are, we can go. Have you a girlfriend you can stay with?'

Cara shook her head. 'No,' her lip trembled. 'Suze moved away and Jackie lives out of town.'

'Then, do you want to come home with me?' Rick said.

Cara looked at him. He'd kicked down a front door to rescue her. She heard the weariness in his voice, and his concern for her. They'd only known each other a week or so, but she felt a sense of connection with him.

She nodded. 'Okay.'

The rest of the night passed in a blur as they drove in silence to his place. The only sound was the music and chatter of the radio. Cara was too exhausted to pay much attention. 'December 10th–almost

Christmas,' said the cheerful DJ before playing the latest Christmas song.

Once at Rick's place, he made her a mug of tea with extra sugar in it for shock. She was almost asleep drinking it. Rick carried her to his bed saying, 'Try and get some sleep. Things will look better in the morning. Give me, a yell if you need anything.' He gently closed the door and went downstairs.

Pale winter sunlight streamed through the window waking Cara. She blinked trying to clear her head. Slowly the confused events of the last evening filtered back in her mind. She shivered, realising how lucky she was that Rick had been passing and rescued her. Downstairs a radio was playing, Cara drew in a few panicky breaths as she remembered the events of last night.

Deliberately, she slowed her breathing and concentrated on listening to the radio chatter. One of her favourite songs was on and she hummed along. The song ended and she heard, 'Here is the local News and Weather for today December 10th.'

The tenth! Ten was important—but why?

Jackie suggested they have their fortunes told. 'Come on Cara. Madam Estella is the real deal, gypsy ancestor and all. It'll be fun.' Jackie wheedled and somehow Cara had agreed.

Madame Estella owned a dimly lit shop filled with lots of New Age items: crystals, candles, incense, books. The deep purple walls were hung with Macramé wall hangings, Egyptian inspired jewellery and Indian anklets and necklaces of silver bells. An oil burner wafted incense. Pan pipes played, faint but persistent.

Jackie insisted that she had her fortune told first. Cara browsed through the rack of crushed velvet embroidered kaftans. The vibrant orange one washed her out. The purple one suited her better with her fair skin and blonde hair. She tried on a couple of floppy, felt hats, feeling a bit out of sorts and nervous. The assistant was wafting a spray of Patchouli around and humming vaguely to herself.

Jackie came out of the beaded curtained cubicle smiling and gestured for Cara to go through. To her surprise Madam Estella was an ordinary looking middle-aged woman with permed grey hair. She wore a twin set and pearls with a tweed skirt and sensible shoes. She could have been a typist or a school teacher. The fortune teller gestured for Cara to sit and watch as she shuffled the Tarot cards. When she'd finished shuffling the cards she gazed at Cara through her turquoise cat's eye glasses.

'I have to get rid of the old energy,' she explained before handing them to Cara and inviting her to shuffle them too. 'Pick ten cards and hand then to me,' she instructed.

Cara did so, and Madam Estella set out the cards into a Celtic Cross design. When the cards were placed Madam Estella turned them over one-by-one.

'Ahh, very interesting.' This was followed by a long pause as she scrutinised the cards. 'An unusual spread.'

'What do they say?'

One red tipped fingernail pointed to the *Knight of Wands* among the cards. Cara stared, fascinated. She'd never seen such cards before.

'There's a man.' The fortune teller began, tapping the card with her nail.

Cara snorted. 'And is he a double dealing, cheating low life, like most of them?' Her recent marriage breakup still smarted, she had been so trusting and so deceived.

The fortune teller pointed to the *Ten of Cups*. 'A strong and harmonious relationship,' she said. Next, she pointed to *The Fool*. 'Crazy wild adventures, but with a good man, with dark hair and dark eyes.' She paused adding, 'and he'll come for you in a ten.'

'Ten minutes, ten weeks, ten years?' Cara didn't believe a word of it.

'The cards don't say, but he's going to be important to you. You'll go on a life journey together.' Madam Estella said with a confident smile as she gathered the cards together and put them back into the pack.

'There are good men, you know,' she said quietly, giving Cara a searching look. Cara nodded, her dad had been a good man. Two years since the car crash and she still missed her parents. They'd been a happily married couple. Yes, there were good men.

A song blared out from the radio as Cara realised that she was daydreaming. *Rick had come for her.* He'd rescued her from the fire. Today was the tenth. That was either a weird coincidence or—was he the one? She was still wondering when he knocked on the door.

'Breakfast in a few minutes, and I've left you some clothes outside the door.' She heard his footsteps retreat and went to investigate. He'd left a pair of jeans, a jumper and a pair of trainers. Passing the dressing table, she glanced in the mirror–her face was grimy, her blonde hair smoke stained. She'd never looked worse. Cara found the bathroom, quickly washed her face, squeezed some toothpaste onto her finger and ran it around her teeth. Taking a few calming breaths, she ran her fingers through her hair. It was the best she could do. Dressed in the tight jeans, and Rick's too large sweater and trainers, she went down stairs.

'They told me you can't return to your flat, it's too damaged,' Rick said. 'I've taken the day off to help you.'

Luckily, she had some money from her parents as everything she owned was either smoke or water damaged. Cara went into the store where she worked to let personnel know what had happened. She bought jeans and some tops, and a navy skirt and a couple of white blouses for work.

When she returned to work next day she was overcome by the support of management and staff. Her department manager said, 'We're glad to have you back safe and sound. If you need to take time off we'll understand.'

It brought a lump to her throat as she said huskily, 'Thanks.'

There was a report of the fire in the local paper and everyone was talking about it. Jackie was curious. 'So he rescued you? Your mystery man?'

Cara nodded.

'So, do you think he's the one?'

Cara glanced at her workmate, grinning. 'He must be. Remember "it's in the cards!"' She made air quotes with her fingers. Now, she was asking herself the same question–could he be the one?

She stayed on at Rick's place. They were so in tune with one another, almost finishing each other's sentences. Nights out were great, but so were nights in sitting together, drinking coffee and talking. One evening as they snuggled together kissing, Cara's breath caught shallowly in her throat as Rick deepened the kiss.

She returned he kiss whispering, 'Come to bed.'

In the bedroom he cradled her in his arms and looked deep into her eyes. 'You're sure?'

She kissed him hungrily.

'Yes, I want you to make love with me.'

Cara wound her arms around his neck and pressed her body against his. She felt him respond to her as he slid his hand up to unhook her bra. She tugged at his belt to rid him of his jeans. They undressed hurriedly. He was a playful, yet demanding lover and Cara responded instinctively, allowing her body to flow under his hands. He knew when to tease her and when to allow her to let go. She moaned as she climaxed, shaken at how her body had responded to him. Cara twisted her hands through his hair and pulled him down for a deeper kiss. She'd reached heights she'd only ever dreamt of. Then she moved her hips until she heard his hoarse groan of contentment as he climaxed. Afterwards, they lay together, fingers touching.

'Wow,' Rick said giving her a loving look and dropping a kiss on her nose.

She giggled. 'Wow yourself.'

She snuggled closer feeling thoroughly loved.

A bit later she kissed his shoulder saying, 'So tell me your hopes and dreams.'

'I've always wanted to go to Australia,' Rick said. 'I almost did when I was sixteen, but my mum wouldn't sign the papers.'

'I did too,' Cara smiled. 'We had a workbook in primary school all about Australia. My dad said he'd wanted to go, but my mum wouldn't. He'd sometimes get a far-off look in his eye and say, "one day, perhaps you'll go, pet."'

They fell asleep in each other's arms still talking about what seemed like an impossible dream. Australia–the lucky country.

That winter the rain was endless, unrelenting day after day. As if that wasn't depressing enough, Rick's soon-to-be-ex-wife and her boyfriend mounted a harassment campaign against them. Following Rick about, banging loudly on the front door in the middle of the night, and repeatedly parking their car outside the house and blocking the driveway. It was even more baffling as she had taken off with his supposed "best friend" and she hadn't given him any grief until Cara moved in permanently. It took the freedom out of their relationship always having to be on guard.

After a day of extra harassment, they sat opposite looking each other in the eye as they sipped a coffee and discussed what to do next.

'We'll have to move once the house is sold,' Rick said. 'And that last couple seemed really keen.'

'And you'll have to split the proceeds with your ex fifty-fifty?'

'Yes.'

Cara nodded, a plan forming in her mind. 'How about moving right out of town and leaving all our troubles behind?' She grinned teasingly at him.

'What's on your mind?'

'We could just move towns,' she said adding, 'but let's make it an adventure! What if we moved countries?'

He looked puzzled until a slow smile spread across his face. 'Australia?'

Cara nodded vigorously. 'Yes, Australia, you've always wanted to go, I've always wanted to go—so let's go!'

'It can't be that easy,' Rick said doubtfully. 'There's tons of paperwork.' He remembered the screed of papers from when he was sixteen.

'Well, I'm great at paperwork!' Cara said. 'Let's find out more.'

A week or so later the house sale was finalised, and they were in Manchester. Standing in the foyer of Australia House and looking at the colourful posters showing sun-drenched beaches with smiling tanned Aussies, Cara nudged Rick, 'That could be us!'

The offices were busy, as various officials spoke to people at the counters. They gave their names to the receptionist and waited to be called. Eventually, a blonde girl called Robyn took them through the steps needed for migration. She discussed their work and experience at length and then shook her head.

'I'm sorry, you wouldn't qualify for assisted migration, you don't meet the criteria.'

Cara gasped loudly and bit her lip. Rick squeezed her hand. Cara's voice quivered as she said, 'Thank you for explaining it to us and thank you for your time.'

She turned away quickly so that Robyn couldn't see the tears of disappointment in her eyes and brushed them away with the back of her hand. They were half way across the office when they realised that Robyn had come out from behind the desk and followed them.

'Wait,' she said quietly. 'There could be another way.'

She opened a door into a smaller office with more bright posters on the wall as well as a table and chairs, and motioned for them to sit down. They sat opposite her holding hands and almost not daring to breathe as she handed a leaflet to them. It was headed *Unassisted Migration to Australia.*

'You are British citizens?' Robyn asked.

They nodded, 'Yes.'

'Well there is another option, you can just pay your own way and go.'

'What—just turn up?' Rick said hardly daring to believe it.

'That's right. But you'd need to act quickly, as there is a cut-off date.'

Cara looked up from the leaflet she'd been scanning. 'It finishes in December!'

'It's already June, that doesn't give us long,' Rick said.

Cara squeezed his hand. 'We could do it though.' She smiled across at Robyn. 'Thank you, thank you, I can't tell you how much this means to me, to us.'

'Just doing my job,' said Robyn smiling at their enthusiasm. Rick shook hands with her and Cara hugged her.

'I hope you make it!' said Robyn.

'We will,' Cara said. 'All thanks to you.'

'Send me a postcard!' Robyn grinned as she ushered them out of the office.

They talked excitedly on the drive back. 'There's so much to organise,' Cara said. 'How much the fares will cost, where we'll go— Sydney or Melbourne, and what to take with us.'

'We'd better keep it quiet,' Rick said. 'We don't need my ex trying to stop us!'

Operation Oz, as Cara called it, was underway. Cara found out all she could about Australia through one of the big Australian banks as they weren't able to go through the government's migrant services.

Finally, they settled on moving to Perth in Western Australia. It wasn't as big as the other capital cities, and coming from a small town they thought they'd feel more at home there.

'We can always go to Sydney or Melbourne later, once we find our feet.' Cara said.

The house sale went through, and it was time to pack for Australia. Suddenly, the move felt real. What would they need for the rest of their lives? Cara sifted somberly through her family photos, knowing she couldn't take them all. Furniture, clothes, ornaments, books all had to be sorted and decided on. Her old teddy bear, Mr. Ted, had to travel in her suitcase. They sold the large furniture and moved into a furnished rental flat. Most of their things were packed and sent by sea to Australia.

One day Rick said, 'We'd better get married. It will make it easier.'

It wasn't the romantic proposal Cara had dreamed of, but it made sense. If it wasn't to be the wedding of her dreams, she was sure Rick was the man of her dreams.

Theirs was a quiet wedding at the Town Hall Registry Office. Cara wore smart bell-bottomed trousers, a pretty voile blouse and a baker boy cap. Rick wore purple flares, a purple and white striped shirt, an Egyptian love symbol on a chain and pink tinted glasses.

'You look prettier than I do,' Cara teased.

He kissed the tip of her nose. 'Never!'

Cara wished her parents could have been there, but in the interests of secrecy Rick hadn't invited anyone. The wedding felt a bit bleak. Jackie, who lived outside the town, and her dad were their witnesses. Cara felt Rick's hand tremble as he put the ring on her finger, but he squeezed her hand and smiled at her and said 'I do' in a firm voice. They went out for a meal afterwards, their only celebration as they went back to work the next day.

'We'll have a proper honeymoon when we get to Australia,' Rick promised.

Cara travelled to Liverpool to be sure that no-one could learn their plans when she booked their tickets. She found a scheme called Ship/Jet. A flight to Singapore and then a cruise to Perth. Those ten days at sea would be their belated honeymoon. The weeks passed quickly, the days getting greyer and colder. In the chilly early mornings and evenings, they sat with hands cradled around steaming mugs of coffee, listening to the honking geese migrating, knowing that soon they would be joining them.

Gatwick airport was filled with excited chatter as people surged around finding the correct gateways for their flights. The public-address system boomed out with instructions and information. Cara clutched Rick's arm. Her eyes sparkled with excitement as she glanced around her at the throng of people.

'This is it! We're finally on our way.'

They watched wide-eyed as the flight crews walked through the airport nonchalantly trailing their wheeled suitcases. The airline they were travelling with had hostesses wearing smart Black Watch tartan uniforms.

Delay followed delay–their early morning flight was announced, then the departure time changed. All around them people slumped or muttered or argued as tempers flared. Children whined, and babies cried. It was about five in the afternoon when the worn-out passengers could board the plane. The delay had been explained as a faulty part that needed replacing. Most people were too exhausted to care, the day in the airport having taken its toll on them. The flight crew buzzed about, serving meals and calming tempers as the plane's engines hummed. Many people slept. Hours passed.

A waft of smoke drifted through the cabin, Rick glanced out of the window and squeezed Cara's hand. He looked alarmed. Stewardesses edgily paced the aisles, clearing them of anything in the walkway.

'Fold your tray tables up now. Please stow your bags in the lockers.'

Stewards began to open the lockers and stuff bags into them, making sure that the walkways were clear.

The captains voice came over the PA system as the No Smoking sign went on.

'We will be landing in Singapore shortly. Please fasten your seat belts and remain seated.'

Rick checked where the nearest exit was, although he hadn't flown before he had a distinct sense that something was wrong. He held Cara's hand sensing her tenseness. The plane made an approach to the runway and then at the last moment it climbed steeply. Babies swinging in their net hammocks began to cry. A collective groan went up from the passengers. The flight crew were buckled into their seats, white faced and tense.

A screech of engines as the plane made another approach to the runway, the smell of smoke getting stronger as the plane made its descent. Cara glanced past Rick out of the window and saw a row of fire engines and a couple of ambulances lining the runway. She sat white-faced and sweating, clutching his hand as she re-experienced the fire at her flat. Surely, she hadn't escaped that to be engulfed in flames now? A picture of Tom charred and screaming came back and she shuddered. Rick had rescued her then and he was with her now. They'd be alright. Her nails dug into Rick's palm but he scarcely noticed. He was holding his breath and willing the plane to land.

The aircraft skidded across the runway, almost collided with a fire engine and juddered to a halt. A billow of smoke surrounded the plane and the acrid smell of burning intensified.

'Quickly, quickly.' The cabin crew pushed the passengers out of the plane. A fleet of transfer buses drew up to take them away from the aircraft. They were thrust into the buses which raced away. Cara glanced back, one of the plane's engines was cascading red and orange sparks. She shivered, watching as a fire engine pulled closer.

Amongst the chaos in the Arrivals Hall, Rick's arms encircled Cara and held her to him. 'We're safe,' he whispered as he smoothed her hair and kissed her forehead. She clutched his hand; their adventure had nearly been over before it began.

Eventually, a tour company representative assembled the Ship/Jet passengers and escorted them to buses to take them to their ship. The air-conditioned bus was a relief after sweltering in their heavy clothes. Leaving the UK in winter, they hadn't expected it would be steaming hot on the other side of the world. They'd a lot to learn.

Singapore's traffic congestion was unbelievable. Cars, buses, trucks all assumed they had the right of way. Rick gestured to an open back truck, with suitcases piled haphazardly in it.

'There's our luggage.'

Some cases looked about to tip off the truck while others had damaged corners or were half open. Cara could only hope that their cases were safe. A heavy shower of tropical rain hit the ground and rose again as steam, while the traffic somehow wound its way onward.

The ship had seen better days but they were happy to reach it. Officials checked everyone's paperwork and Rick and Cara gazed about them listening to the mix of excited chatter of young Aussies returning home and excited Brits at the start of an adventure.

'I wonder if anyone else is chancing their luck and just arriving in Australia, hoping to stay?' Cara whispered to Rick. He gave her hand a reassuring squeeze.

Finally, they could board the ship and find their cabin. It was a tiny, windowless space deep in the bowels of the ship, but it was all they could afford. At that moment it was a relief to have a bunk to collapse on.

Their days at sea took on a pattern: an early breakfast, followed by a stroll around the deck before lunch then another stroll. Afternoon tea served on deck and then it was time to get changed for dinner. As they sailed southward the sea became rougher, the ship plunged up and down with the waves. Fewer and fewer people were present at their shared table. Many stayed in their cabins, too seasick to care about meals.

Instead of the ship feeling crowded, there was space. Cara and Rick could stroll along the deck easily. They'd formed the habit of taking an after-dinner stroll, it was good to be in the fresh air and they were on a mission. They were stargazing–hoping to spot the Southern Cross, the same star constellation depicted on the Australian flag.

'Once we see that, we'll know we are on the other side of the world!' Rick had his arm around Cara's shoulders and she leaned into him as they gazed skywards. Her uptilted face was pale in the moonlight. Stars twinkled above them while music drifted out from the disco. They leant over the rail, felt the soft sea breeze in their faces and talked about their future in Australia.

Faintly, Cara could hear the song *Will you still love me tomorrow?* She looked at Rick–would he still love her tomorrow? He must have sensed something and bent to kiss her muttering, 'tomorrow and all our tomorrows.'

She relaxed into the kiss, enjoying the feel of his lips on hers. When the kiss ended they, both looked skywards and there it was, the large star with the smaller ones that formed the Southern Cross.

'It's a sign,' Cara said. 'We're going to be ridiculously happy here.'

The days and nights passed swiftly and soon they were being guided into the port of Fremantle by the pilot boat. The passengers crowded on deck, some laughing and chattering about where they'd go and what they'd do. Others silently scanned the horizon, perhaps wondering what lay ahead.

The sky was a perfect, cloudless blue as Immigration officers boarded the ship to check the passengers before they disembarked. The skyline of Fremantle looked so much like the port of Liverpool that Cara felt her stomach flip. She bit her lip nervously and squeezed Rick's hand. This was it!

The ship made slow progress gliding into its berth and docking. The gangplanks were let down and finally they set foot on Australian soil. Rick pointed to a large sign which said 'Welcome to Fremantle' as they shuffled along the sprawling customs line.

Eventually, they were at the front of the line, the officer checked and marked their suitcases with a cross.

'On holiday?' He grinned at them. 'How long are youse stayin?'

Cara gulped nervously as Rick said, 'Permanently.'

There was a long moment of silence. Rick clutched Cara's hand as she scuffed her feet tensely. The official grinned and stamped the passport.

'Welcome to Australia, then.' He shook Rick's hand and winked at Cara. 'Have a nice life!'

She could have kissed him. Instead she let out a huge breath. 'Thank you.'

They moved away, and Rick opened the passport to let Cara see the round official stamp which said Department of Immigration Fremantle Permitted on November 10th to enter Australia. They'd made it. She thought her dad would have been smiling approvingly. Hand-in-hand Cara and Rick walked out into the sunshine to begin an exciting new chapter of their lives. Their Australian story played out under the Southern Cross.

Years later they wondered at their daring, as they'd no home, no jobs, knew no-one and had no back up plan. Yet, it had worked out for them.

They'd stayed in a motel for a few days. Within two days they'd found a flat, and by the end of the week they both had jobs. A year or so later they built their first home. Something they'd have been hard pushed to ever achieve in England. Australia had been good to them. Indeed, it was their lucky country.

They sat on the deck of their home, star gazing and reminiscing.

'We've made a good life here,' Rick said, as he lifted his champagne glass and toasted Cara. 'Thanks to you my darling.'

She shrugged his compliment away. 'Nothing to do with me,' she said airily. 'It was in the cards! You were my destiny, just like coming here was.'

Rick shook his head, he didn't believe in Tarot cards and all that stuff, but hey, they were happy together. It was all anyone could ask.

Flowers from the Heart

P.L. HARRIS

Jade squinted at the bright light as she dragged her weary body to a sitting position in the bed. Alex's decision to put work above their anniversary weighed heavy on her heart. He'd practically sold his soul to his boss. When would it stop? When would he realise she was a flesh-and-blood woman just wanting her husband back? Her chest tightened, the growing distance between them a constant barrier in their marriage.

'Ouch,' she mumbled, twisting, working the sleepless kinks out of her body. As she wiped the crusty sleep from the corner of her eye, her nose was accosted by the honey-sweet scent of flowers.

Her breath caught in her throat. Flowers covered their bedroom. Potted honeysuckles. *Her favourite.* Jade's eyes widened. The warm, rich, golden colour of the honeysuckles glistened under the rays of sunlight streaming through the plantation shutters.

What   the   ...

Her gaze scanned the room. Twelve beautiful, potted bunches of honeysuckles. *Oh my God.* Her heart pounded inside her ribcage like a full-on stampede.

Tears welled in her eyes as Alex walked through the door, shirtless. With his chiselled body, he was a fine specimen of the perfect man. *Her* perfect man. His smile touched her deep in her soul.

'About time you got up, sleepyhead,' he said with a sexy smile.

Alex's eyes shone with love, deep unconditional love. Her skin tingled as he brushed a stray hair from her cheek with his hand. Sitting beside her, his leg brushed hers and a flutter shot through her body just as it had the first time they'd held hands. Her heart felt ready to burst like a bubble. *How could I have doubted his love?*

'You thought I forgot our anniversary, didn't you?' Alex pried, an eyebrow raised in question.

She nodded. Jade's own foolishness overwhelmed her.

He pointed to the scattered flowers. 'Honeysuckles. I know they happen to be your favourite. Twelve pots, one for each year we've been married. I know you love the honeysuckle because it reminds you of happy memories of your childhood home, but have you ever looked into the meaning?'

Her mind blanked. 'Actually, no. I've never bothered to look.'

Alex held her hands in his, running his thumb softly over her knuckles. 'It has an interesting meaning. It means bonds of love.'

He smiled and her heart melted all over again.

'Fitting, don't you think, for our twelfth anniversary? A reminder that we'll be bonded together, for all eternity, by love.'

Shame filled every part of her body. Shame that she could have allowed herself to succumb to her false doubts. She hiccupped, and tears flowed freely down her soft cheeks.

'Hey, enough of that. This is a happy day remember?' He reached for a tissue.

'I'm just an old romantic at heart,' she said between sniffs. 'I thought you'd forgotten.'

'Never, but thanks to work, I'm not able to be here tomorrow for our real anniversary,' he whispered, brushing a lone tear from her moist cheek with his thumb. 'But there's no way I could leave without showing you how much I love you.' He tugged her forward, bent his head and delicately pressed his lips to hers.

Butterflies ran rampant in her stomach. His kiss ricocheted through her body, all the way to her big toes.

Alex held her hand in his, the warmth of his skin blended into hers. 'I'm sorry I haven't been around much lately. I want you to know that things are going to change around here,' he said. A sincere smile spread across his face. 'I've been working hard these past few months to secure this promotion. After this trip, you and I are going to reap the rewards of my hard work.'

She no longer feared his rejection. She basked in his devotion.

'I had no idea what to give you for our twelfth anniversary.' Alex reached under the pillow and withdrew a small white box. 'I wanted to make it special.'

Jade raised an eyebrow, stunned by his admission. Her heart swam with love for this man.

Her trembling fingers slowly undid the green bow.

'This present signifies our old life, blending with our new life together.' His eyes glowed with love.

She wiped her damp cheeks with the back of her palm, her focus blurred through the tears.

'Hey,' Alex whispered. 'Enough of the tears, unless they are happy ones.'

She laughed a hearty laugh. Relief soared through her body. 'They are.'

She lifted the lid and her breath caught in her throat. Two beautiful, matching rose gold rings, each with their own diamond, were laid delicately next to each other in the box.

'Oh my God,' she gasped, her hand darting to her chest. 'Alex, they're the most beautiful rings I've ever seen.'

His smile beamed with happiness. He eased one on his right ring finger and one on hers. The metal warmed against her skin. Jade held her hand up, admiring the precious gem. The blazing sunlight bouncing off the diamonds shot coloured rays around the room.

She shook her head, unable to put her voice into words.

'Diamonds are forever, or so they tell me, and you're mine, Jade ... forever,' he paused, engulfing her trembling hands in his. 'Now every time you look at the ring, you'll remember that you will always have my heart and my love.'

'Oh, Alex,' she threw her arms around his neck, the trickle of tears down her cheeks was an emotional sign of her love for this man. 'I love you so much.'

They fell back on the bed laughing, their bodies tangled together.

A sharp crack of thunder shattered Jade's happy memory. She curled her legs up on the couch and pulled the woollen rug tighter around her shoulders. *Miserable day. Matches my miserable life,* she thought.

It had been a year since she'd lost Alex and she was still as numb today as the day the police had broken the news of his death, destroying her reason for living. She had hoped the sleeping pill she'd taken last night would have helped her sleep through the day, but here she was, at 10 am, wide awake.

Wednesday, July 1st. Her thirteenth wedding anniversary.

The same day, a year ago, when her life had turned to shit. The day her world irrevocably changed forever.

The rain began to pelt the Colorbond roof. Typical Australian winter. Her heart was as icy as the frigid air outside. Cold and broken.

Alex. His name crawled into her clouded mind, conjuring memories of her laughing, funny, beautiful husband. Just as quickly as they came, they shrivelled into black nothingness as if they were never real.

Alex was gone.

Dead … never to come home again.

The sudden shrill of the doorbell pierced her skull like an ice pick. Burying her head in the blanket, she muttered, 'Go away.' She'd already fielded calls from her mother and aunt, she wouldn't make it through the day if she had to see anyone. Eyes closed, she pressed her hands to her temples wishing she could rewind time.

The doorbell shouted again, this time with a more persistent ring. Her blood began to boil and she threw the blanket off storming towards the door. 'For God's sake, don't people know when to fuck off?'

Furious at the interruption, Jade grabbed the cool metal handle and flung the door open. 'What?' she yelled.

She froze in the doorway, the air instantly evaporating from her lungs. Her chest burned.

'Excuse me, lady,' the boy said. 'Delivery for Mrs Walder.' He thrust the bouquet in Jade's direction.

No, it can't be. It's not possible. Alex?

'Who are those flowers from?' Her eyes glued to the boy standing on her porch with a bouquet of golden honeysuckles.

'I don't know, lady.'

'Take them away,' she blurted. The exquisite flowers ripped her heart out, deadening it all over again. 'I don't want them.'

What kind of twisted joke was this?

All the blood left her face as she watched him place them on the porch. 'I'll put them here, just in case you decide later you want them.'

Before she could say anything, he turned and hightailed it back to his car.

Want them? She felt the blood drain from her face. Refusing to look at them a moment longer, she turned and began to retreat inside when her eye caught the edge of a card. She glared at the crisp, white envelope and her lips thinned. Someone was messing with her head in a big way. Alex was dead.

Rage surged through her veins like bubbling lava. She grabbed the card and gave the bouquet one almighty kick, sending it sprawling across the porch. Her ears rang as the pulverising slam of the door reverberated through her head.

She threw the card on the coffee table and buried herself in her blanket again, ignoring the persistent nagging in the base of her neck. *Open it, open it.*

'Oh for God's sake. All right, you win,' she barked and she snatched up the card. When she withdrew a short hand-written note, she stilled once more. All the blood left her face as she read Alex's words.

Bonded together for all eternity by love. I love you, always. Alex.

She sat stunned, the air draining from her lungs. Jade's eyes kept re-reading his words. Mixed emotions ran through her body. Rage, anger, sadness, longing, disbelief. Was this for real? Who the hell would pull a stunt like this? She couldn't imagine anyone in her family stooping so low.

It was several minutes before her gaze dropped to the name on the bottom. *Flowers from the Heart Florist.* Fuming, she stomped toward her bedroom. 'Well, Flowers from the Heart, I guess you're going to hear from this woman's heart right now.'

Jade stared at the sign above the florist's door, her mouth so dry she could barely swallow. *Nothing says love like flowers.* 'Love sucks.'

She tightened her jacket around her waist, hoping it would warm her cold skin. Jade forced the door open and marched towards the counter. She stopped, the image of a man, almost the size of Arnold

Schwarzenegger in his prime, stood with his back to her. He fiddled with several colourful buckets in the fridge. An image she didn't expect to see.

'Excuse me, can you please tell me who sent these flowers?' she asked as she placed the card on the counter.

He spun and she stared open mouthed. His pink *Peppa Pig* apron was a stark contrast to the tanned, muscular man. He smiled and the warmth that shone in his eyes was a welcomed change.

His brow creased. 'Jade?'

Her belly clenched as he spoke her name. 'Yes.'

'It's Deacon ... Deacon Bailey from primary school.'

Holy crap. It can't be. Last time she'd seen Deacon, he'd been a scrawny little boy with mousy brown hair and freckles. Now, he was this tall, muscular man wearing a girly apron who worked in a florist.

A soft giggle rumbled deep in her belly and she struggled to keep a straight face.

He looked down at his apron and grimaced. 'Oh, damn. I know I must look pretty silly wearing this. My niece, Georgia, gave it to me for my birthday and she was just in, so I thought I'd better do the uncle thing and wear it. Seems I forgot to take it off.'

'Oh, I think it brings out the—' She stopped, inwardly cursing herself for making a joke. Betrayal swamped her heart.

'Deacon, I had no idea you'd moved back to town.'

He shrugged. 'Kinda had to, after Mum fell ill. Joe and Katy have their hands full with young Georgia. I was the unattached one so it seemed like the right thing to do.'

'Sorry to hear about you mum,' Jade said. Bitterness bled into her chest. *At least with multiple sclerosis, when the time comes, you'll get to say goodbye.* Thanks to the car accident, she'd been robbed of her last goodbye to Alex.

'Thanks,' He replied, placing a bucket full of daffodils on the floor. 'Now, what can I do for you?'

Shaking the cobwebs from her head, she pointed to the card. 'I want to know who sent these flowers to me.'

His gaze scrutinized the card. 'My business partner usually takes care of deliveries but I'll check the computer.' His fingers punched away on the keys and then his eyes widened and his cheeks paled.

'What? What is it?'

'Um, it looks like your husband left a standing order for a honeysuckle bouquet delivered on this date every year.'

She gasped, her chest burning. 'Alex,' she whispered and her heart shattered all over again. Tears welled in her eyes. She barely heard his voice, under the heavy wave of sorrow drowning her heart.

'I'm really sorry to hear about his sudden passing,' he said, worry etched in his expression. 'But he has good taste.'

Her eyebrow shot up. 'Excuse me?'

Mortification bled onto his face. 'That came out totally wrong. I meant he has good taste in flowers. Honeysuckles. They mean bonds of love.'

Oh God, please stop. She prayed that she held it together long enough to escape.

'That's one of the reasons I became a florist. I love that every flower has a meaning and can show another person how we feel.'

I don't want to feel, damn it. Frustration coursed through her veins. She snapped. 'Have you ever lost the most important person in your world ... the person that was your reason for living?'

'No, I haven't, and I would never presume to understand what you're going through,' he said, his voice soothing against her sharp outburst. 'But what I do *know* is that you can't turn back time and life is too short to waste. I'm reminded of that every time I look at my mum. I've no control over this disease while it eats away at her. All I can do is make her comfortable and spend as much time with her to show her how much I love her.'

The sadness in his eyes touched her heart. It was as if he knew a little of what was to come.

'She has no control over the rest of her life, but you and I do. Back in Year 7, do you remember what you said when I asked you why your mum named you Jade?' he asked.

A smile worked its way across her face and she nodded. 'Yes. It comes from the Spanish word that means 'jewel' and wards off bad spirits, but mostly it was led to believe that if you put jade near a baby's stomach it would cure colic, so she did. My mum still believes to this day that's what cured me and why I'm still alive. So, she re-named me after the miracle gemstone.' A lone tear slid down her cheek.

Deacon sighed. 'Life *is* a miracle to be celebrated. What do you say I flip the sign on the door to Closed and make you a coffee? Most people say my coffee is the best this side of the Swan River.'

His gentle smile beckoned her to stay. She was already here so what difference did it make if she stayed for coffee or not? 'Sure, black no sugar.'

They sat in silence. Jade sipping her coffee as the mug warmed her cold hands.

'Tell me about Alex,' Deacon said as he refilled his mug.

Jade felt light fill her chest and once she started talking it was like a free-flowing river releasing all the pent-up heartache she'd stored over the past year. 'I'm sorry for dumping this on you,' she said realising how much time had passed. 'I should go so you can get back to work.'

He shook his head. 'It's okay. He sounds like a lovely guy, wish I had met him.'

'I wish you'd met him too.' Jade could feel her facade slowly crumbling.

'At least you have those memories and you should celebrate them. He wouldn't want you to be unhappy. Take it from someone who knows. Life is too short to waste.'

Happy? I was the happiest when I was with Alex.

'Alex obviously loved you very much. These flowers he sends you prove that even in death, your love is eternal and never forgotten. You and Alex will always have a special love that transcends time. No-one can ever take that away, unless you let them, but he would never want you to spend the rest of your life mourning him. No-one would wish that upon anyone, I know my mother wouldn't want me to waste the rest of my life mourning her.'

Tears stung her eyelids and she swallowed hard, as if her throat was knotted and she could barely breathe around it. She'd been dead inside for so long, but Deacon's words were slowly melting her frozen heart. Even through his tough-guy exterior, she sensed he had a heart of gold.

He bent and picked up a bunch of daffodils from the bucket. 'Do you know what the daffodil means?' he asked as his strong hands fiddled with the flower head.

She shook her head and fiddled with the silver rings on her right hand. She'd worn Alex's ring with hers since the accident, entwining their love together.

Alex will always be with me.

'Chivalry, rebirth, and new beginnings.' He pulled a lone flower from the bunch and held it out towards Jade. 'Life is all about new beginnings, Jade, and if you'll let me, I'd like to be that friend that helps you find your sparkle again. The one you used to have in middle school.'

The tears she tried hard to suppress ran freely down her cheeks in endless streaks. She smiled and took the daffodil from his hand.

She'd always love Alex, but maybe it was time to let a little light back into her heart.

The Colour of Fear

PRIYA CHIDAMBARANATHAN

It was a sunny Sydney morning and Akila sat in her apartment watching dust motes drift around the room. She was weary and home sick, tired beyond words or understanding. Her two-year-old son, Adi, raced his red Hot Wheels car up and down and round and round their glass-topped coffee table in an endless loop. And she watched him listlessly.

It had been a few weeks since she moved to Australia from India. And in this quiet country where no horns honked, and no neighbourhood vendors called out their wares, she longed most of all for noise; for someone to make sense of the voices screaming in her head. She was tired of the quiet.

Into the sharp stillness of her yearning, came a scream. One that tore through the silence and scattered the dust motes.

Akila froze and looked towards the door, where the sound had come from. Silence settled again like a gentle blanket.

She waited a moment, listening and waiting. And then heard running feet, and a voice cry out, 'Help! Help! Police!'

In a split second, Akila decided to answer the call. She turned on the TV and, leaving Adi in the house, locked the door and flew downstairs. At the foot of the stairs stood Suganthi, her Sri Lankan neighbour. A slender, graceful woman, she held the stair railings with one hand and a toddler with the other. There was no one else on the dark landing. The door to the other house remained firmly closed.

Akila hardly knew her beyond exchanging brief hellos and smiles when they crossed each other in the corridor.

'*Enna aachu?*' she asked hesitantly in Tamil, the language that helped bridge a divide confounding their respective countries for centuries. *What happened?*

'*Veetulle thirudan,*' replied Suganthi, her voice trembling with anxiety and fear. A thief in the house.

Akila froze, wondering what to do. It was obvious she was expected to do something. But memory and fear held her in an immovable grip. A thousand possibilities, the flash of knives and the stench of blood threatened to overcome her. She forced herself back to reality. She was here in a gloomy passage looking into the terrified eyes of a woman she barely knew. Taking a deep breath, she prepared to face her demons. But first she needed to understand the situation.

She asked Suganthi, 'Who? How many?' noticing her own voice trembling.

Before she could go on, the door opposite her opened and a frowning male head looked out. He was one of a group of young men occupying Apartment 1B, whom she hardly knew. But now she was happy to not have to face the demons alone.

'Hi!' she called out as he looked enquiringly at them. 'This lady says that there is a thief in her house. Can you help us please?'

He looked very reluctant to help them out, even more so at the possibility of encountering thieves. 'Are they still inside? How many are there? We should call the police.'

Akila breathed again. Of course, the police should have been her first thought.

'There were two men standing inside the bedroom when I went in. But I think they went out of the window as soon as I screamed. I just took my son and ran,' said Suganthi.

'Okay. So most probably they went out ... that's good. We don't need to worry they will come out here. Let's wait till the police come.' He must have realised that he would be the one making the call and invited them into his house. But Akila declined saying she had to go upstairs and check on her son, while Suganthi said she would wait in the corridor for her husband.

Akila climbed the steps two at a time and arrived, panting, on the first floor. She unlocked the door with trembling hands. Everything was just the same as it had been a few minutes ago. The familiar high-pitched voices on ABC Kids had cast their spell on Adi. He sat completely still on the brown suede sofa, eyes locked on the TV, unaware that she had left or re-entered. For this she was grateful.

She scooped him up, his eyes still fixed on the TV, and switched it off. Ignoring his howls of protest, she carried him out the door. Suganthi and her son sat on the foot of the stairs and the crying stopped when he saw them. The door of 1B was closed.

Akila sat down heavily beside Suganthi and handed her a phone, asking if she wanted to call her husband. Suganthi took it gratefully. Once her call was over, the door to 1B opened.

'Umm ... I have called the police and they said they will come as quickly as they can,' the man announced as he came into the corridor. 'Have you called your husband? Do you want to call him on my phone?' he asked holding out his phone.

'Thank you so much but I have used her phone to call and he said he will come in fifteen minutes.' Suganthi rose from the step indicating to Akila.

'Okay then. No need for thanks. It was my duty to help you. Let me know when the police arrive and I can talk to them. Are you sure you are okay here? You can come and wait inside my house if you want to?' He seemed to have grown more confident and hospitable now that the police were on their way. And there no longer seemed to be any danger of thieves bursting out of the door of 1A.

'No, no, you have been a big help. Thank you. I will let you know once the police come. I just want to wait here for my husband so he doesn't have to search for me,' responded Suganthi.

'Okay, I will just be inside.' He scuttled back inside his flat.

The two boys, who had been eyeing each other carefully, had now progressed to showing off their respective cars and then racing them down the stairs. The sound of their delighted laughter echoed through the building. Their mothers looked on indulgently, happy to have something to smile about.

Suganthi then told Akila what had happened. Her husband had left for work a little later than usual that morning while she had been in the living room with her son. She had gone into a bedroom to put away some clothes when she saw two men, one standing in the room and the other climbing in through the window. That was when she had screamed. She ran into the living room, grabbed her little boy and gone out of the door as fast as she could. The men had been startled too, climbing out of the window as she screamed and left the room.

Suganthi paused a moment as if reliving the horror of the experience. It seemed such a violation and shock that could never be completely forgotten.

'But how did they come in?' Akila wondered.

'I think they opened the window and cut the fly screen,' replied Suganthi.

'But how did they get into the compound? The fence seems quite high.'

'It's not that high. It can be climbed.'

'Thankfully they did not hurt you. You did a good thing when you picked up your son and ran outside.'

'Yes, I am lucky to have escaped.'

Suganthi seemed to have calmed down after telling her story. Akila offered to take them back into her flat for a cup of tea but Suganthi just wanted to wait for her husband to come back. They sat a while in silence, each absorbed in their thoughts, trying to make sense of what had just happened.

Suganthi burst out after a pause. 'You know, we moved here because the war in Sri Lanka had become very bad. There were bombs exploding everywhere, we couldn't travel in a bus or even walk outside. Every day we lived in fear. One of our friend's son was recruited by the Liberation Tigers of Tamil Eelam when he was just fourteen. They knocked on the door one night and took him away. That's when we decided to move. We applied for a Permanent Resident Visa and came here. I thought we would be safe.'

She paused for a moment then continued. 'But after today, I don't know what to believe. I am afraid to go into my own house now.' Her eyes filled with tears.

Akila gave her a hug and patted her shoulder. There was nothing to say. She had come to this country to escape too. But she had slowly realised that you could never be completely safe anywhere. That your fears follow you like bad breath.

Suganthi's husband, Ilango, bounded up the stairs from the underground parking garage. 'Suganthi!' he cried.

She rose up and stepped towards him, a graceful goddess even in this stressful time. Akila watched her, knowing she could never be that graceful in any circumstance. His breathing returned to normal, once he saw her whole and fine. Their son rushed into his father's arms.

The police arrived at the same time. Two uniformed officers came in, eyes squinting to adjust to the dark corridor, guns bristling. They asked everyone to step away from the door and went in carefully. In the hallway, the adults waited in silence while the children played catch.

The policemen came out saying that the house was empty, and nothing seemed to have been disturbed. They started asking the couple about what had happened and ushered them into the house.

Akila took this as a cue for her to leave and climbed up the stairs with Adi who was reluctant to leave his new friend. She went inside, closed the door, and curled up on the sofa with him.

Akila went to Suganthi's flat the next day carrying *Kesari*, an offering made to Gods or guests, to cement deals and relationships. The sweet dish made of semolina, sugar and ghee was Akila's way of offering friendship.

Suganthi was happy to see her and welcomed her in, receiving the sugary dessert with pleasure and exclamations. Akila was shown around the spotless house and the window through which the burglars had entered the previous day. It had now been partly boarded up by Ilango. The real estate agents had been apathetic so Ilango had taken his own precautions. He had left for work after locking everything and entreating Suganthi to be careful.

The boys, who had become best friends in the space of a morning, greeted each other with shrieks of delights, chasing each other round the room.

'How are you doing now?' Akila asked.

'Better now. I couldn't sleep last night. Ilango was not happy to leave me alone today but he couldn't miss his meeting. He wanted me to go to a friend's house. Maybe I will go later.'

'What did the police say?'

'They came and looked around. Checked for fingerprints but didn't find anything. They are not very hopeful.'

'Yeah. A similar thing happened to us in India and the police were the same there. Even though we were hurt quite badly.'

'Oh?'

'I was at my parent's house, Adi was a tiny baby at that time. A masked man tried to come into our house one night, when my father came home. He held a knife to his throat.' Akila was miming a knife with one hand.

'My God!' said Suganthi with a horrified face.

'Yeah! I came out and saw them standing in the doorway. As soon as I saw them I went and grabbed the knife.'

'You tried to grab the knife?' asked Suganthi, her eyebrows raised.

'Yes. I know it's a stupid thing to do. But at that time, I just felt this blind rage. I was so angry at that man. I kept screaming at him and abusing him, trying to grab the knife from his hands. My father was holding it as well and finally, we sort of bent it.'

'Weren't you afraid at all?'

'At that time, it was just instinct. I thought *How dare he come into our house. How could he bring a knife in here?* And only later when I started to think, I felt afraid.'

A female voice rang out suddenly singing *Om Shakti Om Shakti,* a popular song praising Goddess Shakti. It was Suganthi's phone and as she answered it, went into a bedroom, still speaking.

Akila looked around the lounge room which was the exact same shape as hers but could not look more different. While hers had the sparse emptiness of necessity; here there was richness. Heavy wooden furniture, a TV console and a dining table, set off against two dark blue couches and art everywhere—on the wall and on most surfaces. The boys sat on the floor with toys strewn around them.

Akila marvelled at the house and wondered how Suganthi could keep it this way with an active toddler around. She could barely manage to cook and keep up with other chores.

On one wall was a pen and ink drawing of a reclining Ganesha. It was unusual and gave her a jolt because she had last seen one like that in her parents' home. Blood-spattered and broken. It had shattered when their front door had crashed down, and the crash jolted everything in the room. It had lain on the floor, among the wreckage. She wondered who that intruder was and why he had come. Two years after the incident, there were still no answers to all her questions.

She had shouted at him, abused him, asked him all those questions, all the while she tried to pluck the knife from his hands. But he hadn't said a word. Hadn't let go of the knife. Those black, glittering eyes still stayed with her, sometimes appearing in her nightmares.

But she and her father had managed to bend it backwards until it clattered to the floor, useless. Her mother had thrown a plastic chair at the intruder, bringing him to the floor. She had called to her mother. 'Ma bring a rope. And call the police.'

As she tried to push the door shut she felt pressure on the other side. Terrified, she had thrown herself against it and driven the bolt home.

But the person on the outside had not given in that easily. The door shook as he shoved harder and harder. The bolt slowly started to loosen and the door jolted. No-one inside the house had moved. Even the man on the floor.

With one last heave, the heavy teak door had crashed to the floor, ripped from its hinges. That was when the Ganesha had slowly slid to the floor. And glass splinters glittered.

Another masked man had stood in the doorway, a dark silhouette framed in the yellow light, his double-edged knife was pointed straight at them and glinted in the light. Akila wondered what he would do. She felt her muscles tense.

He hesitated for a moment, looking around and then called his companion, '*Vaa da, polaam. Podhum.*' *Come let's go, enough of this.* Hearing this, the boy on the floor had risen up, and stepping over the Ganesha to get to the door, left a blood-stained footprint on it. They disappeared into the darkness without ever saying what they had come for.

Akila and her parents were left with a door-less house, shivering in the wind that blew through. They hardly dared move, until they were sure that the two men were not coming back. They moved into the living area as a bedraggled, huddled mass and separated into different strands.

Another family might have taken this time to reconnect, maybe even to hug. But this family was made of sterner stuff. They each went to separate corners, to recover and lick their wounds.

Akila went straight to her son to make sure he was okay. Once she saw he was fine, she turned back to the living area to see if her father might need help. Her mother, always one for action, was on the telephone calling someone. Her father limped towards the kitchen which was on the other side of the living room. He refused all offers of help, saying he was fine, and left a trail of blood on the shiny brown tiles. Akila stood in the doorway, watching him for a moment. With his stooped frame and shuffling gait, he looked broken.

In the bedroom, her son lay still and wide-eyed, staring at the ceiling. He seemed to have known something was wrong and stayed silent the entire time. She wanted to lift him up straight away and feel the warmth of his new body. She held him and gently rocked him in her arms until he fell asleep. Even then she didn't want to let go. This was her one point of sanity in a world that had suddenly grown insane.

By the time Suganthi returned from her phone call, Akila felt chilled. Reliving the terror of that moment always left her unsettled.

'Sorry, it was my mother from Sri Lanka. She is a bit worried about me, so I had calm her down,' she said apologetically.

'Don't worry, that's okay. I was just watching the boys. But how are you so calm after what happened yesterday. If it had been me I wouldn't have wanted to stay in this house alone. I would have asked my husband to move,' said Akila.

'I am scared, but if I let my fear control me how can life go on? I could sit here brooding over what has happened, but I choose to move on. Moreover, I have seen so much more in Sri Lanka. This is a small incident. It was scary, yes, but I can't afford to spend my time thinking and worrying over it.' Suganthi paused for breath before continuing.

'I have seen people die. A bomb exploded in a bus in front of me. People have been killed at gun point right before my eyes. My cousin disappeared without a trace one day. Even now we don't know if he is dead or alive. And yet I have survived. How do you think I did it? I can't afford to sit down and weep. If I did, I don't think I would be able to get back up. My solution is to keep moving without stopping.'

Akila thought back to her family's reaction to the violence in their lives. They had survived, limped slowly back to normalcy, but every day had to cope with the fear that suddenly clouded their lives. They had dreaded the night and all its imagined horrors. Once the shadows lengthened, every dark corner, every whispered movement seemed like a potential threat. Her father had become a ghost, roaming the house at night, unable to sleep. He drew every curtain, checked and re-checked the locks and could not be calmed. He stood at the windows, a pale shadow lit by moonlight, watching the road for any would be intruders.

Even getting up at night to go to the toilet was a minefield loaded with possibilities. They longed universally for the night to pass quickly and daylight to brings its comfort. Their faces grew drawn and tired, their eyes darker. But slowly they recovered and were able to go out without looking over their shoulders. They were able to sleep at night again.

Akila had longed for escape and she thought Sydney was her way out of this house of fear and memory. She had longed for the day she would leave.

There was relief at first when she landed in the new country. The wide tree-lined roads, the brick fronted homes and pretty gardens offered her an illusion of safety. But fear remained her firm friend in this new country too. She still stayed awake at night, listening for footsteps, imagining intruders.

And now she could see that there could be so many different responses to violence. She had much to learn from this brave woman, who spoke about violence in such a matter-of-fact way and took fear in her stride.

'Where did you get that Ganesha from? It's a very unusual drawing,' she asked Suganthi. The atmosphere had grown dark and heavy and she wanted to lighten it up.

'I drew that, actually. A long time ago. I think I copied it from a picture in a magazine.'

'Oh! It's a beautiful drawing. We have a similar thing in my parents' house. That's why I wondered. It got ruined during that incident though, the one I was telling you about. And it's a very unusual drawing. That's why I asked.'

'Oh yes. Sorry you got interrupted while telling that story. What happened?'

'Well after that, there was another person outside, who broke the door down and came in. He didn't do anything, though. He just called the other guy and they left. My father was hurt quite badly. He couldn't use both his hands for some time. I was lucky and just escaped with a few cuts. But mentally, it took us a very long time to recover. It made us very conscious about security. But also more fearful. Especially my father because he was the one who was closest to it—to the knife.'

'I can understand. I know how much fear can take over and become so much a part of ourselves that we don't even recognise what we are doing. I know it took me a very long time to process the experiences I had in Sri Lanka. I don't think I can ever fully recover from it. But what has really helped me process it is through art. I love painting, have always loved it since I was a child. But I only realised how therapeutic it can be after I started practising it when I moved here. At first, it was a way for me to get over my loneliness and boredom. But slowly I realised that it has actually helped me heal.'

'Are all of these your paintings?' asked Akila looking around at the room filled with paintings and art.

'No, not all. Some of them are mine and some of them I have bought,' replied Suganthi waving her hand around the room.

'This is exquisite.' Akila stood before a small, but detailed rendering of Shiva Nataraja in all his dancing, long-limbed glory. Arms flung out, toes pointed while all around him the flames ranged around the universe. It was the Lord of the Universe in brilliant colour. It was a powerful painting and Akila stood before it stunned.

'Where did you get this from? Did you paint it?'

'No,' Suganthi laughed. 'I stumbled on it online by accident. She's a very new artist, I had never heard of her before. She is just starting to exhibit and sell her work online. Her name is Sunitha Rao.'

'Okay, I will look her up. I love this painting. So which of these paintings are yours?'

Sunitha waved her hand around. 'Most of these are mine. This is one of the first ones I did,' she said pointing to one of Krishna, a traditional Tanjore style done in gold leaf.

'It's beautiful. How did you learn to do this?'

'Oh, I went for some classes that a local artist was offering here. There are plenty of options to learn nowadays. Even online if you can't get to a class. I got interested in art only after I came here. It was a way for me to stay sane. I had to find a way to process all my trauma and grief. I was so lonely and lost. All my family and friends were in Sri Lanka.'

'I was lucky to be here, in this country, and still I wanted everything I had left behind. I am sure you can understand that feeling. In the first few days I felt like I was going crazy. And so this art kind of saved me. This is what has kept me sane and able to function normally.' Suganthi raised an arm towards the painting. 'This is the art that I can display. When I first started, I had a lot of anger and most of the things I did at that time were a way for me to express that. A slot of slashes and cuts and red and orange. I nearly ripped the canvas in two once,' she said laughing. 'But now I've found my place, I know what I want to paint and I do that.'

'They are all beautiful. You are very talented.' Akila gasped as she looked around her with fresh eyes. There were paintings of all shapes and sizes around the room and she was fascinated.

'I wish I could do something like this.' The words were out before she realised it.

'There is nothing stopping you if you want to. Like I said earlier, there are so many courses teaching you everything you could possibly want to know. If you are interested I could teach you some basics just to get you started.'

'Thank you so much Suganthi. That would be amazing.'

As she went back home that day, there was a spring in her step. Suganthi had opened up more worlds for her than she could have imagined. She couldn't wait to get started.

The Unravelling of Adventure

AMANDA VIVIERS

The Arrival

The flags above flickered as the rusty car weaved through the streets of Nepal. Each house we zoomed by drew deep breaths of wonder, as I remembered the last time I had driven down this back road. The car rattled loudly awakening me to the present and the group of travellers asking question after question.

Trudy asked kindly, 'Hey Melissa, how does it make you feel being back here in Nepal post the earthquake?'

I replied quickly, hoping she didn't hear the vulnerability underneath my smile. 'I'm okay, it will be great to see my friends again.'

Kelley spoke from the front seat of our rented bus. 'Can you remember these roads and the families who belong to this village?'

I spoke slowly. 'Yes, I can. I will never forget every face.'

I could never describe the depth of pain that it provoked with every question. I thought those moments in the airport as people scrambled to secure a flight home were the worst I would face. Returning seemed to bring pain to the surface with every memory. Even more frustrating was the fact that my work sent me back here with a group of women and their constant questions.

The memories of faces unravelled as I watched them sweep by, house after house. The window became a movie screen, seeing cracks through bricks and rickety old bikes travelling with us. The last time I drove through this village was on the morning after the night of terror. I went to the airport with a stranger who had rescued me that Thursday night.

I assumed I would never drive these streets ever again. Divorced, disillusioned and distant. When I land back on Australian soil, I am resigning. How could my management not recognise that this trip with our sponsors was fraught with potential disaster?

The driver spoke sharply. 'Mrs—we are nearly at your hotel, please be ready. Are you happy with my service?'

I smiled. 'Yes, guru you have looked after us well.'

We turned the corner into the overcrowded shopping district, and the crowd of noise shocked my companions into silence. They madly pulled out their phones and cameras, clicking through the windows as we slowed to a snail pace as the car chugged through the market.

A cow walked ahead, and the crowd gathering was demanding all of our attention. The six women surrounding me smiled and laughed outrageously at the sight of traffic stopping mid-market by a big old cow. I leaned back with a crooked stretch looking for my favourite colours flicking miles wildly above. The ticker tape that flew high reminding my Nepalese sisterhood to pray helped ease my anxiety and helped me breathe.

Red, yellow and blue flags wave proudly through Kathmandu asking its inhabitants to look up and remember their freedom. The ticker tape flickering allures me into moments of contemplation, and I settle in to remember why I love this land.

Shops filled with rugs and carved jewellery boxes grab my attention. Fake climbing jackets and beanies made from goat hair snuggled softly into their highest corners. Felted balls rowed the streets, smiling with colourful expression, and Turkish teahouses overflowed with milk and honey.

The streets of Kathmandu are designed for the astute traveller, but what each bar and café doesn't tell you is the rumbles that lie waiting in its soil. The cow continued to call the crowd captive and my guests, that's right my guests.

I scolded myself silently. 'Melissa, remember your present moment. You are here to host these leaders, remember. Their wish is your command.' I coughed out loud at the awkwardness of it all. 'Oh, that's right, yes remember this is a privilege.'

The car moved slowly towards our gated hotel, and I remembered with familiarity the brilliance of our lodging for the next twelve days. The Kathmandu Hotel was a local institution, and I was worried to see it post the earthquake. It reminded me of the Marigold Hotel with its flowers, white walls with golden highlights pulling off its regal flair.

The driver spoke warmly. 'Mrs—the markets are full this evening. Sorry for the delay, your destination is still waiting.' I replied with a smile, 'Oh guru, you are doing an amazing job. And watch out for those cows. They are making their way slowly this evening.'

The rest of the bus laughed out loud at the hilarity of it all, but I remembered and breathed deeply the feeling of pure relief the last time I left this part of town. Vowing never to return ever again.

The gates opened and the wind rushed past our little white bus as I saw the uniformed men running towards us, hoping for a tip or special mention when they helped us disembark after our long journey from Australia.

Knocking interrupted my thoughts of escaping, and the moment had arrived to offload my guests and their luggage, quickly as possible getting them into their rooms for the night.

I shouted over the ambient noise tooting loudly beyond the gates. 'Come on ladies, it's time to get out of the van. Don't leave anything here at this moment, because tomorrow our adventure continues with a different vehicle, but hopefully our same guru of a driver.'

Our driver smiled at me, and we all laughed at the pride he took in his place in our party of seven. He said with enthusiasm, 'I am your guru ladies; your wish is my command.'

We laughed as we unpacked our baggage and essentials, all looking over our shoulders hoping to have a moment to get lost in the markets that promised bargains beyond the gates.

Kelley spoke forthrightly. 'Isn't it time for dinner, Melissa?'

I replied with, 'Just waiting to get us all settled. I promise you will find the most amazing food awaiting us when we have washed up and booked into our rooms with air conditioning.'

Trudy sidled alongside me and whispered, 'You're doing a great job, Mel. Can I call you Mel?'

I said softly, 'No you can't. My name is Melissa.'

The Next Step

The sound of the horns pierced my veil of sleep as I looked around the room, unsure of where I even was. The sound of Kathmandu awaking stirred me into my present. Remembering the hullaballoo of our check-in process last night, I rolled over and tried to go back to sleep.

Trudy was not coping with the shared bedroom arrangement, and Kelley felt the need to control the details of our stay, right down to the dinner details. I stood off to the side, reminding myself calmly that I was indeed forty-five years young and I could handle this group of women.

The hotel clerk was checking in this team of six who had travelled a long distance to come and see first-hand the projects that the not-for-profit ran here in Nepal. What these women did not know was the sheer anxiety I was facing returning to this place that I both loved and hated. Framed by the recent pain of my marriage cataclysmically falling apart after I returned home last April.

The last time I stood here in this amazingly complex country was in the aftermath of the Gorkha earthquake. Over nine thousand beautiful souls lost overnight, and thousands upon thousands were gravely injured. To remember those moments as we stood watching walls and concrete structures groan is more painful than childbirth.

It is morning. And I must shower quickly. If team 'perfection' gets to breakfast before I do, there could be some backlash, especially after the problems from last night.

Shower.
Groan.
Don't forget to wash your teeth with bottled water.
Freak, what was that noise?
Get out.
Get out.
Breathe.

You're okay. It was just the pipes waking up through the 150-year-old walls. Seriously!

Hello, Nepal.
Hello, Day two.

The sounds of cars honking and the market waking echoed behind our hotel gates. I smiled as I walked past the front desk with the same staff still on after the night shift. They wiggled their heads with a wink and a nod, reminding me that they hadn't forgotten the arguments that played out in their foyer last night.

Kelley couldn't help but let the staff know she was displeased at the length of time our check-in was taking, and Kym (the creative, soft soul) was ironing out the creases in her dress as she watched the show unfold.

I tried to walk quickly through the foyer hoping the manager didn't stop me, and stepped hesitantly into the courtyard. The trees swayed, betraying my trust in the land that we walked on. The music lulled me into a state of positivity, smiling at the possibility of the day and its program.

Of course, Kelley was waiting, already choosing her favourite table and seat. I sat down with purpose ready to talk out last night's happenings.

'Hey Kelley, how are you going this morning?' I offered.

She replied, 'Oh Melissa, I'm so sorry last night went a little awry. I just wasn't thinking after the long flight, drive and recovery. Do you forgive my little outburst?'

I smiled. 'Yes, this time I do. What would you like for breakfast?'

The breakfast was full of story and expectation; we walked the buffet trying to ignore the buffalo milk and its curd-filled cousin, the yoghurt. Trying to eat, remembering we were in fact in a developing nation fresh from an earthquake that destabilised every sanitation system across the country.

We quickly rushed to the waiting van for our drive out to the project, and the whole team seemed to be in cheerful spirits, mostly ignoring what happened the night before.

Guru was beaming, with his keys jingling at his crowd of women. 'Come on ladies; my chariot awaits you. Time waits for no-one.'

The Journey

What no one knows about travel through Nepal is that the vans are rarely roadworthy and the roads are barely gravelled. The words flowed quickly as the journey began swiftly. Questions fielding answers that were complex even to the discerning scholar.

The developing world is a difficulty to most who visit their boundaries because they expect poverty and decay, but are often not prepared for the resilience and hope. Each time I take teams of people on the ground to refugee camps and projects, I am always pleasantly surprised at their experience of vulnerability in the most unusual way. The culture in our western world is more displaced than we would like to admit. Village life has sustainability and respect that isn't in a supermarket or the university library shelf.

The penny drops when I take women into rural places and they realise that they are not the hero of this story but the women who provide for their families with nothing to show for it are. Watching women carry a child on one hip and a large vessel of water on the other, scrambling up a hill carrying safe passage for their family's welfare.

A scream from the back seat brought me into the present, and I remembered how bad a driver my old mate Guru was. Cars screeched past the five-lane highway, and horns were shouting a melodic handshake as they interrupted each other's paths.

I shouted above the racket, 'Everyone okay back there?' I smiled slowly saying, 'settle in ladies the day has only just begun.'

Kelley, of course, replied, 'How long exactly is this trip today Melissa?'

And I replied, 'As long as it takes Kelley. As long as it takes.'

Developing nations are difficult to understand when you have only ever known flowing water from taps and doctors' surgeries offering free services. They often swing from a land of the fast Internet to a complex mix of slavery and degradation. Whenever we take people out to the field, it is often an awakening that cannot stop.

Our van rattled on freeways for another four hours, and then as we turned off the tarmac we settled into the rhythm of rocky pathways as we made our way up mountains to villages removed from city life. The further we moved away from Kathmandu and its facilities, the more I started to relax into the rhythm of my job this trip, remembering why I did love my life despite all the pain of transition.

Trudy leaned forward and softly asked me, 'Tell me Melissa, are you going okay? This journey must be bringing up all the stories from your last trip to this nation.'

She caught me off guard, and I began to describe to her the last terrifying twenty-four hours before I left this forsaken place. The deep breath started with these four simple words: I will never return.

The Memory

It was a night in Kathmandu, for some reason I remembered that the clouds overtook the stars that evening and the eerie sense of mystery settled into village life. My Nepalese guide had taken me on a tour of the city, and the next day I was to go out and visit projects for my office back at home.

It was my job to make sure that the funds for projects were spent appropriately and the domestic staff led the programs with care. I travelled the world with my career, and this trip to Nepal was my first to this nation. I was expectant and cautious with the warnings that had been released by my government, to travel with caution.

My husband, Dave, didn't want me to continue with my work. He always reminded me that it absorbed all of my passion. He often rolled his eyes at my adventures and couldn't take another sob story about a part of the world needing our help. He believed Australia needed the finances just as much as the overseas aid. He was not impressed at all by my compassion and empathy. He tried to demand my attention, and I just couldn't shake the feeling that someone else was meeting his needs.

The memory of that night came flooding back as I retold the story to Trudy on our long journey towards a little village east of Kathmandu. Once the floodgates were open, I couldn't stop the tale tumbling out.

I was waiting for my dinner in a café on the corner of a night market. A sweet American institution that understood the power of well-brewed coffee and the comfort that inspired a lonely traveller became my refugee after a long season of travel. After a day of acclimatising to the altitude and the atmosphere, I could only stomach a muffin and a flat white. My guide stood outside waiting for me as the windows began to shudder.

Our staff training for emergency evacuations was evident, our information was up-to-date, but nothing will prepare you for the sight of humanity heaving as it tries to save whomever they can in the wretchedness of the earth shaking.

Women and children began to scream as the memories of growing up in an earthquake zone taught them the importance of swift action in the midst of movement. I looked from the left to the right of the café, and suddenly glass began to shatter and bodies began to launch themselves towards the exit.

In the midst of the chaos, I forgot the name of my guide. I'm not sure if it was the shock or a momentary forgetfulness, but I screamed out hoping someone would help as I felt the ground move like a giant rope had flicked from the universe proving its might.

I looked across the courtyard to see centuries-old buildings sway and cracks forming from the ground up. Dust began to fly and buildings fell like a stack of dominos betraying their history and architecture.

My sweet guide found me amidst the rubble and gently carried my hand towards an opening in ruins. My guide led me through the pain and the unfolding commotion as I saw family members searching for broken pieces of history for their kin. We moved quickly because the likelihood of more aftershocks was a very present danger.

As we ran towards the corridors that promised another opening, we found many people backed up in between piles of broken pieces of life formerly known as Kathmandu. Old grandmothers dusted lightly by grey particles sitting on the floor sobbing at the heaving state of their locality. Children stood behind us shouting for their parents, and men lifted beams of wood searching for any signs of life underneath.

I stood silenced by the shock of the commotion that surrounded me, unsure if I could ever erase the scene unfolding. My guide pulled my arms again, and I shook my head vowing that if I ever made it home to my husband that I would never return to this place ever again.

He called me towards another place of safety behind the walls that betrayed their majesty with cracks teetering with every groan that burped out of the earth.

As I walked out into the open field beyond the pillaged market, I began to breathe again as I saw a soccer field promising space away from swaying buildings. As I walked tentatively towards the opening, I started to sob, watching families covered in dust walk my same path.

Guru interrupted my introspection with Trudy and said softly, 'Excuse me Mrs, we are nearly arriving. Sorry if my driving has been a little crazy. I did my best, don't you think?'

I replied hesitantly, 'Oh guru, you have done well.'

The People

As our van rattled into the driveway of our school in this far off land, we watched young children scamper across the horizon, buoyant at the opportunity to meet with strangers from a far-off land. I stepped out of the van and gathered myself in the midst of my revelations to Trudy, regaining my composure for those around us.

Standing off in the distance were the mothers and grandmothers noting our every move, nodding in agreement, whispering to each other and giggling at the sight of white women holding their handbags tightly to their chest.

The Australian women peered towards the gaggle starting to gather, extending a hand of acceptance as they met for the first time, wanting to make a good first impression. The children did not hold back their amusement at our arrival. They shouted at each other, talking animatedly in their language, smiling cheekily at our displacement in their everyday.

The staff member, Moses, with a darkened face and yellowed teeth welcomed us with wide open arms. 'Ladies, welcome to our village. Thank you, you have come such long distance to visit with us. Can we get you all a drink of water?'

Kelley accepted with a big open smile. 'Yes, please. I would love a drink of water.'

Kym stood with her camera in hand and a tear dripping from her cheek. She had noticed a small child carrying a baby on its back, and the eyes of the children pierced her veneer. She was moved deeply with compassion.

Moses walked us proudly across his village and settled us onto straw mats outside the community centre, handing bottled water to each traveller. Every gulp cleansing the fear from our lips of the moment we found ourselves present. Children were looking after children. Women were wearing clothes that obviously were their only option, and shoes so worn through that some of the holes were patched with string and rope.

They smiled vigorously at our group of women, and soon we began to laugh with them as well. Language became a barrier, but our eyes and smiles grew a bridge to walk between us.

Each week the women in the village had committed to come together, forming an encouragement circle, holding each other accountable to a microfinance bank with each other. Moses spoke in English explaining that they would hold each other responsible for contributing a small amount to the fund, and then they would help each other start a small sustainable business. They were changing the village one loan at a time.

Children hung around the edges of this strange meeting, and my team of six women from Australia sat in silence, transfixed by the courage of those who were before them.

Moses asked us whether we had any questions for the ladies, and Trudy began to speak even though her voice shook with fear.

'Moses, can you ask them what they dream of for their life?'

He spoke in their dialect language, and the ladies discussed amongst each other and nodded their heads furiously, agreeing with each other the best answer they could find to Trudy's question. They spoke to Moses and described what it was that they wanted to tell us, and he nodded with understanding and turned back to our group bridging the communication gap between us.

He said softly, 'Their greatest dream, ladies, is for their children to go to school and to grow up to have a better life than they could ever dream. Their collective prayer is that their children would get an education to help them get jobs so that they can provide for the needs of their family.'

We all looked at one another, and Kelley said quietly, 'Moses, please tell them—that is our dream as well. That our children would find their voices and that education would inform them of the great potential of their future.'

He turned to talk to the ladies, and they smiled back across the mats, nodding towards us. Kym looked around and then asked Moses whether she could speak to the children.

Moses nodded and called them out from behind the corners that they were peering from. They sprinted towards Moses, smiling with excitement and intrigue. Kym looked them in the eyes and said, 'Children, what do you dream of doing with your life?'

Moses spoke to them, repeating Kym's question softly with purpose, and one young girl stood up in front of us, and we all took a deep breath.

She stood up so straight with confidence it was clear that she was destined to go far. She spoke to Moses, but stared straight into our eyes. Her passion betrayed her innocence, and she had a clarity that even a different language could not hide.

Moses looked towards us and spoke with an inch of shame. 'This young girl's name is Pranua, and she dreams that no more children would marry in villages here in Nepal. Young children are sold sometimes as young as six years old from family to family as a negotiation for debt and money. She believes that it is her generation's responsibility to stop this from happening in her lifetime.'

Breathe deep.
Confusion abated.
Sit in the discomfort.
How could this be still happening in our day and age?

Time stopped that afternoon as we listened to the echo of generations reverberate across the hills that shadowed us, and the confusion sat heavy in our hearts as we listened tentatively to story after story of slavery.

The moment came as pink started to flare across the horizon to load our women back into the van. They walked back to sit down and put on their seat belts. The trip home was awkwardly silent, and we sat reflecting as we pulled away with women holding arms with other women, waving goodbye.

The Adventure

The plane rattled and hissed as I looked across the cabin at the group of women journeying home after twelve days visiting projects in rural Nepal, moments of frustration and long awkward silences as they grappled with the stories that deeply marked their souls.

Trudy walked down the aisle towards the bathroom and stopped, looking down at me. 'Hey Melissa, I think there is more to your story than what you have shared with us. Tell me why you came back to Nepal after the trauma of your last visit and the earthquake.'

I shuffled over into the empty seat beside me and beckoned that she sat down next to me so I could tell her the rest of my story.

I was lucky to be evacuated out of the natural disaster pretty quickly because of the Australian Government. However, as I waited at the airport in Nepal for three days, trying to get on a plane, I was surrounded by foreigners trying to escape the sheer terror of the aftermath of such a colossal earthquake. The aftershocks were constant, and the sanitation quickly began to be compromised as sewerage pipes broke and people searched endlessly for their loved ones.

Nepal lost thousands of people that late night in April last year, but I realised in a moment that I was returning to a loveless marriage and a husband who wouldn't have even understood the danger I was putting myself around.

As I stepped on the plane, I vowed I would never return because fear overtook my heart and I was determined to reframe the way I lived my everyday life back in Australia.

I landed back in Adelaide, stood at the luggage carousel as my bag travelled around and around. I stood there for probably two hours watching my bag circle that black pathway, and I realised it was the same as my marriage. Just going around and around, not going anywhere.

He didn't pick me up that day when I arrived back home. So I got into a taxi which drove me home and told him it was over. The saddest thing is he didn't fight back; he said nothing.

Little by little, over the next few months I remembered the faces of women and children from that night as they searched and looked for family members. It broke my heart that he wouldn't have been looking for me and that I meant nothing to him after so many years. I was so grateful at that moment that I hadn't had any children. Who would want to bring children into that kind of degradation?

Week-by-week, staff meeting after staff meeting, I began to

remember why I had travelled there in the first place. I started the divine adventure and believed I could live beyond today. To help women and children find their voice and to encourage them that many people in far-off nations like Australia wanted to help them.

Despite the fear and the shame I felt at my marriage breaking down, I realised that my life had meaning beyond my current circumstances and I desperately wanted to make a difference beyond the pain I faced walking towards divorce.

It became apparent that he had checked out of our marriage years before. Sometimes life can take you to far off places to help you unpack the darkness found in the hearts of those closest. Little by little, I decided to believe again and to take the time to rebuild my core by rebuilding the courage of those faces I saw running away from me that night in Nepal.

Trudy smiled and said, 'I know that this trip was terrifying for you to face but your courage has changed me.'

I looked into her eyes and questioned whether she truly meant what she was saying. Didn't she see my fear? Wasn't she aware of my brokenness and inconsistency?

She smiled again and said, 'Melissa, the fact that you faced your fears, despite the craziness of your last year, and took six women back to the land that nearly broke you and now you are advocating to help them find their voices is the greatest adventure anyone could ever hope.'

The aeroplane loudspeaker came on and loudly encouraged us to settle back into our seats as we were preparing to land. Trudy shrugged and walked back to her place. I sat in silence thinking about what I wanted this new season of my life to represent.

How often do we get the chance to begin again? How many people would give anything to have the adventures that are a part of my job description?

As we landed, perspective dropped into my lap and I could not ever walk the same again. Healing had been found in that moment, and that far distant land held my heart. I knew what I had to do.

I walked with confidence off the plane and towards the baggage carousel. Picking up my bag, I saw Kelley with her family holding her and gushing over her homecoming, and I breathed profoundly remembering why I began this work in the first place.

She looked over at me as said, 'Thanks so much for everything you did to help us understand the plight of those amazing people. What's next for you Melissa?'

I smiled as I walked my luggage towards the taxi rank and said casually, 'I'm going home to sell everything I have and I'm shifting to Nepal, Kelley. I think I am ready to give everything I have to the people who have my heart. My days in Australia have come to a close and it is time for a new and glorious chapter.'

Little by little.
Fear buried by courage.
I stepped into my greater tomorrow.
Goodbye Australia.
Hello, the rest of my life.

The Wash

LISA A. WOLSTENHOLME

March 2012

'Clara Reid,' the prison warden bellows, heaving open a thick metal door leading to a tiny office.

A man sitting behind a grey Melamine desk looks up at me, glasses tilted on his nose.

'Welcome Clara. Please—have a seat.'

I sit opposite. 'Thanks. Nice to meet you Mr Cox,' I reply as butterflies jostle for position in my stomach.

'Anthony. Call me Anthony,' he says, offering his hand.

I shake it, hoping he can't feel mine trembling.

'So, Clara, how are you feeling about your work placement?'

'A bit nervous,' I admit, 'but I'm looking forward to it.'

'You've been highly recommended by your Uni supervisor. I hope you know what you've let yourself in for.' He tosses me a grin, raising bushy brows. 'We'll start with the two-hour group session. You'll be observing at first, taking notes about the inmates in the program. We'll debrief afterwards.'

'Okay,' I reply, feigning a confident smile.

'We start in half-an-hour, so let's grab a coffee and I'll show you around.'

The butterflies start performing backflips.

Anthony and I sit in the middle of a large room with cream walls, grey carpet, and plastic chairs arranged in a circle around us. I glance at the walls adorned with posters about drug and alcohol abuse and tacky motivational quotes like, 'It may seem like a mountain, but we'll help you climb it.'

I balance a notepad on my lap and clasp my pen like it's a lifeline. Anthony tucks in his shirt and pulls a whiteboard marker from his pocket. 'Ready?'

'Uh-huh,' I reply, twisting my fingers, almost dropping the pen.

'Most of them do this to score brownie points to get a shorter sentence,' Anthony whispers, leaning towards me, 'although a few genuinely want to sort themselves out.'

A lasting memory of Jake's face flashes in my mind—pasty and covered in spots and sores. It reminds me of why I'm here—my dream of becoming a novelist swept away when he overdosed on heroin a week before my sixteenth birthday. Discovered by a morning surfer face-down in the wash on Scarborough beach. I couldn't—no—wouldn't write after that. Instead, I made it my mission to figure out why my only brother had taken his life. But six years of studying psychology at Uni have barely scratched the surface.

I hate the fucking sea.

'Clara—' Anthony whispers, pulling me back. 'They're arriving.'

I straighten and turn to watch figures dressed in navy pants and grey, short-sleeved shirts trundle single-file into the room. Wolf-whistles ring out as I eye each man.

'Guys,' Anthony says. 'Manners.'

I can do this.

Mumbles, and a chorus of, 'sorry,' intertwine with scraping chairs. I count eleven men, each taking a seat in our circle.

'Alright. Let's start by—' Anthony is interrupted by another man darting into the room. 'Michael—you're late.'

'Sorry Tony,' Michael replies, scurrying to a seat opposite.

Michael looks across at me. 'I'll make sure I'm not in future,' his lips curling around a thick accent I can't place.

Penetrating blue eyes, so much like Jakes, lock me in like a tractor beam and the hairs on my arms stand tall.

'Okay guys … this is Clara,' Anthony announces, pulling me away from Michael's hold. 'She'll be helping me for the next six weeks, so be nice. Right, who wants to go first?'

A youthful-looking Aboriginal man puts his hand up. 'I'll go, Anthony.'

'How are you doing today, Adam?'

'Ah man … I'm tired, y' know. Fitzy kept me awake all night with his farting!'

Laughter erupts around the room.

'That's enough.' Anthony frowns. 'Adam, do you want to start again?'

'Yeah … sorry,' he sniggers. 'I'm feeling good. Gonna do some community service today.'

'And what are you looking forward to the most?'

'Decent food.'

Several of the men jeer.

Anthony shakes his head and grins. 'Okay. Who's next?'

One-by-one the men share how they are and what they are looking forward to. I jot down each one's name, and features such as curly black hair and tribal tattoo as an aide memoir.

'I'm looking forward to this,' Michael says when it's his turn.

'Oh?' Anthony says.

'Well … I haven't seen a decent bit of skirt for nearly 18 months.'

I shrivel as Michael and the others regale in his comment.

Anthony shakes his head.

'Sorry Clara …' Michael says, locking eyes with me for the briefest of moments before looking away.

'How do you feel the session went?' Anthony asks me across the desk in his office.

'Okay, I think,' I reply, making some final notes.

'They push the boundaries, but you can pull them up and they will toe the line. They're not a bad bunch.'

'I was expecting worse, to be honest.'

'This lot are not hard-core criminals, just made some bad choices.

And don't worry about Michael—he likes to act-out.'

'What's his story?' I ask, feigning indifference.

'Strange, really. From a well-off family. Went to Uni and had a promising life but was charged with drunk and disorderly offences before he finished. His parents pushed for this rehab program.'

'Really?'

'Guess they'd had enough. Couldn't get him off the grog, so thought it best to get him banged up and into rehab.'

If only we'd done that with Jake.

April 2012

'What are you writing?' Michael leans over my seat from behind, his warm breath brushing the back of my neck.

Startled, I try to flip over the notepad in my lap and it drops to the floor. 'Nothing,' I reply. 'Work stuff.' I scramble to pick it up almost butting heads with Michael as he reaches down to get it too.

Our fingers lightly brush as he hands it back, his eyes boring into mine.

I grab the pad and look up at the clock. 'You're early—' I stammer, the room constricting around me.

'I write, y' know,' he says, crouching in front of me.

'Really? Like what?'

'Dunno … stuff. Life, y' know?'

'Written anything recently?' I tuck a strand of hair behind my ear.

'I started my life story, but I guess it's still a work-in-progress,' he chuckles.

'I can relate.' I lower my gaze, praying he can't see the heat rising in my cheeks.

'What're you working on?'

'Nothing much,' I sigh. 'Can't seem to get the right words out.'

'I'd like to read your work sometime,' Michael says, his eyes pulling me in as if I'm diving into an azure sea. I don't even notice the other men filing into the room.

May 2012

My gut twists as I set up the room, adopting Anthony's seat like a throne as the men walk in.

Michael's voice emanates above the mumblings. 'Where's Tony?'

'He's sick, so I'm running the group today.' The temperature in the room seems to sky rocket.

I hear sniggers circle like Chinese whispers.

'Doesn't mean you can take the piss.'

'Yes Miss,' come the chants as I shrivel like a withering leaf.

I clear my throat, straighten my back and glance over at the warden for peace of mind. 'Let's check in. I'll start—I'm feeling confident that we'll have a productive session.'

Michael fixes his gaze on me, but I can't hold it, afraid he'll see how he's unhinged me.

He's the last to check-in. 'I'm not sure how I feel today, Clara.'

'Oh?'

'You intimidate me.'

What?

'You feel I'm intimidating?' A shiver meanders down my back as snorts dance around the room.

'Yeah. Like … if I say something wrong you might report me.' I swear his eyes are glinting.

'This is a safe space, Michael,' I reply, trying my best to take control.

'You did ask—'

'Do you have anything else to say?' I snap.

He tosses me a wink.

Breathe, Clara. Just breathe.

The rest of the session passes more smoothly, and our discussions around coping mechanisms seem to have been reasonably well-received.

I start packing away chairs as the men file out of the room, but as I turn to grab the last one, Michael blocks my way.

'Did you need something, Michael?'

He inches closer, putting a hand in his pocket. 'Here.' He pulls out a folded piece of paper and thrusts it towards me.

'What is it?' I grab the paper and step back.

He cocks an eyebrow and walks away.

I glance around to see if anyone saw this clandestine moment, my fingers trembling as I unfold the paper and read the note:

'Clara,

'Sorry for being a pain.

Michael.'

That's it?

'I need to tell you about Michael and show you this—' I hand the note to a snuffling Anthony and recount Michael's comments during the previous session.

'Always pushing the boundaries,' Anthony replies, tutting. 'He's a funny one. Doesn't like to be thought badly of. Apologises whenever he gets the chance.'

'Do you think I should say something to him?'

'Ordinarily, yes—but he was released on Monday.'

My heart cracks, just a little …

October 2015

A friend request pops up on my Facebook notifications. A picture of a shamrock appears next to the name Michael Moran. Curiosity bites and I click on the picture.

Scrolling through, I find photos of the Michael I'd met during my prison rehab work.

I shouldn't, should I?

But I can't help myself and click 'Accept.'

'You finished Uni—that's great.'

I re-read Michael's message over-and-over, contemplating a reply, settling on, 'Thanks. How are you?'

A beep rings out as Michael's response comes just as I hear my front door shut.

Dan, my boyfriend, calls out, 'Clara … you home?'

'In here.' I snap my laptop shut.

Within seconds he's at my side, arms encircling me. 'Hey,' he says, kissing my cheek.

'Hey back.' I twist round and smile up at him, hiding the niggle deep in my gut. 'How was your day?'

'Better now.' He pecks my forehead and heads off to our bedroom.

My intrigue to see Michael's reply builds like a rumbling volcano, but I need to make dinner, continue as normal.

But after Dan has left for work the following morning, I rush to my desk and fire up the laptop.

'Not bad,' Michael's message reads. 'I'm working. Driving forklifts. Haven't had a drink since rehab.'

'That's great.' I type back, gnawed by parasitic guilt.

I rifle through papers strewn across my work desk, filling time, my eyes falling onto a picture of Jake and I fishing together by the Swan River. Even now, eleven years on, the hole he left in my life is cavernous.

'Like two peas in a pod,' my mum used to say, marvelling at the bond between us.

I adored him—my protector, my confidant. We'd spend hours poring over books and writing letters and stories. He was my biggest champion, encouraging me to write more. So why did my letters of love and support matter less than his next fix?

Tears trickle as memories of happier times are bulldozed by the image of his bloated, grey body lying on a cold slab, my parents falling apart as I stand numbed beside them.

By lunchtime, boredom has taken hold. I turn to my laptop and indulge in social media to find out what bullshit is happening with so-called 'friends.' As soon as I log in, a message pops up.

'What have you been up to?' Michael writes. 'I see on your profile you're in a relationship.'

Annoyance and excitement lock heads as I finger the keys. 'I'm in private practice now.'

I hold my breath waiting for his response.

Dan is out for the evening and I have our unit to myself for a few hours. I haven't been able to get Michael out of my head, so I power up the laptop hoping for a fix, much like a child sneaking a lolly from a candy bar.

'How's business?' comes Michael's message.

'Fine,' I reply, an unwieldly excitement bubbling in my veins.

'How's the partner?'

'None of your business.'

'Sorry.'

'No—I'm sorry. Bad day,' I reply.

'Wanna tell me about it?'

'Just boring. Not sure I'm cut out for listening to people's woes.'

'Don't wanna help people?'

'I used to. Anyway, how's yours?'

'Boring!'

I chuckle, lightened by his comment. 'Sober for 3 years—that's great. Sounds like you've turned your life around.'

'Wouldn't say that. Been a hard slog. I still wanna drink, but every day I don't is a blessing.'

'You found God?'

'Nah. People like you save me.'

A pang rises from my gut. 'The program saved you—I didn't even know you,' I type with fervour.

'I want you to know me.'

My fingers freeze over the keys, my heart now racing.

'Clara?'

'Got to go.'

Dan wraps his arms around my waist from behind as I apply the finishing touches of makeup.

'You look great,' he says, nuzzling my neck. 'Not sure I want you going out now.'

'Jealous?'

'Always.' He kisses my cheek and leaves the bathroom.

He's a good catch, isn't he?

I take an Uber into the city and meet up with my girlfriends in a trendy Northbridge bar.

'Watch out, straight jacket's here!' Tiffany calls as the other three cheer and giggle.

Our sisterhood of five huddles together, moving in unison towards the crowded bar.

'How's practically old-married-couple life?' Tiff mocks.

'Very funny!' I reply. 'Dan's having some mates over to watch the game.'

'Glad you got a pass-out,' Anna shouts above the din.

We take our drinks and find a spare table, chatting merrily as we catch up. The night progresses quickly with wine and mixers readily consumed. The desire to dance the night away soon beckons.

We leave the bar and walk the buzzing streets to the Mint nightclub, passing cafes and bars all still alive with animated conversations and pumping music. Flick, my bestie, links arms with me as the other three lead the way.

'Clara?' A voice carries from across the street. I turn to see who it is and spot a tall, red-haired man grinning and waving at me—Michael.

I gasp, my pulse zooming from nought to sixty.

He strides across the road towards me, and I can't help noticing how good he looks—dark pants, crisp white shirt, and slicked back hair.

'Shit!' I whisper, bowing my head.

'Who's that?' Flick asks, gawping.

'An old client—'

'You avoiding me, Clara?' Michael calls as he nears.

'No—err … hi,' I reply, my legs threatening to buckle.

Michael eyes us both. 'You out on the pull?'

'Of course not!' I glare at him. 'I'm out with friends.'

'You look good.'

'I'm Felicity.' Flick thrusts her hand towards Michael, cutting through the spark.

'Michael.' He barely grasps her outstretched hand, eyes locked with mine.

'Clara, we need to go.' Flick says, tugging my arm.

'Um … gotta go. Nice to see you.'

Flick's hold tightens, and she pulls me away.

'You too, Clara. Talk to you on Facebook.'

I turn to look at him, and he nods as I toss him an apologetic smile.

Dan is asleep when I get home.

Still tipsy and wide awake, I grab a glass of water from the kitchen and plonk myself down on the sofa.

My mobile chirps. Texts from the girls litter the screen with messages and photos from the night. I swipe through, giggling, then open Facebook. Michael's online and almost immediately a message pops up.

'Good night?'

'Yes, thanks.'

'Hope you behaved.'

'That's none of your business.'

'You have a boyfriend. Wouldn't want you to do something stupid.' Before I can reply, he follows up with, 'unless it's with me.'

'You can't say that!'

'I just did.'

'Go away.'

'Why?'

'I don't want to play games.'

'I didn't ask you to.'

'Goodbye Michael.' I'm about to lock my phone when another message pops up.

'Don't go.'

Don't reply, Clara.

But alcohol has made me impetuous. 'What do you want from me?'

I watch three dots wave, then stop, then wave again as he types and re-types. 'Answer me, dammit!' I yell out, then look around, breath held, in case I've woken Dan.

'To know you more.'

I shake my head, thumbs hovering over the phone keys.

'I can't.'

'Why not?'

'I have a partner.'

'Is that really the reason?'

'Yes.'

'Is it serious?'

'Of course!' I fidget from imaginary lumps in the sofa, my breath ragged.

'I'll leave you alone, then.'

Michael's status flips to offline.

He's unfriended me from Facebook. Why am I not relieved?

THE WASH

December 2015

The girls and I are going out for a Christmas meal at a swanky riverside restaurant. Dan drops me near the Bell Tower and I walk towards the Lucky Shag bar to meet them.

I'm tottering along on too-high heels and smoothing down my party dress when a voice calls out from a nearby nook, stopping me in my tracks. A pair of sea-blue eyes stare up at me.

'Michael?' I gasp.

He squints into the still-bright light of early evening. 'Clara?' His face crinkles into a smile. Stale whisky wafts on his breath and paled skin peeps from beneath wisps of red stubble.

'Are you drunk?' I ask, noticing a bagged bottle on his lap.

He sits upright. 'Oops,' and puts a finger to his mouth. 'Shhh. Don't tell anyone.'

I should leave, ignore him like all the other vagrants, but—

I stoop to grab hold of his arm, but he flails as I try to pull him up.

'Leave me be.' He turns away from me.

'GET UP!' I yell, glancing around in case passers-by have noticed.

He sighs, easing himself onto unsteady legs. 'Where are we going?'

'To a café to get you sobered up. Why have you started drinking again?'

'Dunno,' he mutters, stumbling along beside me.

Luckily, the nearby café is still open. I guide Michael to a chair and go and order us coffee. A mother at a nearby table stares at me, clasping her toddler close to her chest.

'You're an idiot,' I tell him when I return, shaking my head.

'You look nice. Where are you going?' he slurs, placing his booze carefully on the floor between his feet.

'Shit! Stay there.'

I step away to text Flick, making the excuse of running late. When I return, the waitress has brought our order and Michael is hunched over the table sipping his drink.

'Can we get some water too?' I call over. She rolls her eyes but returns moments later with a filled bottle and two glasses.

Michael's head droops over his coffee, avoiding my glare. He finishes his drink and looks up at me through long eyelashes. 'Sorry …'

'For what?'

'This.' He gestures to his empty cup.

'For coffee?' I pour a glass of water and push it towards him.

Without protest, he guzzles it in one go, sliding it back for a refill.

'What happened?'

'I messed up,' he replies, staring at the floor. 'Lost my job.'

'Oh.'

'And the girl I'm into wants nothing to do with me.'

'I'm sorry—'

'Are you?' The furrow in his brow pierces any feeble defences I might have.

'You know I am.'

He nods. 'Well, thanks for rescuing me. You can go now.'

'I didn't rescue you,' I snap. 'Why would you say that?'

He shakes his head. 'Doesn't matter.'

My phone beeps, breaking the awkwardness now hanging like a storm cloud between us.

'Are you coming or what?' Flick's message reads.

'You'd better go—boyfriend's waiting.'

'I'm not leaving until you've sobered up.'

'There's no need.'

Anger bubbles and I glare up at him from my screen. 'You'd do the same.'

'Would I? Anyway, I need to go—'

'Go where?' I slam my phone on the table.

'I need to piss. Is that okay?'

'Fine.'

He gets up and wanders over to the back of the café. I watch him sway a little as he walks, eyeing his torso and ruffled hair.

By the time Michael returns, I have refilled his glass and disposed of his stash.

'Are you hungry?' I push a menu towards him.

'No.'

'When did you last eat?'

'Dunno. Stop treating me like a kid, will ya.' He rolls his eyes.

'Then stop acting like one!'

'I'm not hungry and don't need a caretaker.'

I scowl at him. 'Okay, well drink up and we'll go for a walk to clear your head. The café's closing soon.'

He gulps the water then gets up, his chair scraping across the café's decking.

I follow him out and we make our way towards a footpath running alongside the river.

The sun is setting, casting a myriad of purples and burnt oranges across the sky, the ripples in the river twinkling in response.

We walk in silence for a while, reminding me so much of the times I spent with Jake in his rare sober moments, trying desperately to understand why he left home and holed up with junkies who wanted nothing more than to live hard, drink and shoot-up. Trying to convince him that our parents would help. That *I* could help.

But he's not Jake, is he.

Eventually, Michael veers off towards a grassy bank, plopping himself down and sprawling out. He pats a spot next to him.

I sit beside him as daylight blinks a final goodbye.

'I love the water, how it ripples ...' Michael says, sounding a little more coherent. He pushes himself up into a sitting position. 'You okay? You look ... sad?'

I want to tell him to mind his own business, tell him that I should go, but Jake's image taunts me. 'My brother—Jake—he ... loved the water too.'

'Loved ...? What happened?'

'I couldn't save him.'

Michael listens without interruption, and when tears prick the corners of my eyes and trickle down my cheeks he folds his arms tightly around me. I curl into his chest, sobbing.

'What time will you be home?' Dan's text, sent at 11:03 pm, appears on my phone screen.

I glance at my watch—1:37 am.

Shit!

I pay the taxi driver and walk the green mile to the front door.

'Clara?' Dan's voice carries from inside.

Within moments, the door's flung open.

'Where were you? Flick said you didn't make it,' he barks.

'Oh ... I ... err—didn't make the meal. Met up with Tiff later.' I brush past him and into our bedroom.

'And you didn't think to call me?'

'I was really drunk ... sorry.' I can't look at him. Can't let him see my guilt.

He walks away, swearing, as I head for the shower.

The following day at work I log into Facebook. There's a message from Michael.

'I'm sorry,' it says. 'Going to AA. Don't hate me.'

He's always sorry.

January 2016

Dan has asked me to marry him. I should be over the moon, shouldn't I?

April 2017

Dan and I have been married for just over a year and we're buying a house together. It should be exciting for us, but cracks have been forming ever since Michael appeared, and I am slowly retreating into a shell, anticipating my next loss. Those cracks are now ravines.

Work frustrates me. My friends know I'm unhappy, but I just smile and say, 'It's fine. Just need to pull my head in.'

Much of my free time is spent out of Dan's way, holed up in the office trying to write, but only managing one or two lines before frustration kicks in and I flee to spend time with one of the girls. Dan says nothing.

On the way to work one morning, I pass by a familiar face at the train station.

'Hi,' Michael beams as we cross paths.

'Michael,' I breathe, stopped in my tracks.

'Been a while.'

I nod.

'How are you?'

'Good.' My voice wavers. 'You?'

'Sober,' he chuckles. 'And working.'

'That's great.' Uneasiness lingers. 'I'd better go. Gonna be late.' I toss him a smile. 'Nice to see you,' and walk away.

'Clara?'

I twist around to look at him. 'Michael—I'm married now. I … I can't do this anymore.'

He doesn't call after me.

August 2017

Dan's face flushes crimson as I look up at him through tear-drenched eyes.

'This is bullshit, Clara. You'd rather spend time with your friends than me!'

We have been fighting for hours and I've run out of excuses.

'I'm sorry,' I reply. 'I never meant for it to get like this.'

'Really?' he replies, eyes fiery.

'I love you, but it—it isn't working. I'm so sorry …'

He punches the wall, roaring as plaster and fist collide.

I slope away to the bedroom as he whispers, 'I love you too,' and start packing.

The winter chill has set in and I hurry to the station to catch the train to my new rental apartment.

As I walk along the overpass, a man calls out, 'Spare any change?' I glance down at him—a straggly beard covers his mouth and chin, his face ruddy from the cold.

'Clara?' He smiles, and I notice a cracked front tooth and wisps of grey in his beard.

'Michael?' It takes a moment for recognition to kick in. 'What are you doing here?'

He clambers up until we are face-to-face. 'Long story. Wanna buy me a coffee?' No protests, no whiskey bottle this time.

We find a café and sit at a table away from everyone else.

'What's going on?' I ask softly.

'Lost my job again.'

'Drink?'

He nods, head dropping.

'Michael …' I reach over and squeeze his hand.

He looks up, tears pooling in his eyes. 'They've given up on me.'

'Who?'

'Everyone. I fucked up too many times.'

'I'm sorry …'

I'm preparing dinner when the kitchen door creaks open. Michael appears wearing only a bath towel. His torso is lean, his skin sallow, but unleashed desire courses through me.

After eating, we spend the night talking, touching, deepening this strange, long-held connection between us. The Universe has given me another shot, only this time, I won't fail.

The note on my bedside table reads, 'I'm sorry.' Michael has gone.

December 2017

As I flick through the local rag, my eyes fall on a large notice in 'Obituaries':

'Michael Joseph Moran, beloved son. Died 29 November 2017 aged 34. Funeral to be held at Immaculate Heart of Mary, Scarborough on 13th December 2017 at 2 pm.'

My cup smashes into tiny pieces on the floor.

I feel numb and barely register the priest's words or the dedications from friends and family sparsely occupying the pews. But the sobs of Michael's nearest and dearest echo around the cold, cavernous church. As the service ends and the congregation leaves, I dutifully make my way to the entrance towards an elderly couple who seem to be Michael's parents.

'I'm so sorry …' I offer, shaking the man's hand. 'I'm Clara. I … I worked with Michael at the prison.'

The woman, her puffy eyes widening, reaches into her handbag. 'This must be for you, then,' she says, pushing a crumpled envelope towards me.

I take hold of it, staring at my name on the front. 'Oh … thanks,' I mumble, and stash it in my bag.

I quick-step out of the churchyard desperate to contain whatever is threatening to burst out as my head starts to spin like an errant Catherine Wheel.

I wish Jake were here to hold me and tell me it'll all be okay. But he's gone too, nothing but a weathered headstone on a patchy grass bed to identify him. I can't bear to see the same for Michael.

So, I walk the short distance to the church on the Esplanade and make my way to Jake's grave.

Why do they always leave me, Jake? Why?

My bag drops onto the sandy shore and I tip-toe, still fully-clothed, into the Indian Ocean, wading until the water reaches my neck.

I can't do this anymore—can't face another loss, so I give in, ready for the sea to claim me. A king wave surges over my head, swallowing me whole and tossing me around until the undercurrent grabs me in its unforgiving pull …

Water fizzes up my nose and I gasp back to life, spluttering.

The sea has spat me out and the wash has carried me back up the shore to safety.

Sodden and covered in sand, I stumble back up the beach to where I left my bag and sit.

With cold, trembling fingers I pull a letter out of the envelope given to me by Michael's mother and read it:

Dear Clara,

Leaving you sleeping that morning was the hardest thing I've ever done. I wanted to come back to you so many times, but I just couldn't live with myself if I let you waste your life on me.

I had so many opportunities to quit the booze, but guess I was beyond saving. Your brother and me—well, we had choices, and we had people who loved us enough to keep trying, but we still took the easy way out.

I've messed up so many times and now my chances have run out. Guess I've got the ending to my story now, eh.

It's been an adventure, though, and maybe one day you can write about it for me, only with a much happier ending.

I just want you to know that I'm so glad to have known you, Clara. And whatever you may think, you did save me in many ways, if only I could've saved myself before it was too late.
Love always,
Michael.'

'I love you too,' I whisper, and the dam wall holding back my grief for Jake and Michael finally bursts.

Darkness falls as I arrive home, my head lighter, my heart steadied, as if the cage I constructed to harbour my losses has been thrust open and washed clean.

I make myself a coffee, flip open my laptop and begin typing with a renewed passion.

There is only one person left to save—me.

Adrenaline Junkie

KELLY VAN NELSON

Hayden's heart raced as Carmen walked in the room. His hands shook as he gulped down a cup of ice-cold water, which did nothing to quench his dry mouth. She looked stunning, dressed in a trouser suit that perfectly accentuated her curves. The navy fabric complemented her blue eyes, which were staring at him now with a piercing intensity he'd never experienced with any other woman in the past. He liked the elegant gold studs in her ears and the strands of blonde hair that escaped her bun and curled around her heart-shaped face. He ran his fingers through his own dark hair to smooth down any loose ends. Hopefully she was just as observant as he was and noticed the trouble he'd gone to with his appearance. Taking the time to shave down to a baby-smooth chin was a concession he made only for her.

'Thank goodness we were lucky enough to get a table without a reservation,' Hayden said as she crossed the room that was packed with diners. 'This place has gourmet food to die for. Even the sausage and mash has Michelin stars.'

A flicker of a smile crossed her face. She wasn't one for letting her emotions show, which made the challenge of breaking down her barriers just that bit more interesting. She was always so poised; as if downplaying her incredible looks to avoid unwanted attention. Her sculptured cheeks were always devoid of make-up and there was never any hint of cleavage showing. It was unusual to meet such a beautiful woman who downplayed her looks the way she did. He wished he was alone with her now, ripping off her underwear and touching her wherever he wanted. It was torture sitting here with his lust building. They hadn't consummated their relationship yet but he knew it would be explosive when they did.

He thought back to the last time he'd been so infatuated by a woman. Brooke Robinson had been something special and their time together was one wild adventure. Vivid memories flowed like it was only yesterday, and not three years ago, that he had met her.

She sucker-punched him from afar when he spotted her amidst the crowd at Hillarys Boat Harbour on a blistering hot Saturday afternoon. The heel of her strappy white shoe had caught between the slats of the wooden boardwalk that sat on stilts above the water, connecting the restaurants, bars, and craft shops. The sudden jerk made her coffee fall and brown liquid splashed on the leather of her footwear.

Hayden crossed the few metres from where he'd been nursing a cold beer while he enjoyed passing the time people watching. 'You okay?'

'Brings a new meaning to Skinny Flat White when you don't get a single sip of calories.'

Hayden laughed, enjoying her humour and the strong lilt of her British accent, which he couldn't quite narrow down to a specific part of the UK. 'Can I buy you another?'

'Not sure I can move.'

The woman gave her foot a wiggle, but her shoe was well and truly wedged in the gap.

'Take off the shoe. Maybe I can get it out in one piece.'

Hayden watched her long fingers unhook the buckle of her strap and the most perfect bare foot slip from the shoe. Her toenails were painted a pale shade of lilac with a tiny daisy on each of them. They were a masterpiece, better than anything he'd seen hanging in the local art galleries of Western Australia. He could barely stop staring at them as he knelt to ease the shoe free. He handed it back to her.

'There you go.'

'Thanks. I'm Brooke by the way.'

'Hayden.'

Electricity sizzled as they shook hands and he instantly knew from the stirring in his loins that she was the one. Blondes always attracted him but this one was something else. Her long wavy locks looked soft and natural in colour; not the harsh peroxide that was so brittle you could start a bushfire if you lit a match within a kilometre radius of it. She had a willowy figure shown off to perfection in denim shorts, and the gypsy multi-coloured top with enormous sleeves made him think she might be the kind of carefree spirit he loved. And that pout. It was coy and sexy with perfect pink lips that just begged to be kissed.

Hayden bought her a fresh, overpriced coffee in a trendy establishment with decadent furnishings and the best ocean views. It was a small price to pay to hear her life story.

Brooke told him she was born in the north of England, in Newcastle-upon-Tyne, which put him out of his misery trying to second guess the origin of her accent. She was a working-class Geordie who had done well enough in her education to claw her way out of a crime-riddled government housing estate. Qualifying as a nurse had provided her with a golden ticket into Australia.

'Which hospital are you working at?' he asked when she'd finished talking about her background.

'None yet. I only arrived two weeks ago, so I've just been checking out Perth city since then. I've a new job lined up in Mandurah though, starting next month, so I'll be moving down there.'

'So, you don't know anyone?'

'I know you.'

Hayden grinned. His life in comparison was ordinary. Since leaving school, he'd worked in the same deadbeat job as a debt collector for the government, chasing overpayments from people on benefits who couldn't afford to put food on the table. The depressing work was enough to drive a man to insanity. He tried to offset this mundane existence by spending his downtime appreciating untrodden territory where nobody but die-hard hikers like him would think to explore. He quickly established Brooke loved the outdoors too.

As they chatted several boats cruised in and out of their pens, expensive toys paid for by Western Australia's mining boom, then the huge commercial ferry pulled in. Hundreds of tourists offloaded their luggage and bicycles after a weekend on Rottnest Island, the spectacular playground forty-five minutes offshore from where they were sitting. Its outline was visible across the turquoise ocean, a magnet attracting the next wave of visitors to enjoy some relaxation time there.

'I'm beefing up my fitness training for this week-long Cape to Cape walk that's coming up soon.' He watched her remove the plastic lid from her coffee to blow on it. 'It goes from Cape Naturaliste Lighthouse to Cape Leeuwin Lighthouse. Trekking and cycling around Rottnest would be perfect as part of my exercise ramp-up. I don't suppose you have a bike?'

'One of the first things I bought when I got here.'

'See, I knew as soon as I met you we'd have so much in common. You up for a day trip?' Hayden beamed, glad that he'd worn his favourite sports t-shirt and khaki shorts. He guessed she was in her twenties, certainly younger than him by a few years, but he regularly pumped up a sweat at the gym to keep in decent shape.

'When?'

'How about tomorrow? I've got a couple of things to do first thing over there on the island but we can meet around eleven outside the main bakery if you get the mid-morning ferry. There's only one bakery and it's close to the main jetty where you get off. It would be cool to hang out again.'

'Let's do it. Give me your mobile number in case anything changes, otherwise I'll see you there.'

They swapped numbers, and he told her about the ticket booth at the marina entrance where she could book the ferry. Reluctantly, he said goodbye and watched her stroll off. He could have talked to her for hours, and it seemed an impossible task to have to wait a whole day before he saw her again.

The early morning ferry was busy as it made the crossing from Hillarys Boat Harbour. Hayden took a seat next to an Australian family with an excited toddler in a Batman t-shirt. The boy kept moving from his father's knee to his mother's as if playing musical chairs. Hayden couldn't wait to get away from them and onto the sanctuary of the island and was pleased the ferry pulled into the jetty at Thomson Bay bang on time. A delay would have been unbearable but thankfully rush hour congestion was not a problem that the Indian Ocean suffered from. Hayden had purposely departed on the ferry before Brooke to have time to steady his nerves before she got there. First date butterflies were something he'd never been able to manage well. His confidence in approaching Brooke was smoke and mirrors. He'd spent years fumbling through awkward interactions with the opposite sex.

After his black mountain bike was offloaded from the ferry, he slung on his backpack and cycled into the main square in the settlement centre, nestled amidst low-rise self-catering accommodation. He set his front wheel in the metal bike rack, pleased at the peace and quiet that was a result of cars being prohibited on Rottnest. The only methods of travel around the island were on foot, bike, or on the circular shuttle bus.

He grabbed a takeaway coffee from one of the restaurants and settled down on an empty bench to take in his surroundings. The Rottnest Island Authority had done a good job of preventing too much commercialisation with not much more than a grocery store, an ice creamery that sold every weird flavour under the sun, and the large bakery. Sympathetic development of an A-class reserve, done so to protect the island's nineteen square kilometres of natural beauty. A group of quokkas meandered around on a large patch of grass next to him. One wandered too close and he hissed it away. Tourists seemed to love the native marsupials that carried their young in a pouch like kangaroos; but to him they were no better than flea-infested, oversized rats. Long ago he'd realised some quokkas were skittish and wild while others seemed to relish human company. He preferred to enjoy nature that was more predictable than animals. Smart trees that never failed to adapt to the seasons and shed their dead leaves in the breeze, the treacherous rips that were invisible to the naked eye but were guaranteed to be present under the ocean surface, or the phenomenal sunsets that left their burnt-orange trail across the sky, night after night on the western side of Australia.

He finished the last of his coffee and tossed the cardboard cup in the bin next to where he sat. Spreading his arms along the back of the bench he leaned back to watch families, couples, and individuals like him gradually fill the square until eventually the area was a swarming beehive. The tranquillity of the museum beckoned to him, so he wandered over to the original limestone building housed inside the old mill and hay store. The main wooden door was propped open so he stepped inside.

'Morning.' An elderly lady with cropped grey hair and kindly eyes greeted him. 'It's a gold coin donation if you would like to look around. This place has such marvellous history. It was built by Aboriginal prisoners in 1857.'

Hayden didn't care too much about hearing stories of criminals who wound up caged behind bars, but he rummaged in his backpack and pulled a dollar from his wallet. 'I'll definitely take you up on that.'

'Are you alone?'

'Sure am. I'm just over for a day of cycling and thought I'd check this place out before I get started.'

'Let me show you around. It won't take long. You're the first one here.'

Hayden relaxed as they wandered around. He was given a history lesson as they checked out artefacts housed in glass cases and exhibitions of photographs and information displayed around the walls. He didn't want to hurt the curator's feelings by telling her he already knew all about the old prison, indigenous inhabitants, and ship wrecks. There had been numerous family holidays spent here as a kid; before his father ran off with another woman and left him with a depressed mother who depended on her only son to change every plug in the house. He knew every inch of the island better than he knew the corners of his own soul.

When his tour was finished, Hayden thanked the lady and headed back to the main square. As he walked there he spotted the next ferry had moored at the jetty and people were busy disembarking as their bikes were offloaded by the crew. His phone beeped with a text from Brooke.

I'm here.

He wiped the message and sat on another bench outside the bakery and waited. Moments later she caught his eye, waving frantically with one arm as she steered her red bike towards him with the other. He remained seated, rooted to the spot as he drank her in. Her glorious long, golden hair was loose today, popping out beneath her helmet to grace her shoulders.

'Hey.' The smile she gave him was enormous.

'You look amazing.'

'In Lycra shorts?'

'Trust me, you look good. Shall we get straight to it before it gets too hot? It's going to be another summer scorcher today.'

Brooke nodded.

'There's a fantastic swimming spot up past Geordie Bay. We'll head that way first.'

'Geordie Bay. That's an ironic place to visit for a Geordie like me.'

She chuckled as they fell into formation, him up front, her tailing him. There were so many beautiful routes to take around Rottnest but he chose the remote track that took them out of the settlement, through woodland, and up past Herschel Lake.

'Wait,' Brooke called from behind him after they'd cycled a few kilometres. He stopped and turned as she climbed off her bike after coming to a halt on the shore of the lake. Piles of natural salt gathered at the water's edge beside her feet. 'This is breathtaking.'

A huge bird glided past them. 'Check that out,' said Hayden, getting off his own bike and walking to her side. 'It's an Osprey.'

'I've never seen anything like it.'

Hayden pulled out his phone and breathed in her heady scent as he leaned in next to her to take a selfie. She smelt of clean laundry, as if she'd dipped herself in an excessive amount of fabric softener. 'These salt lakes are a Rottnest phenomenon. The island is small but there are several more lakes like this one.'

'You'll have to send that snap to me.'

'Later. There's no phone signal here.'

'I never dreamed this place would be such a wildlife haven.'

'Wait until you see more of it. Every beach is unique and has a different name. The Basin and Little Salmon Bay both have mind-blowing snorkelling but they get packed in summer. I prefer the quieter coves.'

'Let's go then. The faster we cycle, the more we get to see before the ferry sails back tonight.'

Hayden couldn't wipe the grin off his face. Her enthusiasm was infectious, and he couldn't wait to get to the spot that was his favourite place in the whole world.

They left their bikes on the ground behind a tall, prickly bush and weaved through the fauna, clapping their hands as they went to send any snakes into hiding. The view was stunning as they rambled through bushland, curving around a cliff overlooking glinting ocean. They clambered over a steep section to find a lagoon nestled behind it, enclosed on all sides with jagged rocks. When they reached the edge of the lagoon, they dropped their backpacks onto a small patch of pristine sand.

'Unbelievable!' Brooke lifted her long hair and twisted it into a ponytail secured with an elastic band from her wrist.

Hayden noticed the dampness around her neckline. 'We should swim to cool off.' He pulled off his t-shirt and watched as Brooke followed suit and peeled off her vest. Her cerise and white polka dot bikini top was strapless but she had fresh tan marks where her vest straps had been, a sign of foreign skin still adapting to the wicked Australian sun rays.

He bent to rummage in his backpack and pulled out rubber reef shoes, black neoprene gloves, and his diving knife, which he strapped to his thigh over one leg of his shorts.

'Wow, you came prepared.'

He nodded towards the ocean. 'This is Australia. There are all kinds of predators out there. When you get into the water, stick close and follow where I stand. There is long sea grass underwater and some sharp rocks that can scratch your feet. If we can get to the far side, there's a submerged cave with a tiny tunnel leading from the lagoon to the ocean. If you're up for the challenge, it's pretty cool to swim through.'

'My middle name is Adrenaline Junkie.'

'I'll wait for you on that flattish rock over there. It's right beside the cave.'

Brooke nodded and Hayden gave her one last smile before lowering himself into the water. It was cold at first but the sharp needles were refreshing, putting him on high alert for the adventure ahead. The water only reached his waist, but as he waded out, it became deep enough to swim across.

His middle name was Adrenaline Junkie too. A rush was pumping through his veins by the time he clambered onto the flat rock on the other side because he knew he'd finally found the perfect girl to share this experience with.

Hayden shook his head to get the image of Brooke out of his head. The ending had been abrupt, but even though it had been three years since she'd gone from his life forever, he still replayed every moment of his relationship with her every day. It was over with Brooke and it was driving him insane thinking about her all the time. He knew the only remedy was to find another woman to replace her. It was about Carmen now. She was the lucky one.

Carmen caught his eye again and the stare lingered longer than necessary before she averted her eyes. She fiddled with a jacket button on her navy uniform and he guessed he was getting under her skin. That was how this relationship was meant to be; two people so in tune with the moment they could read exactly what was going on inside the other's mind. He wanted her, and from the way she watched him so intently, he suspected that she knew it.

He looked down bashfully and placed his hands over his groin under the table. Any obvious desire visible through his pants would make her jumpy, not because she'd experienced it yet, but because she knew exactly what he was incarcerated for. It took a lot of patience to chip away at her defences. Based on his history, it would be understandable for Carmen to be afraid of their relationship becoming physical. For three years now, he'd been working on gaining her trust by behaving impeccably in her presence. His reward for acting with demure restraint was usually an extra minute of yard exercise time or throwing him a rare smile in the corridor, but it was slow progress. Eventually, he was sure she would slip up on her endeavours to avoid being alone with him.

Grabbing her was the monumental event he was waiting patiently for. He was still an adrenaline junkie, only these days the rush that he craved was fuelled by narcotics. Amphetamines, benzo's, or whatever he could get his hands on. The drugs would heighten the thrill he'd have when that window of opportunity came with Carmen. It would be all-consuming, frantic, and there would be no coming back from it.

It would make his time with Brooke pale in comparison. With her, he'd enjoyed several leisurely hours in one of the world's most incredible secluded locations, turning every fantasy he'd ever had into reality, before he finally slit her throat with his dive knife. With all his careful planning, he'd nearly gotten away with it too. He'd indulged in a handful of crazy trysts before but nothing where he tipped things right over the delicate line between life and death. For so long, he'd been strong in resisting the urge to take his desires to another level, but Brooke was his weakness. He'd intentionally chosen her as the one to satisfy his needs because she was a new arrival to the country; someone nobody would miss straight away. Meticulous details had been thought through. Making sure they travelled to Rottnest Island on different ferries. Ensuring he'd been seen by the Aussie family with the Batman brat. The curator had been another witness of his solitary visit to the museum; just another tourist enjoying the island. He'd doubled back to sink Brooke's bike too before he cycled back to Thomson Bay for the last ferry home. It was that stupid *'I'm here'* text she'd sent him when she first got off the ferry that directed police attention onto him. He'd filled her bag with rocks before tossing it into the ocean and thought her phone had been in it. But it hadn't. It was found in the sand next to where they had stripped down to their swimwear. That message led investigators to him and they'd found the photo on his own phone of them by the lake. Before he was caught, he'd gone to delete that selfie so many times, but could never manage to trash it. Just looking at her face had excited him, over and over again. So exuberant. So trusting. His biggest misjudgement of all, though, had been thinking the ocean would pull her body far out to sea after he pushed her over the lagoon edge into the waves. Instead it washed up on Geordie Bay five days after he'd killed her. He cursed the great whites for not being around when he needed them most. He knew sharks were unpredictable and hadn't solely relied on their hunger, but his miscalculation of the riptide had cost him dearly.

With Carmen, their time together would be short. At best, he would only be able to grab a few intense minutes with her behind the silver shelving in the laundry room, or in the food storage cupboard just off the main kitchen, before an avalanche of her prison officer colleagues descended upon them with their batons and cuffs. He would need to be quick when he screwed the screw. Still, it would be long enough to see the rollercoaster of emotions that would pass over her face. The anger he hoped Carmen would feel when she realised she'd finally been cornered, then resignation when he had his way with her. What a kick to reverse the power she asserted over him every day when she locked him in his cell after communal meal times like this or put him through an impromptu strip search. She was a nosey bitch, always entering his personal space to look for contraband. He would put his mouth over her nose so she could smell his breath. Maybe he'd even bite her nostrils. He would relish the build-up of her discomfort and get off on making her scream. With pain or with pleasure, it was all the same.

Finally, before he was hauled off to the slot, he would wrap his hands around her neck and squeeze. He would enjoy watching her gasp for breath before sadness etched itself forever on her beautiful face. And he wouldn't blink in those final predictable few seconds as the light in her eyes went out.

He looked at Carmen and ran his tongue over his lips. It had been euphoric with Brooke, and it would be even better with this one.

The adventure worth getting a life sentence for.

Rock the Boat

LIA ELIADES

She said yes, although she knew it was a terrible idea. Oh, sure it sounded great, cruising around the world in a luxurious catamaran. She would be crazy to say no. Her husband was a seafarer, went out every day to pull up the cray pots or fish, no matter how rough.

He loved the sea and it loved him. But for Ingrid, it was a totally different story, even though her Viking ancestors most definitely sailed the seven seas; she had no stomach for it. Seasickness was something that drains the goodness out of the hardiest.

They had been invited by friends richer than them, and more generous than they could ever be. Todd and Janet were Kiwis, and they had adventurous hearts and minds. Janet was fluent in French and Italian and went to all the best schools. She found Todd on one of her many travels abroad. Todd was a rebel, with a spirit to achieve and it served him well. They were a perfect, balanced match, one social and engaging, the other more introverted and learned, but put them together and they created a magnificent united front, one to be admired.

Ingrid and her husband had been having difficulties since the betrayal. She supposed he thought that this might bring them close again. That with a bit of luck and time away, Ingrid would find a way to forgive him even though he was never man enough to admit his actions.

Never giving Ingrid what she needed most—a proper apology that would allow her to find a way to release the despair, hatred and rage she found swirling around her heart at the most innocuous of times. It could be so simple.

The TV anchor looked somewhat like the other woman, the mention of the town or the pub, even having to drive through the town on the way to the city; yes, it was painful.

If she had been ten years younger, Ingrid was sure she would have told him to stuff it up his jumper, and she would have waltzed out without a look back over her shoulder. But she wasn't. And here they were.

The thought of travel always excited her and although she knew she got seasick, she thought that being at sea for long enough would conquer it. She also had a sneaky suspicion that it was the lingering smell of bait and fumes that made her sick, not the rocking of the boat.

Gavin said it was all in her mind.

'Hmph,' Ingrid thought. 'Yeah right. Just like you cheating on me was in my mind.'

Oh, there were moments of contempt. Times when she really hated him, and she tried hard not to, didn't want to. But there it was time and again. The desire to harm him in some way, to make him feel the pain that she felt. The wish that it never happened was the one that was strongest in her; she just wanted it to not have happened. And it should not have.

She gave him everything—her best years as they say.

How dare he? When I gave up everything to help him, to be with him by his side through his grief and his troubles.

And now here she was, jailed by his cruel, unthinking actions. A prisoner of her own thoughts. He was guilty of the crime. It should be him being driven mad by repetitive thoughts, debilitating despair and spite.

There is no doubt about that. But to be fair, the deep hurt was blown way out of proportion by something from her past that almost killed her because it touched on her primal wounding—the loss of her father: the abandonment, the unanswered questions, and the deep sense of despair, confusion and hurt. His betrayal heaped on her early one, brought her to a place where she contemplated how she might bring her legacy to an end. She never, ever thought about killing herself before. She was sure there was always so much more to do and see. But this created a finite edge for her to peer over—an empty canyon where she saw and felt nothing but a desire to no longer exist.

Ingrid was too depressed to even muster the energy to kill herself, and now here she was, about to set sail for foreign lands.

Ingrid had packed her kit bag, bought some new things that a sailor needs for a journey of this kind. She had to admit that she was a bit excited. Knowing that Gavin was happy as can be to be going away, leaving all of his troubles behind once again, and seeing the guy that she fell for all those years ago shining through, broke her heart and lifted it at the same time.

Todd and Janet had made all the arrangements. Ingrid was told that she will need to pull a few ropes and do some night-time watches, but for the most part, the boat is computerised and state-of-the-art. Her biggest job was to look pretty and pour the champagne or the wine.

Since the betrayal, Ingrid had kept her distance from Gavin, but here they would be sharing a cabin and a bed. The proximity would either heal the wound or make it fester and weep. Weeping was something that Ingrid had become very adept at. The reality of being soaked by salty waters was commonplace to her now. It seemed like a poultice. She could cry her salty tears and let them fall over the side of the Catamaran, becoming one with all that water. Maybe it would help to purge them or set them free and she could escape the hellish halls of her mind. The internal struggle to love or hate, to crush or cuddle, to repair or wrench free from this mental anguish, woe.

Purgatory.

They flew to Sardinia. Ingrid used to love flying with Gavin. Holding his hand as they took off and resting her head on his shoulder to allow the weariness from all the travel preparations to overcome her and slumber deeply until the stewardess called out asking if they wanted something to drink.

When they arrived at the marina, the crew was already there and helped Ingrid to board. The sun made her feel more alive than she had in a while. The glint of light on the water reflecting in her eyes and the eyes of the young man who grabbed her hand and her heart at the same time as she stepped from the dock to the Catamaran.

'*Buongiorno!*' he said, and under his breath, '*Che bella!*'

Ingrid heard these words loud and clear, as if he shouted them into the cavern of her wounded heart. But he didn't shout. He spoke them in a hushed manner to himself, preoccupied with her long neck and thin, fine fingers. Her white shorts and blue and white French shirt made her feel more like a sailor. The new crisp white Superga sneakers gave her away, though.

Gavin called up to her from their cabin. 'Wait til you see this honey, come on down.'

Ingrid shot a glance towards their young seaman then quickly looked away and down with a wide smile appearing on her face and a tickle in her stomach. Without picking her head up, she climbed down into the place that would be their home for the next six weeks at least.

Gavin grabbed her hard around the waist and pulled her to him in a strong hug. She leaned her upper body back into a bow leaving only her waist touching him. He laughed nervously and pulled her one more time, then released her. She smiled. He might've taken that as a good sign, but she knew that this was a smile that came from a place she had not felt in some time. Something in her was coming alive once again, and it had nothing to do with Gavin and everything to do with her getting her power back.

It wasn't just the recognition from the young man of her classic beauty, but being on foreign soil, hearing a language that touched her soul, reminding her that this was the place she once wanted to live, many years before she ended up in Australia.

Yes, Italy held so many of the things that she valued: excellent classic style, architecture, mysteries, catacombs, great masterpieces— right there out in the open and in museums, artisan foods, bread, cheeses, wines, the hills, the olives, the liquorice; she loved all of it. The language soothed her soul. The churches allowed her spirits to soar to the heights of the domes that graced them. The small villages, the winding constricted roads that run like veins throughout beautiful piazzas and gardens. Yes, she felt very much at home in Italy.

The sea was so salty that she floated easily. She was buoyant and held by the dense molecules of the water. Yes, that was it—she felt buoyant. Maybe she would fall in love again, maybe there could be repair, and a rekindling of love. Let's see, yes maybe.

The stores had been bought and the fridge and cool storage filled to overflowing. The drinks took up more room so that the floor of their cabin became a storage place. Beer, wine and champagne everywhere. But who was going to complain about that? Tomorrow they set out to sea, and they shall see how good Ingrid is at keeping the bilious liquids and thoughts down where they belong.

The winds and weather are on their side as they set off. They have had some training and practice at reading the weather, the winds, and the charts of the local waters. So far so good. Cutting through the waves like a pair of shears zipping through silk in one fluid motion, no snagging. Todd had told her it would be smooth sailing on the Cat. Ingrid didn't believe him at first, but now she did. She felt terrific and alive once again.

The day was perfect. Ingrid is on deck preparing dinner for everyone. The excitement and high of the successful day of sailing creates a buzz that only gets mellowed by the drinks that are swallowed and the way the sea swallows the sun leaving them awash in a pool of purple light. They decide to anchor for the night in a small cove, settling in just as the stars decide to turn themselves on like small night-lights for all the frightened children of the world. There are so many of them, and the sound of water lapping and running the length of the yacht is as hypnotic as is the sky.

The quiet conversation consists mostly of the next day's adventure and where they will attempt to sail. Todd and Janet put themselves to bed, leaving Gavin and Ingrid on board sitting in chairs facing each other. She has her bare feet perched up on the arm of his chair. He reaches over and grabs her foot and starts to rub it, massaging the little toe first and moving up to the big toe. She used to love this, and she forgets for a moment and allows herself to enjoy the thought of the benefits of reflexology massage—of how feet hold all the organs; represented there in the bottom of the foot, up near where the toes meet the ball of the foot, sinuses, along the arch, the intestines. And then he did it—pressed on the place where the heart sits, and she swears she could feel it wrench and ache. Ingrid's foot jumps from his hand and falls to the floor, along with her high spirits. Yes, her heart was still broken and hurt, and he was responsible for this never-ending ache.

Ingrid wonders if she will ever get over it. She shoots Gavin a look. She can't help it. Then she quickly looks away. He sighs, gets up and goes to pee over the edge of the boat. She hates that. Why do men do that? Why do they think it okay to just whip it out and spray wherever they feel? She listens as he empties his bladder into the pristine sea that she bobbed about in earlier. Now he has spoiled it with his beer waters. She imagines walking up behind him and giving him just the slightest of pushes. Kerplunk—it would be easy. Or hit him over the head with a champagne bottle. Yes, that is good and heavy. She would have to strike him on the side of the head to make it look as though he struck his head as he fell over into the water and drown.

Ah … but it is too calm tonight. No-one would believe it. Her negative fantasy comes to an abrupt halt when Gavin speaks.

'I'm going to bed. Are you coming?'

But he knows the answer and descends dejectedly.

She waits until she hears the light click off and then waits a few counts more until she can hear his steady breath. Ingrid strips down to her bra and panties up on board so as not to wake Gavin, and she can just slide into bed without disturbing him. She just can't risk having him awake and then have to rebuke him once again. She is not ready to be intimate with him, even though they had a great day and she felt some stirrings of love returning to her heart. She was tortured by her rage at him, at all men.

Ambivalence kept her captive for months on end, now it was going on nine months and still she couldn't shake it. Initially she wept and wept and moped around the house in her dressing gown, staring into space, then weeping some more. Then she became territorial and voracious and fucked him with a fervour that scared him. She wanted to show him what he gave up, have him miss her and feel her passion like a searing heat. She wanted him to burn like a rocket upon re-entry to Earth. Yes, she wanted to shatter the fantasy world he created with this other woman and make him fall to Earth with an ungodly thud. She wanted to make him suffer the way she had.

The sad part was that she hated herself for it, hated that she was too weak and depressed to do anything but fall on the ground and not get up for a good six months. She was despondent and unable to do anything but obsess about the details that she didn't have. Calculating all the late nights he was out working, supposedly. All the phone calls, cloaked conversations and the presents that came unbidden. All the lies, the pompous callous actions. He thought she was stupid. He mocked her. His existence mocked her.

How could he disrespect her so? Had he not cared for her? No thought of her? She could not reconcile with the fact that he did things without any regard or respect for her, and after all she had done and all she was to him and his broken family. She rescued all of them, and this is how she was re-paid?

Well, fuck him.

Ingrid grabbed a beach towel and settled on the lounge chair. Breathing fitfully, she twisted and turned and tried to sleep. After some time, she woke up feeling the chill air and crawled down to the bunk knowing that sweet sleep was close by now.

She slumbered as she slipped into a dream where she is being rocked in the arms of the young man who helped her board the boat for the first time. He is stroking her hair and telling her in Italian how beautiful she is, tracing all of her imperfections and making them all okay. Although her Italian is not fluent, she understands everything that this young man says to her for some reason. She weeps with her head in his lap and he strokes her back in wide, sweeping movements from her shoulders down to her buttocks as though he is trying to smooth out all the wrinkles of time. Purging the hurt from her, the magic begins to work, her weeping subsides, and she feels herself relax. All the sailor's knots that bound and gagged her for the past months unfurl like sails billowing in the breeze, and finally she can breathe again.

She rolls over and lets him run his hands down her body from shoulder to top of thighs and back up again. She starts to arch and bend under his hands. She feels a pulse where only the dim light of a firefly had been before. There is a heat between her legs and a fire in her stomach that tells her she has more living to do, and she wakes herself with the passion still pulsing.

Normally this would have been the start of a fantastic session of lovemaking with her honey, but he has spoiled that for them. This will just be an opportunity wasted, one set aside until she can find a way to forgive him. Which infuriates and frustrates her further.

'Damn you!' She felt the anger rise to the top of her throat again.

There were voices up above now. Ingrid was groggy and moribund, but she dressed and attempted to put a believable smile on her dial. Coffee drank and course set, away they went out of the cove and into the sea. The day started out as planned and predicted, but in no time and without warning things started to change. The mood, the boats relationship to the sea, and the weather darkened.

The steady vessel became a bucking bronco and caused Ingrid to quell and squirrel. The bile began to boil and roil along with the waves. First came the feeling at the top of her throat, the anxiety causing her to feel like swooning. She knew this feeling. It happened when the realisation of the infidelity came. She was going to get sick and she never wanted to, always tried to keep things down. She had done it with her emotions for the past nine months now, kept it down, tried against might to push it back down, or to the back of her mind, and here it was again sitting at the top of her oesophagus and attempting to escape once again.

The emotional sea wins. As she ran headlong to the boat's edge and released black and green bile into the turquoise sea, it was ugly and made her churn and cough up another bucketload. The choking and the back wash were the worst. The smell at the top of the throat coming up and out the nose brings one more vocal burst of brutality forth. It was like self-punishment punching at her soul, begging her to escape the violence that has been done to her. Yes, it was like a violence and a death.

Everyone left her to her own devices. They were busy steering the Cat and managing the course. Gavin looked at her once, but he has never been good at comforting her when she was sick. There was so much that he wasn't good at. She wondered to herself, as she hung over the railing regarding the spittle spots on her pristine Supergas, what she ever really saw in him.

She was nauseous at the thought of all those years wasted, all the labours, only to have it pouring out of her on the deck of a million-dollar Catamaran. She was done. There was nothing left. Nothing to hurl, no slings, no arrows, nothing to release. She had been emptied.

Finally, as the breeze and spray of the sea covered her face, she leaned out further and felt herself free, finally free. She has escaped her ambivalent mind and decided to get off this boat at the next port, to get out of this marriage to a man she can never learn to trust again, and to get started with a new life of her own.

She felt exhilarated now with the tempest as her ally, the wrath of the gods agreed with her, hurling thunderbolts and lightening and throwing water about cleansing her of the poisons that tried to kill her. All of it being washed away in the most dramatic way. She was never in more danger and never in more control than in that moment, and like Ahab in Moby Dick, she dared the beasts and her demons to take her, but she knew they couldn't. She was in charge now.

Ingrid drew her forearm across her mouth and dragged a beautiful smirk onto her lips. She had an escape plan. A way out. And she was ready for what was to come next.

Not What She Expected

JEAN FROST

Isn't it funny how some childhood memories are all but forgotten until you do the same thing again as an adult? Maybe this is déjà vu? That sudden giddy feeling you experience when you think you have done it before?

This is the feeling I got when we glimpsed the ship's funnels over the rooftops of the shops facing the wharf. You see, it's not the first time I have been on a ship. I am a 'Ten-Pound Pom.' As a child, this is how I came to Australia, sailing on a ship called the Castel Felice, way back in 1968. I haven't been on one since and to say I was a tad nervous is an understatement.

Take my suitcase, for instance. I had packed it three weeks earlier, then the night before we were due to sail I woke up around midnight with the uneasy feeling I had left the little bottles of shampoo and conditioner behind in the bathroom cabinet. Mumbling that I was silly, I rolled over and buried myself in the bed covers where I tried to go back to sleep. After tossing and turning, I went to check. Sure enough, they weren't there.

When my travelling companion, Kathy—who is also my sister-in-law and best friend, yelled from the seat beside me, 'There she is,' I almost peed my pants. Almost, but not quite. Instead, my head jerked up, eyes darting from the passport I had been checking for the third time since getting into the backseat of our car, to the windscreen where Kathy's neatly manicured finger was pointing.

'Where?' I cried as I struggled to release the seatbelt. By the time I had found the button and scooted forwards to where I could see, there was nothing except blue sky and sunshine.

'Damn,' I said slapping the consul. 'I was too slow and missed it.'

Within seconds Kathy's arm snaked around my shoulder as if she was trying to soothe a spoilt child.

'You didn't miss much,' she said.

When she saw that I wasn't convinced, she grinned.

'Come on Sue. I'm not even sure it was our ship. I could have been wrong. You know it does happen occasionally.'

Hearing the last sentence made me smile again. Kathy was such a terrible liar.

We continued to sit there wedged in the gap between the front seats like two corks stuck in the neck of a wine bottle until the car pulled into an empty space in front of the passenger terminal at Fremantle harbour.

'Get a load of that,' I said stepping out of the car and gaping up at the huge ship that loomed over the roof of the passenger terminal. 'It's so big!'

Kathy came around from the other side of the car and leaned on the bonnet next to me.

'I hope you're talking about the ship and not one of those stupid guys over there.' She flicked her head in the direction of a group of young men dressed in silly sailor costumes laughing and poking fun at one another. It was obvious they were planning to have a buck's party on board as one wore a white bridal veil, but as Kathy was being Kathy, couldn't pass up the opportunity to have a little fun especially when it was at my expense. She lifted her voice just loud enough for my husband to hear. 'At least not while your husband is still here.'

'Oi! I heard that,' said Kevin, the craggy, black-haired man I call my husband.

He came from behind the car and nearly threw my suitcase at me. I rolled my eyes and turned to thump Kathy hard on the arm. She was always saying stupid things, but as Kevin was her younger brother, he should have known her better. Unfortunately, he was so gullible and believed every word she said. I decided now was not the time to dwell on the negatives as I was eager to get on board and start my holiday.

Finally, after saying goodbye to our husbands and promising not to hang too far over the guardrails when we were at sea, we wheeled our suitcases through the main doors of the passenger terminal with an excited rush. Yahoo! We were free. Albeit, it was only for four days. Still, it was four days of freedom with nothing to worry about except what to eat and, more importantly, what to drink.

'Passenger or visitor?' barked a rotund, middle-aged woman dressed in an official uniform. She had positioned herself in front of a pair of glass doors, and it was her job to stop unauthorized people from going any further. I quickly showed her my ticket as I was too scared not to comply and, without a second glance, she ushered us through to the main passenger lounge.

'Health card anyone?' a female voice called over the din.

Immediately my eyes fell on a group of people crowded around a tall, curly-haired red-haired woman waving a wad of blue paper. Right at that moment, I really can't say what came over me, it was as if someone had flicked a switch inside my brain. All I could think of was, is this free stuff being given away? If so, I knew I had to get some.

'Yes please.' I called back, dropping my suitcase on Kathy's foot and barging my way through to the front of the crowd. Once there, I held my hand out eager to see what special treasures they were going to give me. It turned out, it was only a thin blue card which everyone had to fill out for Customs explaining where you had travelled in the past six months. Talk about being disappointed. Maybe that's why I pocketed one of the pens that had conveniently broken away from the short-frayed cord that tethered it to the wall.

A little payback for getting my hopes up, I justified to myself.

After that, we went to sit on one of the plastic chairs which faced the windows looking out at the harbour. It was time to relax. We had got there on time. All we could do now was wait until our names or ticket numbers—whichever would be used to identify us—were called.

Time ticked by at an agonizingly slow pace from when the first passengers were called until it finally being our turn. I felt one more minute wouldn't hurt.

I held my phone aloft, 'What do you reckon? One for the road?'

Kathy appeared out of nowhere, her head squished in next to mine as I pressed the button to take another selfie. I added this one to the others and, with swift, sharp jabs, SMS'd that we would be out of reach for the next few days. We would miss everyone madly, with plenty to talk about when we got back. Then I posted it on my Facebook page.

The scene that confronted us on the other side of the doors seemed a little over the top. Big muscle-bound security guards decked out in all the right gear stood ready to pounce on suspicious travellers while Customs officers checked the contents of randomly selected suitcases on long metal tables.

I stood there wide-eyed and too scared to move as a Customs official beckoned Kathy over to a walk-through body scanner. I was horrified but also fascinated as he first pointed to a white plastic tub (about the size of an ordinary laptop) and then to Kathy's pockets. Without hesitation, she placed her phone and wallet into the container. Then, as if she was stepping through a gateway into another dimension, held her head high and walked straight through the arches of the scanner to the other side. She made it look so easy. There were no flashing lights nor the sound of alarm bells. It was an anti-climax really, not scary at all. I followed her example, repeating everything she did. I even put the pen I had taken from the other room into the plastic tub and breezed through to join her on the other side.

Finally, the ship was right in front of us, all fifteen decks of her, and as I stood there looking up from the wharf, a cool breeze sent gooseflesh up my arms. Was this what it was like when I left Southampton all those years ago? Did my mother and father look up at the ship that would take their whole family to a new land, a new beginning with the same awe as I did now? Of course they would. Who wouldn't have? I chuckled at the silliness of it all.

'Come closer Ma'am, closer,' beckoned a strained voice from behind a black tripod.

Jumping at the unexpected sound of someone calling to me, I peered into the shadows cast by the ship and drew back in horror. The gangway was a mass of colour. Paper flowers in every shade imaginable adorned the metal handrails, then intertwined with wire, coiled their way up to form an archway. It was clearly meant to put you in the holiday mood, all it did for me was made me feel a little more anxious than I already was. If only I had lost a quarter of the weight I had put on over the years I might have felt a little better about myself. I might have even looked forward to laying by the pool.

'Come, get your photo taken with the Captain,' the voice mumbled from behind the tripod again. Standing a little to the left of him was a cheesy cardboard cut-out of a generic Captain with his arms arched ready to drape over the shoulders of anyone who dared to stand under them.

Kathy grabbed my arm and squealed with delight as she pulled me forwards.

'Isn't it great? You get under that arm,' she indicated to the empty space closest to the gangway where for just a split second I was tempted to do a runner. 'And I'll get under the other. It might be the only chance we get to have our picture taken with the Captain, and I told all our friends I would post one as soon as I had one taken.'

I took a deep breath and put on my best smile. In the end, everything worked out fine, and we laughed and panted our way up the gangway until finally, we stepped onto the deck. Halleluiah. We were on board.

'Welcome, welcome. Can I have your name, please? Look here, hold still, Ma'am.'

It was all done with military precision. I was seriously impressed. Within the space of ten minutes, we had been welcomed on board, checked in, electronically seen and handed our cabin key cards. All that was left to do was join the queue of passengers as they waited to be taken to their cabins.

Our cabin was on Aloha deck about halfway down a brightly carpeted narrow corridor on the left. We had picked an interior cabin over a balcony one, with the idea you only slept in it. So when we finally closed the door after the porter had brought in our luggage, I was ready for a little lie-down.

'Not on your life,' was Kathy's response. 'We have all night to sleep. I want to find the pool deck and order my first drink.'

I must admit since she had put it that way it didn't take much encouragement to get me on my feet. So, within a matter of minutes, we were back out in the corridor and on our way to catch the elevator.

'Excuse me, please. Make way for the bride,' someone called and it was followed by whoops of laughter.

Not sure if I had heard right, I flicked Kathy a sideways glance. Now, I'm not usually a nosey person, but it did tug at the fringes of my curiosity, so I wasn't surprised when I found I had quickened my pace. We had just reached the intersection where the corridor met the bank of elevators when in our haste, nearly bumped into a group of girls clad in bathing suits with flowers in their hair.

'Here comes the bride,' one of the girls sang out, and they all joined in the chorus.

It took a few minutes, but finally, we made it to the pool deck. Then I realized we were quietly sailing out of the harbour. I felt cheated and disappointed. Where were the pomp and ceremony? There was no fanfare, where were the streamers thrown by our loved ones left behind on the shore? Where was the deep, throaty sound of the ship's horn announcing our departure? It was only by chance that we managed to wave goodbye to a group of strangers who had gathered on the South Mole. Without them, we could have sailed out to sea leaving no trace behind us. In a different story that situation might sound very romantic. My husband and I alone on the deck of a ship sailing out of the harbour bound for destinations unknown. But I wasn't with him, I was with Kathy, and she had left me on my own to watch the lights gradually recede into the darkness while she went and ordered another drink.

'Sue!' I heard my name called. When I turned around, I rolled my eyes. Kathy was standing on a chair with a drink in one hand and waving a sheet of paper over her head with the other. 'See what's happening on our last night? There's going to be a wedding right here, and we're all invited.'

Normally, I would have turned beetroot red if someone yelled out my name, and fled the scene. I was used to Kathy's antics and being loud was just her way. So, I casually walked over to where she was standing and helped her down. I couldn't afford for her to break a leg, not on our first night anyway. That set the tone for the night, with loud drunken behaviour from Kathy, and semi-sober motherly concern from me. Sometime after midnight, I gave up making sure she was alright and went to bed.

The next morning I found Kathy sitting in the corner of the dining area wearing the same clothes from the night before. The coffee she guarded so fiercely in front of her was black and smelled very strong.

'Have you eaten?' I asked.

Not because I was concerned about her nutrition, but because I didn't want her to run out on me and leave me to eat breakfast by myself.

She slowly lifted her chin and with eyes shot through with red veins croaked, 'Nope.'

'Huh, well I'm starving.'

I put the plate of eggs and bacon from the bain-marie on the table and was just about to tuck in when I heard, 'How can you eat that?'

'What?' I poked my knife at the orange yolk of the egg. 'I like fried eggs. And they have two types of bacon! English and American.'

Kathy dropped her head forward again and used her fringe as a curtain. I didn't have to be Einstein, I got the message loud and clear, she didn't want to talk. Instead, I read the ships daily itinerary while I ate my breakfast.

Maybe I should have been a little more sympathetic towards her delicate situation. Perhaps I should have banged on the table or cleared my throat to indicate that I was going to speak. When I saw the range of keep fit classes on board, I couldn't help myself.

'Do you want to come to Zumba with me?' I asked eagerly.

Kathy stiffened and didn't say anything right away. She just gripped the table as if holding on to a life raft. Mumbling that she was going to bed, she asked me to wake her around lunchtime. She rose and hurried out of the room leaving me to finish eating alone.

The Zumba class was everything you would expect it to be. Slim bodies gyrating in time to the loud music. The over-enthusiastic instructor encouraging you to 'push it a little further,' even though she can clearly see you are not in the best shape. I started off slow, getting a feel for the music, and by the time the class finished I was swinging my hips and stepping in time with the best of them. When I say 'best of them' there were only six of us, the five girls we passed in the corridor the day before and me. I did enjoy it, though. It took me back to my dancing days when I was a lot lighter on my feet.

'OK everyone, well done,' I heard as I went to retrieve my towel. 'You all picked up those moves quick, so there shouldn't be a lot of trouble remembering the steps. All we need to do is work out when the extra girls are to start, so it can all come together as you progress down the aisle.'

What? Down the aisle? I didn't know what the instructor was talking about, but I was intrigued, so I moved a little closer pretending that there was something wrong with my shoe.

'Ah, there you are. I was wondering if I might have a word?'

Oh no, how embarrassing. I had been caught eavesdropping and it looked like I would have to come clean.

'Umm, Sorry?' I said trying to sound nonchalant.

'You picked up the steps easily,' the instructor said. She pointed at my feet. 'Have you danced before?'

I brushed my sweaty fringe out of my eyes tucking the stray hairs behind my ears. 'Yes. I have all my medals in ballroom dancing and even tried a little swing. But as you can see …' she followed my gaze to my thick thighs, 'that was a long time ago.'

'Well, you are light on your feet and still have good rhythm.' Her smile was warm, and she said every word as if she meant them. I knew I carried a lot of weight, more than I should. 'Look, are you aware there is going to be a wedding on our last night at sea?' she asked waiting for me to respond. Then she went on. 'As it happens the bride wants to dance down the aisle in a Flashdance kind of way. She has a video of their rehearsals but needs a few more people to join in. Would you be interested?

This was not what I was expecting. Of course, I was interested. Who wouldn't be? The instructor made arrangements to meet us all later in the day to watch the video and get better acquainted with each other. It was almost twelve o'clock, so I thought it was time to wake Kathy for lunch.

You know there's something ironic about going on a luxury cruise where there are five-star restaurants, and end up having an Aussie barbeque by the pool for lunch. Kathy was doing her best impersonation of Julius Caesar, laying on a sun lounge dangling hot chips over her open mouth while I sat in the shade next to her rearranging the fried onions in my hotdog.

'So what did you get up to while I was asleep?' Kathy managed to ask through a mouthful of potato.

I hesitated for what felt like a long time, debating on whether to tell her about the whole Flashdance thing, or not, but in reality, it was probably only a heartbeat.

'I told you this morning I was going to Zumba.'

'Oh, I forgot. Exercise.' She rolled over to look at me. 'You do realise this is a holiday on a cruise ship, not a stint in a health camp?' She signalled to a passing waiter, ordered drinks, and carried on telling me I needed to relax more all in one fluid motion. It was a great shame that she wasn't born into money as this kind of lifestyle suited her.

'It's fun,' I answered before biting off the end of my hotdog. 'And it lets me eat things like this.' I held up the half-eaten bun and watched a few limp onion rings fall out and splatter on the floor. 'I'm going again this afternoon. I'm helping them with a Flashdance thing. Do you wanna come?'

You know the little lines that form between the eyes when someone frowns? Well, Kathy's resembled the Grand Canyon when she looked over her sunglasses. 'I don't do exercise remember? And I'm not into group dancing.' She let her eyes roam around the pool area, stopping only when they fell on the group of partygoers she had been drinking with the night before. 'I'll just lay here and wait for you to finish.'

'Alright, but you can't tell anyone.' I moved a little closer and lowered my voice. 'It's a secret. Okay?'

I made her swear her most excellent pinky swear and when I was sure that she really meant what she said, I left to go back to the gym.

Talk about having to find my feet after so many years of not using them correctly. I stepped on people's toes, knocked over gym equipment, even bumped into walls on several occasions, and still, they wanted me there. I'm not sure if it was through necessity or because we had struck up a kind of friendship, but I felt I was part of their group. By the time we had finished with the rehearsals, we were following the lead of the person swaying and stepping in time with each other and the music.

The morning of the wedding arrived so quickly. I woke early, dressed quietly, and told Kathy I would meet her for lunch in the Horizon's

Court. Then I left the cabin so she could go back to sleep. To my surprise, the breakfast area was crawling with people. It was apparent they had risen early to make the most of their last day at sea. I carefully navigated my way around the queues of bleary-eyed passengers as they waited their turn to pile bacon and eggs on their plates, while I grabbed a cup of tea and two bits of cold toast. I found a sunny spot out on deck where I could watch the crew ready the pool area for the wedding ceremony. I sat with my back towards the sun and ate slowly, concentrating on every bite, chewing it over and over until there was nothing left, then I washed it down with sips of hot tea.

I must have looked a picture of tranquillity sitting there lapping up the sun. But I wasn't. My mind was in a whirl. I knew the routine—step here, step there, but what if I stuffed it up? Inside I was a bundle of nerves, and I needed to calm down so, I took a walk around the ship.

'Hello, you're early,' the instructor said as the glass doors of the gym whooshed closed behind me.

I had planned to do a few more laps before heading to the gym, but it seemed that my feet had a mind of their own.

'Yeah, I know. I couldn't sleep,' I explained.

'Well, I'm glad you're here. I have your costume.' She held up a pair of fawn coloured shorts and a green shirt with a palm tree print. It was what the crew wore on our first night at sea. 'I also had this strap attached to the underside of the tray as I know you were so nervous about dropping it.' She turned the tray, and to my joy, there was a strap to put my hand in. I did a few laps of the gym using empty water bottles in place of glasses, and instantly I was in control. The small rehearsal gave me confidence that I had done everything I could. I left with the costume and tray tucked neatly into a bag and went back to my cabin where I would get changed.

It had been almost three hours since I came out of the bathroom dressed in the waiter's outfit and Kathy had burst into laughter. And to my dismay, it had been the same length of time as when I had asked the same question, 'Are you sure I look alright?'

'Oh for ...' she said, closing her eyes and taking a deep breath. 'Yes, you look great. I told you a hundred times I was a dickhead and that I am sorry. I didn't realise how nervous you were until you burst into tears. Honestly, you'll be fine.'

'Two Rum and Cokes please love,' a man called from a table near the guardrail.

Kathy tilted her head to the side and smiled. She didn't have to say another word.

'Hey, how're the nerves?' asked the gym instructor as she came to stand next to me. 'I think they are ready to start the ceremony soon. So, if you go over there and start to clear the tables, I will do the same over there.' She pointed to a small area near the beginning of the red carpet and then to the opposite side. 'Now, remember. Wait until I am three steps ahead of you before you join in and as soon as the first bridesmaid steps onto the red carpet we make our exit.' She squeezed my hand for good luck and hurried off to where she had pointed.

Clearing tables was a piece of cake. I had finished my first and was just starting on the second when the soft tinkling notes of piano music floated through the overhead speakers. I readied myself for our cue. At first, no one paid any attention, drink orders were still taken, a woman's laughter was so loud you could have heard it from the front of the ship, even though we were at the bow. But as the music slowly increased in volume and tempo, people stopped what they were doing and looked around.

It was at that moment the gym instructor started to dance. At first, it was only a twirl and a few pointed steps. She paused at another table just long enough to pick up a plastic glass, which had been placed there as a prop, and then continued on. I stood there nervous as hell, sweat running down the centre of my back as I prepared to join in. As the music changed pitch and she stepped onto the red carpet, I followed precisely three steps behind her. It was executed perfectly, neither of us faulted. We were in perfect sync with each other. It was one of those magic moments when everything came together and you know it will turn out fine.

If only my ballroom dancing instructor had been there, she would have been proud. We both exited the red carpet as soon as the first bridesmaid stepped onto it, then we were free to cheer with the rest of the passengers as the bride came down the aisle.

After the wedding ceremony, when all toasts to the bride and groom were finished, I let my hair down. That night it was Kathy who played mother instead of me.

Delayed

TABETHA ROGERS BEGGS

For Ali, who kept this story alive.

"I love airports. They are so full of promise. Of adventures beginning and journeys ending. An emporium of opposites; order and chaos, joy and sorrow, nerves and excitement, earth and sky. It must be why I like writing about them so much."
—Tabetha Rogers Beggs

May 1992

Lexi stepped down from the National Express Coach that brought her from Coventry to Heathrow Airport trailed by Mark and Kevin, two lads she'd been chatting with to pass the two-hour journey.

'Nice arse,' Mark commented to Kevin as they waited for the driver to release the hatch where their luggage was stored.

'Yeah, she'd make a good double-adapter,' Kevin added.

'Come on Lexi, dump your boyfriend in Ibiza and come with us.'

'Tempting,' Lexi said sarcastically. 'But no thanks.'

'I hope he's worth it,' Mark said grabbing his backpack from the driver.

'Oh, he is,' replied Lexi. *'He* is.'

She watched the two lads in their Coventry City football strips head towards the doors of Terminal 1.

Mark turned and shouted, 'If you change your mind, we'll see you in Majorca.'

'Have a good time,' Lexi shouted back politely, relieved to see the back of them.

I'd make a good double adapter?

Lexi straightened up her suitcase, tugged on its short leash and led it into the airport.

Inside, travellers scurried like ants on their way to an international sugar convention.

Bing Bong Bing

'Flight BA766 to Rome is now ready for boarding. Could all passengers please proceed to Gate 9.'

A wave of excitement welled within Lexi knowing in a couple of hours an announcement like that would be the one she was waiting for. She tugged at her case again and headed towards the departures board.

Craning her neck to read down the brag-list of destinations: Rome, Paris, Majorca, Tenerife, Rhodes, Prague, Antwerp, Berlin—her eyes locked on the one she was looking for—Ibiza.

BA8461 - IBIZA - 1600 hours - A22 – ON TIME

Instant glee. A vision of Toby danced in her head—the way his ocean-blue eyes would light up at her surprise arrival, how he'd scoop her into his arms and kiss her like a lost explorer who hadn't tasted water for weeks. In a little under six hours they'd be together again.

The split-flap screen burst into life and the click-clack of little tiles flicked over like a vertical Mexican wave breaking the little movie trailer scene playing through her head. She looked up to check the details one more time.

BA8461 - IBIZA - 2300 hours - TBA – DELAYED

DELAYED? NO!

While math had never been Lexi's strong point, it didn't take her long to work out it was a seven-hour delay.

You've got to be kidding me?

Lexi considered her options: go find Mark and Kevin and let them harass her for a couple more hours; get back on the National Express to Coventry which would kill four hours, there and back; or find a bar and wait it out.

She yanked on the retired greyhound of a case, the same one she'd arrived in the UK with two years earlier and led it into a bar called The Village Inn. She parked the greyhound at a small table in the corner and made her way to order a drink. A bartender about her own age appeared.

'What'll it be gorgeous?' his cockney accent enquired.

Whoa! You are the double of that guy from Take That, she thought as the words, 'a bottle of Sol please,' fell from her mouth.

She watched as he bent down to get her beer from the cooler. His forearms covered in tattoos and his Levi's clinging to his butt like he was packing a couple of honeydew melons.

'You from Oz?' he asked placing the bottle in front of her.

'Yeah,' she said surprised.

'I'm good with accents,' he said. 'We get a lot of Aussie backpackers through here.'

'Yeah, I guess you would.' Lexi did a quick check on the greyhound and sensed him follow her gaze.

'You don't look like you're backpacking, though. Where you headed?'

'Ibiza.'

'Party Island.' He raised his eyebrows. 'Meeting friends?'

'Actually, I'm surprising my boyfriend.' Lexi hesitated. 'Well, sort of boyfriend. It's—'

'Complicated?' Ryan, as his name badge read, rescued her.

'Yeah, sort of.'

'Well, I hope it works out.'

'Thanks,' Lexi returned his smile. 'Me too.'

And if it doesn't I'm coming back to find you Ryan!

Lexi took her drink back to her table and pulled out a packet of Silk Cut cigarettes. She lit one up and watched the other patrons in the bar, trying to look seductive as she blew her smoke into the air in case Ryan was watching. The temptation to look back at the bar was hard to resist, like a serpent whispering, 'Go on, one bite won't hurt.' She was lost in a moment of her and Ryan half-dressed and making out in the cool room when Toby's face cut in. The guilt was as real as being caught in the act.

While Toby didn't have the tattoos, he had mischief in his eyes and a smile that could lure mermaids to shore.

The first Sol barely touched the sides and Lexi was back at the bar ordering a second.

'So, Oz, if you're not backpacking, what's the story?'

'Well I live here now. In Coventry,' she said handing over a five-pound note for her next drink.

'Sent to Coventry, hey? I thought we sent all the criminals to Australia. You don't see many coming the other way.'

'My parents are from there, so I deferred from Uni and decided to check out the Motherland.'

'How long you been here?'

'Couple of years now,' she said taking her change.

'What you studying at Uni?'

'Musical theatre.'

'One of those thespian types, hey?'

A couple of middle-aged men approached the bar and Ryan excused himself to serve them.

Lexi took herself back to her table, reflecting on the conversation.

She scrambled in her handbag for a pen and peeled off one side of a beer coaster to reveal a blank piece of card. She needed to write a note for Toby.

When she'd initially booked the trip, she'd envisaged hitching a ride with some of the Thompson Reps from the hotel Toby and Chris had secured jobs in as the resident karaoke DJs.

She would appear in the entertainment lounge and wait for Toby to spot her. He'd dedicate a song to her, then ask her to come up and do a duet with him. The whole room would be cast in the warm glow of watching their romantic rendition of *Endless Love*.

Now her flight had been delayed, she needed a new plan. She wouldn't arrive until late into the night, which meant Toby and wingman, Chris, would more than likely be asleep.

Maybe she could get the night porter to slip a note under Toby's hotel door. Or better still, bribe the porter to let her into his suite and she'd seductively slip into bed beside him. Lexi tingled at the thought.

She looked at her watch. Only an hour had passed. Another six to go.

Lexi had reached the bottom of her second bottle of Sol and the pub had filled up with temporary tipplers—passengers getting in a last-minute pint before heading for their flights. She stole a glance towards Ryan at the same time he was stealing a glance at her. She felt her cheeks blush as he nodded an acknowledgement while he dried a pint glass with a tea towel and they exchanged a smile.

I bet he has a stunning girlfriend.

She had thought the same about Toby the first time she'd seen him perform at a karaoke night in Coventry. The day Lexi arrived in England from Perth, her cousin took her to a local pub and introduced her to his friends, Toby and Chris. From the moment Toby said, 'You sound like Kylie Minogue,' Lexi knew her life would never be the same. Two years on, Toby still made her want to bust out a chorus of *I Should be So Lucky* every time she saw him.

The hours passed by slowly while the bottles of Sol now amounted to four. She could feel the numbness of the alcohol lulling her thoughts. The ashtray was piling up with all the cigarettes she'd chain-smoked, and her bladder was at bursting point.

Not wanting to drag the greyhound around again, she went to the bar to wait for Ryan to finish serving a young couple wearing matching hibiscus-print shirts.

'American honeymooners, right?' Lexi joked when Ryan got to her.

'Or die-hard Hawaii Five-0 fans,' he laughed. 'What's up?'

'Would you mind watching my case while I nip to the loo?' Lexi asked.

'Anything for you, Oz. Take your time,' he winked.

He's flirting with me. He is absolutely flirting with me.

Lexi sat down on the toilet and rested her head against the cubicle wall. *I Should Be So Lucky* was on repeat in her head.

It had been a big day and she'd barely slept the night before with all the scenarios playing through her head. How was Toby going to react to her 'unannounced visit?' What would people say when she got back and told them where she'd been for the past week? Two days ago, she'd been sitting at her desk compiling examination papers to be sent out for the Royal Society of Arts.

The question of whether this was the arts career she'd envisaged was playing on her mind as her colleague, Paula, bragged about the holiday she was about to take on the Costa del Sol. A light bulb flashed in Lexi's head. She printed off an annual leave form and filled it in. She took it to her supervisor and said, 'I need next week off work.'

'You need to give at least four weeks' notice,' he said bureaucratically.

'Come on John. All the registrations finish this week, and I'm up to date.' She flashed him a cheeky smile and his resolve dissipated. He'd always had a soft spot for her, not just because she was the same age as his own daughter, but also because she was the only one that laughed at his punny jokes.

He signed the form and handed it back to her. 'Okay, but don't go spreading it around that I've gone soft.'

She nodded her agreement.

'Where are you going anyway?'

'Nowhere special,' Lexi said.

'Not chasing that idiot boyfriend, are you?'

She took the form from his hands without divulging anything further.

'You be careful,' he said more Dad-like than boss.

'I will and plus, I never said that's where I was going.'

Lexi returned from the ladies and thanked Ryan for watching her case. She sat down and calculated how many hours she had left to wait.

Still three hours to go.

She slumped onto the table resting her head on her elbows. She was watching people come and go from the bar: families, couples, backpackers with badges sewn to their rucksacks from all the countries they'd travelled to. It made her reflect on all the places she'd been, thanks to the encouragement of her 'flower-power parents,' and all the countries still waiting for her to explore.

From the corner of her eye she sensed someone next to her. It was Ryan with a bottle of Sol in his hand. He put it in front of her while he collected the other four empties and replaced the overflowing ashtray.

'This one's on me,' he said. 'My shift's just about to finish, so good luck with the trip. I hope your man knows a good thing when he's onto one.'

Lexi thanked him as he reached into his pocket and threw a tiny book of matches onto the table with The Village Inn logo printed on it. 'Consider it a souvenir to remind you of your night at the bar,' he laughed.

With Ryan gone and two hours still to go, she pushed through to finish her last bottle of Sol and resigned herself to the fact she was trolleyed.

Vic Reeves and The Wonderstuff's new song *Dizzy* was playing through the pub's overhead speakers. Lexi's head bobbed to the beat.

'Yep, I'm so dizzy my head is spin-n-ing,' she sang to herself not caring whether anyone was watching her. She sparked up another cigarette only to find she'd lit the wrong end.

Oh God, I've got to sober up.

She looked at her watch again. 'Shit!' she whispered under her breath, there was only an hour to go. In a state of panic, she wondered whether she should have checked-in already? She stood up too quickly causing a wave of vertigo and blinked a couple of times to re-focus.

She cleared her table, putting her cigarettes, beer coaster notes, and the little book of matches into her handbag, then tugged on the greyhound reluctant to budge across the sticky dark carpet. It toppled over onto its side, causing a few heads to turn. Lexi fumbled in her high heels to lift it upright again. 'Behave' she grumbled.

Mustering as much dignity as she could, she strutted out of the pub like a drunk trying to act sober.

'Oh god, sober up, sober up,' she kept whispering to herself as she looked around, disorientated, hoping to see an arrow pointing in the direction of the check-in desks.

At the escalator, she ignored the signs warning against taking suitcases on it. With no time to look for the lifts, she hoisted its dead weight to her chest, her arms barely able to reach around its circumference. Even in her befuddled state, she had the sense to question why she'd packed nearly every item in her wardrobe for a trip that would only require a pair of bathers, a towel and a couple of sundresses.

With her case obscuring her view, when she hit the bottom of the escalator she stopped with a sudden jolt, landing like Di Vinci's Vitruvian Man, face-first onto her case.

She scrambled to her feet, got the greyhound back on his wheels, and marched on with the heavy footsteps of inebriation towards the British Airways check-in desk.

In her haste to get there without further calamity, it didn't register that all the check-ins were closed. The whole hall was mood-lit by emergency lighting only, and when the penny finally dropped, she panicked.

At the end of a long chain of empty counters she saw one light with a woman sitting behind it. She picked up pace until she stood in front of the desk signposted Disabled Passenger Check In.

'I'm supposed to be checking in for a flight to Ibiza that got delayed and—' the woman dressed in red, white and blue cut her off. 'Miss Alexis Lloyd?'

'Yep, that's me,' she said hoping to hurry things along.

'Have you not heard the announcements calling for final boarding?'

'NO!' Lexi said about to launch into her excuse but thought better of it.

Lexi handed over her passport, and after a few clicks on her keyboard the woman handed it back with a pre-printed boarding pass.

'Please make your way to Gate A22 immediately, if you're lucky you might still make it.'

'What about my case?' Lexi enquired ready to lift the greyhound onto the conveyer.

'The loading hatches are now closed. You'll have to take all your luggage with you onto the plane. The hostesses will have to find somewhere to stow it.' By her tone, clearly it was no longer her problem.

The woman then reached under the counter and retrieved a fluorescent pink sticker the size of a tea-towel which read LATE PASSENGER and handed it to Lexi.

'Please stick this on your case and hurry to the departure gate.' Clearly some humiliation tactic to ensure passengers were timelier with future check-ins.

Lexi reluctantly peeled the backing off the sticker and plastered it across the greyhound. Now he looked ready to chase the rabbit out of the gates.

'Let's go.' No longer caring that she was talking to her case.

Her high heels clip-clopped along the polished flooring as she ran back to the escalator, this time letting the greyhound ride beside to her. At the top she searched for the direction of her gate and cursed her choice of footwear and non-supportive, but very sexy bra, which her boobs were doing their best to bounce out of. She could hear all the items in her bag jangling as she ran. The greyhound nearly toppled under the pace, but this well-seasoned champion surely had one more race left in him.

Reaching the glass doors of the departure lounge she was confronted by a sea of disgruntled and tired passengers. All eyes burned into her and the bright pink sticker announcing her less than desirable status.

Lexi handed her passport and boarding pass to the pristine airhostess standing at the entrance and tried to catch her breath. The airhostess winced, catching a whiff of the toxic alcohol and cigarette fumes emitting from Lexi.

'Glad you could make it Miss Lloyd.' The hostess said with a tone of sarcasm. 'We're just waiting for the catering staff to finish loading and we'll open the doors. Please take a seat.'

'Yanksh,' was all Lexi managed to say. Her words a jumble.

At the back of the lounge she found a row of empty seats. She parked the greyhound under her feet and sat down. All that running and adrenalin had not helped to sober her up. In fact, it had had the opposite effect, forcing more alcohol into her blood stream and causing her head to spin. With the three spare seats next to her unoccupied she took the opportunity to lie down. She stared up at the ceiling tiles, trying to focus, but felt like they were closing in on her. She turned to the side to count the feet of the passengers in the chairs backing onto hers. She noticed a half-eaten Mars Bar lying near the bin with a string of caramel peaking from the bite of its last owner. She wondered if anyone would notice if she picked it up and ate it. She hadn't eaten since she'd left home ten hours earlier.

No wonder I'm shucking drunk!

Before she could entertain the idea, the hostess called for passengers between rows 15 and 34 to embark. Lexi looked at her boarding pass for the first time to see she'd been allocated seat 20C.

She pushed herself up slowly from her lying position, knotted her long hair into a makeshift ponytail and hoped she still looked presentable. She wiped the mascara from under her eyes, which left black smudges on her fingertips, then lifted the sleeping greyhound up for one last stretch to the plane. She was totally exhausted and the prospect of sitting down and falling asleep felt like the reward for all the inconveniences of the delay.

As she crossed the air bridge into the fuselage she tried with all her energy to ask the airhostess what she needed to do with her greyhound. 'Sorry—I meant my case, not my greyhound. Sorry, it's been a schlooong day.'

The airhostess passed it to a male steward, who took it away. Lexi didn't bother to ask for instructions of what to do when she arrived at the other end.

She zig-zagged down the aisle, too intoxicated and tired to walk in a straight line. She plonked herself into her seat, happy to know the other passengers in the window and middle seat were already in. She forfeited her usual niceties and buckled up her belt, zipped up her handbag and shoved it under the seat in front. Her eyes shut instantly.

Unfortunately, they weren't shut for long as she felt a heavy tap on her shoulder. An elderly passenger was blocking the aisle and looking up at the seat number above Lexi.

'I'm sorry young lady, but you appear to be in my seat.'

'Am I?' Lexi replied, suddenly alert. She stood up, not bothering to double-check her boarding pass. She took it as read—it was her mistake. In her less than coherent state she was bound to have made the error. She grabbed her handbag and stood up to let the older woman sit down.

Lexi stood in the aisle scrambling to find her boarding pass in her handbag when an airhostess asked her to clear the aisle so other passengers could get to their seats.

Lexi walked to the back of the plane and stood in the rear exit door recess between the toilets and the kitchen compartment. She rooted around in her handbag for her boarding pass to tell her where her actual seat was.

Bollocks! Where is it? I must have left it in the front pocket of the seat I sat in.

She was about to walk back to retrieve it when the plane jolted. She popped her head out from behind the toilet cubicle wall to check if the aisle was clear, only to find the airhostess who'd asked her to move wearing the demonstration life jacket and pointing her arms towards the exits. She scanned the rows to find an empty seat, but every seat was taken.

'Cross check and arm doors,' the pilot announced over the PA system. 'Cabin crew be seated for take-off.'

Lexi watched from her hiding spot while the airhostesses strapped themselves in. She peered out of the tiny window of the exit door, as the illuminated Welcome Heathrow Airport sign on the terminal disappeared into the distance. The plane picked up speed, the Rolls Royce engines revved into full grunt, the nose of the plane started lifting. Not knowing what else to do, she star-fished herself like a magician's assistant on a chocolate wheel about to have knives thrown at her and gripped onto the back wall of the recess.

She stretched her neck out to watch the front of the plane tilt on its assent, locking eyes with the airhostess who'd told her to clear the aisle. In her rear-facing, fold-down seat, the airhostess looked horrified. Her telepathic message to Lexi was coming in loud and clear.

HOLD ON!

When the plane levelled out and seat belt and smoking signs were turned off, the airhostess made a beeline for Lexi.

'What? Are you drunk?' The airhostess asked rhetorically.

'Not anymore,' Lexi said candidly.

'Why aren't you seated?'

'I think my seat was double-booked.'

The hostess's anger waned. 'You were the late passenger, weren't you?'

'Yeah,' Lexi said, embarrassed.

'They must have reallocated your seat to a wait-listed passenger thinking you weren't going to turn up.'

'OK,' was all Lexi could muster.

'Would you like a drink?'

Lexi nodded and followed her into the kitchenette.

'Just a big glass of water and a bag of peanuts if you've got some.'

Lexi spent the three-hour flight being fussed over by the onboard staff, doing their best to ensure she wasn't going to sue them for contravening airline safety. As it turned out, the only spare seat for landing was the chief airhostess's one in the cockpit. She gave it up for Lexi and sat with the other staff in economy class. Behind the co-pilots seat, Lexi found the greyhound, snuggly tucked in like a first-class passenger. 'How did you manage that?' She whispered to him.

When the plane touched down at Ibiza airport, Lexi revelled in her royalty status as her and the greyhound were escorted off the plane with the cabin crew. She couldn't wait to tell Toby and Chris about her amusing, if not slightly frightening ordeal, knowing Toby would love her even more for enduring these escapades with such humour.

It was midnight by the time the BA cabin crew wished her well with the mantra, 'Go get your man, you little Aussie hottie.' She'd embellished her love story like a best-selling author and was confident British Airways would foot the bill for the publishing rights of the novel she was sure to write one day.

In the arrivals hall she looked out for the Thompson Reps dressed in their red and mustard-yellow striped blazers. She found two young women holding up signs to the Portinax Beach Hotel. *Bingo!*

'Hi I'm Lexi. Toby and Chris's friend from the UK. Any chance of me getting a lift to the hotel with you tonight.'

The prettier one asked. 'How do you know Toby?'

'I'm his girlfriend,' Lexi responded with pride, even though that wasn't strictly true.

'Sorry, but under our insurance policy we can't take passengers without prior authorisation.' She battered her long dark eyelashes and seemed genuinely apologetic.

While Lexi was disappointed, she was resolved to the fact that rules were rules and she didn't want any of Toby and Chris's new friends to get in trouble. But seriously, couldn't they ignore the code on this occasion? She was a BA celebrity now, after all.

She sat on a bench in the arrivals area demoted to cattle-class status again, watching travellers being rounded up like sheep and ferried onto coaches waiting to get them to their comfy hotel beds. Before too long, the only people left in the airport were Lexi and a couple of Spanish trolley collectors. Eventually, they clocked off too, leaving Lexi alone in the empty shell of Ibiza Airport. Then the lights went out and the doors were locked. No more flights due until the following morning.

You're fucking kidding me!

Lexi woke up on the marble floor, sunlight creeping in from the wall to ceiling windows, a wet patch of dribble circled into the fabric of the greyhound's coat where she'd rested her head, her blue court shoes still in her hand like a lethal weapon in case someone tried to attack her in the middle of the night.

From her position on the floor, the digital clock on the far wall looked like it said S.O.S, but when her eyes focused it simply read 5.05 am.

Lexi sat up, her head fuzzy and her body bruised from the discomfort of sleeping on a cold, hard floor. She dragged the greyhound with weary steps to the universal sign for female toilets. She flicked on a light switch, illuminating the darkness. As she'd hoped, there was a shower and toilets inside.

With renewed hope and quietly crediting herself for resourcefully packing her beach towel, she showered, dried herself off, dressed and reapplied a fresh face of make-up. She hadn't travelled all this way to turn up looking like a dishevelled hobo. She stood back to review herself in the mirror.

Not too shabby. Not too shabby at all.

When she reappeared in the arrivals area, it had burst into life. Lights all blazing and early morning staff flocked to their stations to welcome and farewell new passengers.

With her head held high and the drama of the previous day behind her, she strutted out of the electric doors. Even the greyhound seemed to have a new spin in his wheels. Ibiza smelled of golden sunshine and salty sea. Of endless possibility. Of love.

She climbed into the first and only taxi parked at the cab rank, and in her chirpiest and clearest Spanish, rolled her *r's* as she said, '*Portinax por favor.*'

After a thirty-minute drive and a few mistranslations about the weather, Lexi asked the driver to pull over at the bay she recognised from last year's trip to Ibiza.

She sat the greyhound under a shady tree at the top of the beach where she could keep an eye on it, and in bare feet tiptoed along the cool sand until she stood ankle deep in the Mediterranean Sea. She watched as a new day dawned, the rays of sun skipping like stars across the ripples. She closed her eyes and cast all her wishes out to the cloudless blue skies. 'Remember this moment,' she thought to herself. 'It's rare and beautiful and whatever happens next is all another adventure to add to my life's story.'

In the stylishly appointed reception lobby, with its fresh flowers and tourist brochures, Lexi pulled out the beer coaster with the words she'd settled on last night:

Wakey Wakey
Open your eyes
Come out to reception
For your big surprise!
xxx

'Can you please deliver this to Toby Meyers Room *por favor*?' She handed the note to the well-groomed receptionist, then sunk herself into the plush leather couch to wait for Toby to appear.

With giddy anticipation she waited. She adjusted the neckline of her sundress so it showed enough cleavage to look sexy, not slutty. She unravelled her ponytail and flicked it behind her ears as she rubbed her glossed lips together.

After what felt like an eternity, she saw the receptionist reappear with someone walking behind her. She stood up in readiness for her fanfare finale.

But it wasn't Toby, it was Chris.

'Lexi! What the hell are you doing here?' She wasn't sure whether his tone was excitement or shock.

'Thought I'd surprise Toby,' she beamed. 'Oh, and you of course! Da da, here I am.'

'Wow … well it sure is a surprise!'

'Where's Toby? Still asleep I suppose?' Lexi's eagerness was on full throttle.

'Are you here alone?'

'Yeah! C'mon, lead the way. I know he's grumpy in the mornings, but he'll be fine when I jump on him.'

'Lexi—' Chris tried to say something.

'Chris, I know what you're going to say—Toby won't want to be woken up, but seriously, it's me. He'll get over it.'

'OK,' Chris said. 'Follow me.'

Lexi followed him through a corridor and with nervous energy started to relay her story.

'Wait until I tell you guys what happened last night, you're not going to believe it.'

'Lexi, just let me go in first and tell him you're here.'

Chris opened the door to the hotel room and slipped inside.

'Don't be stupid Chris, that'll spoil the surprise,' Lexi pushed her way through the door.

In front of her eyes, there he was—her beautiful Toby, sleepy blue eyes and messy bed hair. His sun-kissed chest exposed, the bottom half wrapped in a white bed sheet. Every nerve pulsated as Lexi launched herself onto the bed.

'Surprise!' Lexi leaped.

'Lexi!' Toby sat up, rubbing his eyes leaving Lexi face-planted on the warm pillow he'd left in his wake.

Just then the creak of another door opening took all their focus. Lexi lifted her head to see a pretty, petite girl with dark eyelashes appear wearing what Lexi recognised as one of Toby's t-shirts.

'Lexi—' Toby stuttered knowing there was no escape. 'This is Marie.'

'We've already met.' Marie folded her arms across her chest.

'Looks like you beat me here.' Lexi held her gaze.

Holding her battered pride intact, Lexi peeled herself off the bed, pulling down the hem of her dress. She walked towards the greyhound and tugged on his lead once again. With the only swear word she knew in Spanish, she offered it up as she exited the room, '*Adios Gilipollas.*' Loosely translated as, 'Goodbye Shithead.'

The words LATE PASSENGER on the greyhound's pink sticker were the last words the dumbfounded trio read as she strutted back out the door.

An hour later, back in the departure lounge of Ibiza Airport, she didn't care about the black mascara streaks zebra-striping her cheeks, or the fact she was drinking tequila at 10 am. She pulled out her packet of cigarettes and dug down into her bag for her lighter. Her hand found the souvenir matchbook Ryan had given her, and somehow it induced a smirk. She flicked it open and struck a match. As she threw it down on the table the top flipped open and she noticed something was written inside:

'If it doesn't work out, you know where to find me.'

Her heart skipped a beat as she looked up at the departure screen to find her flight home.

BA8462 - LONDON - 1400 hours - Gate 7 – RIGHT ON TIME

Lexi held the matchbook in her hand and pulled on the greyhound one last time. She could already picture the thermometer of The Village Inn cool-room rising a few degrees.

Reunion

JEAN JENKINS

'We'll have a few days holiday at one of the resorts in Port Douglas,' he'd said. 'That way we can relax and get to know each other again. And you can decide whether or not you want to drive back with me and see where I live. Maybe even spend a bit of time there.'

It had sounded reasonable. Not that Maggie cared whether it was reasonable or not. All her adult life she'd been reasonable. And look where it had got her: a boring marriage and now in the closing stages of a divorce.

The flight from Perth to Cairns had been uneventful. The shuttle-bus trip to Port Douglas was a delight with its unfamiliar, lush tropical vegetation. She even caught a glimpse of a cassowary running away on its long legs—a giant bird, surely a relic of the dinosaur age.

She opened the bar fridge and viewed the contents. Hmm. Not a bad choice. From habit, she glanced at the prices of the wines and spirits. She turned the notice over. Cost was no longer of consequence. Her divorce settlement would be generous. Charles had acknowledged he owed it to her.

The smooth sourness of the whisky hit the right spot and she opened the glass door to the balcony. Unpacking could wait. She needed a couple of whiskies and time to contemplate her situation. She had until tomorrow afternoon to prepare herself for meeting up with Pete again. Would it be possible to write off the past fifteen years and take up an innocent teenage romance where it had left off?

She put her feet up on the adjacent patio chair. So much water had gone under the bridge since then. So much whisky too, she half-giggled to herself. Thirty-one-year old Maggie Worth was light years away from schoolgirl Margaret Bennett, who was so in love with handsome young apprentice Peter Heydon, just a couple of years older than her.

She poured a second whisky. It had been a spur-of-the-moment decision. She had three months to fill before the divorce became final. Catching up with Pete by chance on Facebook and learning his wife, Kate, had died three years earlier seemed serendipitous. She had accepted his invitation promptly. It was the time for adventure. She had never been to Queensland before. The agreement was for separate rooms and no pressure—and then, who knows? What did she have to lose?

Later in bed, Maggie retrieved the ring and turned it over in the palm of her hand. The tiny diamond had retained its sparkle all those years. It was nothing like the ostentatious triple diamonds in a twist that Charles had given her. But Pete had sold his beloved trail bike to pay for it. She replaced it in its case and pulled the pillow behind her head to watch the cop drama on TV. Tomorrow Pete would be here. She had nothing to fear. They were simply catching up for old times' sake.

'You haven't changed one bit.' Pete gripped both her hands tightly and gazed steadily into her eyes.

Maggie's heart fluttered in a way it hadn't for years. She swallowed hard.

'*You've* changed, Pete. Maturity suits you.'

He collected his room key and she felt an edge of excitement as they walked close but not touching.

'This is just how I imagined it. I booked our two rooms to be adjacent and overlooking the pool.' His voice had deepened and was more self-assured. She stole a glance at his profile as he continued. 'Give me twenty minutes to have a shower and change and I'll join you.' As he closed his room door behind him, Pete gave the broad grin she had never been able to forget.

Maggie's hands were shaking as she changed into her swimsuit. The years had flown away and she was a teenager again. Except she wasn't, she reminded herself. She resisted the temptation to have a quick whisky.

The first two days were exploratory, with shared amusement at the denied wrinkles and extra kilos. They held hands tentatively, laughing at how whisky and beer had replaced Babycham and cider.

It was on the third day, after a cruise to the Great Barrier Reef, that Maggie knew she was ready to continue from where their teenage romance had left off.

It started to rain as they walked back from the Reef Marina. Pete grabbed her hand. 'We'll need to hurry. This looks like one of our tropical downpours.'

'I love it,' Maggie laughed. 'It's like a warm shower and delicious after all that hot sun. I want to get drenched.' Pete joined in her laughter as they ran. She glanced up at him and was thrilled by the tenderness expressed on his face.

Later, over dinner in the restaurant, Pete leant forward and gently brushed a damp tuft of hair from Maggie's eyes. 'So you'll really drive back with me to Mooloomba tomorrow and see where I live? You'll love my few acres. They're inland from Townsville, where I have my business.'

Maggie smiled. 'Yes, Pete. I want to see those horses you rave about and see Townsville and take the ferry to Magnetic Island. But please understand I need to take things slowly and not be on the rebound.'

Pete nodded. 'It must have been a shock to discover that Charles had been cheating on you all that time.'

Tears filled Maggie's eyes. 'The feeling is still raw.' She dabbed her eyes with her napkin. 'You've never told me about Kate. How did she come to pass away?'

Dessert arrived and the moment was gone. Maggie had asked a couple of times. Pete hadn't yet told her.

Saying goodnight outside her room, Pete held her tightly. 'I don't want to rush you, but I'm finding it hard to keep to my word.'

'Me too,' she whispered, as the old tummy flutters returned, except now she knew where they could lead.

Pete slowly drew back. 'We'll drive to Mooloomba tomorrow. It will all be fine, you'll see.' He kissed her gently on the lips. When Maggie responded with an urgency that took them both by surprise, Pete groaned, suddenly pushing her inside her room and walking away quickly. Maggie sighed. He was still the honourable, dependable Pete she would have trusted with her life. She had been devastated when her father's job meant the family's hasty relocation from Sydney to Perth.

She couldn't get to sleep, replaying in her mind their last meetings all those years ago. 'Stay on in Sydney, and do your last year of school here,' Pete had begged. 'I'll ask

Mum if you can board with us.'

Neither set of parents had agreed, and Maggie and her family moved to Perth the following month, at the end of the school year.

'I've only eighteen months to go on my apprenticeship, Maggie,' Pete had said, on the last day. 'In no time I'll have saved enough to come to you in Perth, or for you to come back to Sydney.'

But it hadn't worked out that way. The letters got shorter and fewer; there were further moves by both families; and, after a while, contact was lost.

By an accident of fate in the guise of Facebook they had met up again. Maggie finally fell asleep, a smile on her lips.

It was only sitting beside Pete in the rattling ute splashing through the wet north Queensland roads with the rain continuing to pour relentlessly, that Maggie started to have misgivings.

Why had he avoided telling her about how Kate had died? Did it still hurt to talk about it? Or had the right occasion simply not arisen? Or was there some other reason? She'd been open about being devastated by Charles's infidelities. Why was she suddenly nervous about travelling alone with Pete to the north Queensland outback?

Maggie felt the ring-case in her bag. Pete hadn't asked, and she hadn't told. The moment wasn't yet right.

The ferocity of the lashing rain began to frighten her. Pete grimaced as they pulled over to a roadhouse for a late breakfast. When Maggie returned from a visit to the restroom, Pete was talking on his mobile. His brow was furrowed and he looked stern. He indicated she should sit at the table while he went up to the cashier, his mobile still close to his ear.

Back in the ute, Maggie detected a change. He seemed engrossed in his own thoughts. 'Is everything all right, Pete?' she asked.

'I'm worried about the rain, Maggie. We may not make it all the way to Mooloomba today. These roads can flood and be dangerous.'

They drove on in silence as the rain became a torrent and the road scarcely visible.

He pulled off the Bruce Highway onto a narrow winding road. Maggie drew in her breath. Where were they going? She breathed out, relieved as they pulled up outside a modest but aptly named Deco Hotel.

'Stay dry in the ute and I'll see if they can put us up for the night.' Pete dashed through the rain.

Feeling a cramp creep up her left leg, Maggie grabbed her umbrella and hobbled to the door of the hotel. She stretched her aching calf and felt it relax. Leaving her soaked umbrella in the porch, she followed the arrow to Reception. Pete, his back to her, was in animated conversation with the man behind the desk.

'Yes, Pete. You're in luck. You've got room number eight at the end of the corridor and the second room is three doors away. Just sign here, please.'

'Thanks, George.'

Pete came towards her, waving two keys. 'We're in luck. We've got the last rooms.'

Maggie forced a smile. 'No worries, Pete. It's fine.'

Later, eating a pub dinner and watching rivulets cascade down the windows, Maggie said casually, 'They seem to know you here, Pete.'

He laughed. 'It's just about half way between Cairns and Mooloomba, and a useful stopping-off point. Of course, it doesn't have the mod cons of the resort, no ensuites etcetera. But we're all great mates here.'

Maggie swallowed her steak. She had no reason to worry.

George came over to collect their plates. 'Hey Pete. A mate of yours is on the phone at the bar. He wants a quick chat about something or other.'

Maggie sipped her wine while consulting the dessert menu. This was Pete's patch and he was obviously well thought of. It was all going to be fine.

As they climbed the carved wooden staircase, Pete put his arm around her. 'The forecast is better for tomorrow. We'll leave early.' His voice sounded forced, different somehow.

She swallowed hard. What was the matter with her? She was probably imagining it.

She pushed the thoughts away as they stopped outside her room. Pete kissed her gently. 'Good night, Maggie. Sweet dreams. All will be well tomorrow, you'll see.'

Maggie felt disoriented. Something had changed, but she couldn't put her finger on it. Well, she thought, she would stick to her guns and not make any sort of commitment until she had a better understanding of the man Pete had become. A few days in the self-contained guest house on his property would provide all the information she needed.

She had a quick shower in the ladies' bathroom and changed into her nightwear. Feeling restless, she read for a while before finally taking a sleeping tablet and switching off the light. She was lulled to sleep by the sound of the rain pounding on the tin roof.

Maggie woke with a start. The bright morning light, unimpeded by the thin cotton curtains, pierced her closed eyelids. It was strangely silent. The rain had stopped.

She stretched luxuriantly, propped herself up on one elbow and looked around. It certainly was different from the five-star resort, but the solid original 1930s furniture was somehow comforting.

She padded over to the wash basin in the corner and filled the electric jug. She would have a quick coffee before Pete came knocking on her door. She drew back the curtains. There were pools of water everywhere.

She brushed her teeth in the wash basin, splashed water over her face, neck and arms and dressed quickly. Maybe Pete had slept in and she would have to wake *him* up with a coffee.

She walked to the end of the corridor. Pete's door was open. She peeped inside. The bed was empty, the bedclothes flung back. There was no sign of Pete. He must be in the bathroom. She walked back along the corridor.

A man was coming out of the gents' bathroom.

'Excuse me, do you know if my friend Pete is in there? He may be having a leisurely bath.'

'No, lady. There's no-one in there right now.'

Pete must have gone out for an early morning walk. She would go to meet him. Maggie made her way downstairs and looked around the bar area partitioned off for breakfast. There was no sign of Pete.

She walked down the hallway to the reception desk. A young couple were fumbling through their bags, looking for their Visa card. No, Clint at the desk hadn't seen Mr Peter Heydon that morning. But the desk wasn't attended all the time. He'd probably gone outside to inspect the condition of the road.

Maggie went out through the open front door. She took a few deep breaths. The atmosphere was warm and muggy, the sky grey and overcast.

Dodging the puddles, she walked round the hotel to the carpark at the rear. Pete's ute wasn't there. Annoyed that he'd gone for a drive without telling her or even leaving a note, Maggie stomped back into the hotel.

This was the day she would see where Pete lived and worked. She would get a sense of who and what her teenage sweetheart had become. But where on Earth was he?

'Will you want breakfast, Miss? Hot breakfast is only served for another twenty minutes.'

What should she do? Pete had extolled the magnificence of the outback Queensland country breakfast. Well, she would sample it and it was up to Pete to get back in time.

The young girl who had served behind the bar the previous evening duly delivered a steaming plate of bacon, two eggs, two sausages, a lamb chop and a pile of baked beans, tomatoes and mushrooms. Pete might still be lucky and share some. Too late. She shrugged apologetically as her plate was whisked away with what she couldn't eat heaped to one side. She helped herself to a second cup of coffee and gazed out at the carpark, as other hotel patrons loaded up and drove off.

Of course. She knocked her forehead with annoyance. Pete must have tried to reach her on her mobile to explain what had gone wrong. Quickly downing the last dregs of coffee, she climbed the stairs and unlocked the door. Her mobile phone was still on charge on her bedside table. Her heart sank. No messages.

She tried Pete's number.

'This number is not in service. Please try again later,' said the irritatingly complacent voice. She flung the phone on the bed and stamped her foot in frustration. What was Pete playing at? She looked at her watch. They had to check out in ten minutes.

A feeling of panic rose in her chest. She walked back to Pete's room and went inside. She opened Pete's bedside drawer. Only the Gideon Bible. The wardrobe was empty, his overnight case gone.

Gritting her teeth and with a swift wipe of her eyes, Maggie packed her toiletries and night clothes and hurried downstairs to reception.

She rang the bell. This time, it was the manager, George, who came to the desk. 'The bill please, George.'

'No bill, Maggie, Pete has paid for the room, and your breakfast. '

Maggie stared at him. 'What about Pete's breakfast? Did he eat his early and pay for that too?'

George shuffled his feet. 'Pete left in the early hours. I was still up, clearing away. He said he'd been called away suddenly and asked me to take payment for everything from his Visa card. Everything is paid for—the room, two dinners, a bottle of wine, your pre-dinner drinks and your breakfast.'

Maggie swallowed the bitter saliva that rose into her mouth. The reunion had been no good from his point of view, and he hadn't the courage to tell her to her face. He had left it to George.

George leant forward and patted her hand. 'It's all right, Maggie. Pete has bought you a ticket on the coach back to Cairns and booked you overnight into a hotel near the airport. I'll drive you to the highway in about an hour.'

Maggie stared back, her mind in turmoil. 'I know it's early, George, but I'd like a whisky.' George took her case and steered her to a quiet corner of the bar with the expertise of someone used to dealing with life's crises.

Maggie had been careful to curtail the number of whiskies she drank on this trip. But what the hell. It didn't matter now. Pete had been so very sympathetic about how she had been let down by Charles. And now *he* had let her down, in spades. What a fool she'd been to think she could go back in time and pick up where her teenage romance had left off. 'Those days are gone, Maggie,' she said to herself. 'A new life is ahead of you, not the dregs of an old one.'

She was silent as George drove her to the highway. 'We'll wait in the car,' he said. 'The coach will be here in five minutes. I phoned ahead and they're expecting you.'

Maggie still couldn't speak. The world didn't make sense anymore. She couldn't wait to be home and forget about her Queensland adventure.

'Thank you, George,' she managed to mumble, as he helped her out of the car. She didn't return his wave as the coach drew away.

After a journey which seemed never-ending, she was at last alone in her hotel room in Cairns, with time to think things over. She would never tell anyone how foolish she'd been and how she had been stood up by her teenage sweetheart, who'd taken off without so much as a goodbye.

After a quick call to the airline to confirm her return flight to Perth the following morning, she had a shower and ordered a room-service dinner. Hunger gripped her as, sipping a whisky, she waited impatiently.

There was a knock on her door. At last.

She opened the door and gasped.

'It's you.'

Pete said quietly. 'I'd like to come in, if you'll allow me, Maggie'.

Her limbs frozen, she nodded as Pete brushed past her into the room.

'I'd like one of those, please.' He pointed to the glass she was holding.

As in a dream, she closed the door and walked over to the bar fridge. This wasn't real.

Pete sat on the chair opposite. 'Please let me explain, Maggie,' his hand shaking as he took a large gulp from the glass in his hand.

It was a flat angry voice that replied. 'It had better be a good explanation, Pete. I didn't come all this way to be abandoned rudely and without a word of explanation.'

There was another knock on the door. 'Room service.'

The robot that was Maggie walked over and opened the door. She took hold of the trolley. 'Thank you. I'll see to that.'

She wheeled it across the room. The voice, still flat, was less angry. 'There's enough to share, Pete. You look as if you could do with something to eat before you tell me what's been happening.'

Maggie spooned some of the soup into a mug and split the bread roll in half.

'Thank you, Maggie. I've had nothing to eat all day.' He wolfed it down.

Maggie eyed him cautiously. Could she believe anything this man said? But she had flown from the other side of Australia to meet up with him again and, looking at him in his dishevelled state and obviously very upset, she had to hear him out. Pete had always remained in a corner of her heart and she had to settle this once and for all.

'Pete, the salad and dessert can wait. I'll pour you a coffee and, when you're ready, please, please tell me what's been going on.' She sat beside him. 'I want to understand.'

Pete took both her hands in his. 'Believe me, Maggie. There's no way I would have arranged meeting up with you at this time, had I known what was about to happen.'

He cleared his throat and looked her straight in the eye. 'Kate became reliant on illegal drugs. I pleaded with her to stop. She went into rehab a couple of times, but never succeeded in staying off the damn stuff for long. She became a shadow of the beautiful woman she'd been. I no longer recognised her.'

'Oh, Pete, I'm so sorry.'

Pete took a sip of coffee. 'It was dreadful, Maggie. She died of a drug overdose. I agreed to help the police track down the dealers as I had some idea of where she obtained her drugs. The gang were part of a mafia organisation operating in this part of Queensland and had eluded the police for years. We got them all—except for Tony Marcellone, the leader. I'd established personal contact with him but he somehow got away. The police believed he'd gone interstate, possibly overseas. Rumour had it that the gang had a stash of hidden money in the area. Further investigations proved fruitless and the trail ran cold. It all seemed in the past. Believe me, Maggie. I thought it was all over.'

Maggie withdrew her hands. 'You're saying that this Marcellone fellow turned up again?'

Pete clenched his fists. 'We were in the roadhouse on the way to Mooloomba when I got the call from Marcellone. He'd come back for the money. He needed my assistance. The deal was half the stash if I helped him—and my life in danger if I refused or told the police. He was desperate and in deadly earnest. He wouldn't seek revenge if I agreed. My world came crashing down. You came out of the rest-room looking beautiful and smiling and happy and, unwittingly, I'd placed you in danger.'

Maggie shook her head. 'Pete, why didn't you tell me?'

'I had to think fast, Maggie. I immediately contacted the police and they asked me to play along. It was their chance to finally get Marcellone. I felt I owed it to Kate. They promised to protect me and you. And Marcellone had no idea you were with me.'

Maggie nodded. 'So we went on to The Deco Hotel. What was all that about Room Number Eight?'

'Those were my directions from Marcellone—to book myself into that room and wait for further instructions. Marcellone even made a call to the bar while we were eating dinner to check I was there. He said he'd call my mobile at midnight with my instructions. I imagined I'd be told where to go to collect the money. I got the call and it wasn't what I expected.'

'What do you mean, Pete?'

'The money was hidden under the floorboards under the wardrobe in Room Eight. Marcellone couldn't risk going there himself, as he was easily recognised. I was to retrieve the money and drive it to a certain location nearby at 3.00 am. I thought I could deal with it and be back well before you woke up and we could drive out to Mooloomba as planned. I paid for everything on my Visa Card and told George that if I wasn't back by breakfast he was to book you on the coach to Cairns and on your return flight to Perth, where I knew you'd be safe.'

'So what went wrong?' Maggie's eyes were wide, her heart pounding.

'Marcellone kept changing the meeting place. I think he guessed something was up. I drove all over the countryside and began to feel desperate. Maybe I wasn't going to get out of this alive. I wished I'd not got involved, especially as I had met up with you again—something I'd thought never possible.'

Maggie was on the edge of her chair. 'So, what happened?'

'When I finally met up with Marcellone, instead of taking his half and letting me go, he took all of the money and held me captive. Thank goodness the tactical armed police were at hand.'

Maggie clutched her chest at the thought of the danger Pete had been in.

Pete drank the last drops of coffee. 'They were magnificent. After a long stand-off, I got rescued without a shot being fired. Marcellone is safely under lock and key. Maggie, it really is all over. I'll understand if you want nothing more to do with me. I wanted you to know that I hadn't deserted you and would never have let you down in a million years.'

Pete gently caressed her cheek. 'I couldn't believe my good fortune when I caught up with you and discovered you're single again. I'd tried so hard to track you down. I loved Kate, but you were my first love and there was always a part of my heart that was yours alone.'

He kissed her. 'The rain has stopped. Maggie darling, will you drive out with me to Mooloomba tomorrow?'

The flutters came back with a vengeance. Her answer was to take the ring box from her bag.

Pete gasped. 'You kept it.'

Maggie silenced him by placing her lips firmly upon his. The time for talking was over. She had a feeling that the real adventure was about to start.

Stage Fright

TEENA RAFFA-MULLIGAN

He'd choose her. Of course he would. Nina didn't look at Mr B, leaning casually against the desk at the front of the classroom. Didn't want him to see how much she wanted to be the one to represent the school in the public speaking competition. Or how confident she was of being chosen. It felt big-headed.

But really, who else? Most of the boys kept their mouths shut hoping to stay under the radar. They didn't want to be called on to answer questions or give their opinion in case they got it wrong. The unlucky ones who didn't escape Mr B's eagle eye tripped and stumbled over the words or mumbled their way through responses. Except for Luke.

Nina's face warmed at the memory of yesterday's drama session. His Romeo to her Juliet. Everything was going fine till Mr B suddenly said, 'How about some action?' right when they'd got to the point in the script where the star-crossed lovers kissed. It was debatable which of them had been most fazed. One minute they were standing side-by-side reading from their textbooks, the next they were on opposite sides of the room looking anywhere but at each other while the rest of the room cheered them on for the required action. Embarrassing didn't begin to describe it. Now she couldn't look him in the face without that awful heat rush.

Nina straightened her pen and lined it carefully up beside her exercise book. Luke was probably her main competition. He'd present a sound argument with plenty of expression, but so would Patricia, with her clear speaking voice and immaculate every-hair-in-place-neatly-pressed look. But Patricia didn't get called on as often as Nina to share her opinions on the novels they were studying or read her essays aloud to the class. Neither did Luke.

So there wasn't really any doubt about who Mr B would choose to enter the local round of the Youth Speaks for Australia competition. Nina knew it. Everyone else did too. She could feel their eyes on her, hear her whispered name rippling round the room.

'Nina ...'

She looked up at last.

'Would you like to be our representative?'

'Yes, Mr B.' It was an effort, but she kept her voice steady. Best to keep her cool, not seem like a little kid that just got promised an ice cream on Sunday. The smile, she couldn't stop.

'Excellent.' He beamed back at her, then gave her a studied look over the top of his horn-rimmed glasses. 'You realise it's a big commitment? Not only do you have very little time to think about the topic and prepare a speech, there won't be much opportunity to practice in front of an audience. Are you up for the challenge?'

'I'll do my best.'

'As always,' said Mr B with an approving nod and she cringed inwardly.

Consistent A grades and good behaviour had already earnt her a minus in the popularity stakes. She'd seen the 'Miss Goody Two Shoes' looks often enough to know that adding teacher's pet to the mix wasn't a plus.

A dramatic puking sound came from the back of the room. No guesses for the identity of that clown.

'Outside, Roberts,' boomed Mr B. 'We don't need your stupidity.'

The culprit swaggered out of the room with a snigger.

Mr B dusted both hands together and straightened. 'Right, then. It's only two days away so we'll have our work cut out to prepare for it but I'm sure you'll do us proud. Okay everyone, back to work. Take out your Albatross Book of Verse and turn to page 63. Nina, come and see me at the end of this period—what do you have next?'

'Science, Sir.'

'I'll clear it with Miss Brown for you to miss today's class and you can let me look at your timetable for the next couple of days, so we can factor in the time to work on your presentation.'

It wasn't easy, but Nina waited until dinner time to share her news with the family.

'That's great!' Dad beamed across the table.

Mum's brow furrowed with anxiety. 'Will you be able to stand up in front of all those people and give a speech, love?'

'Of course she can,' Dad said without hesitation.

'If I win this heat I get to go into the state finals and the winner goes to the national finals in Sydney. Mr B thinks I've got a good chance.'

Mum's forehead smoothed. 'Well, if anyone knows, he would. Are we allowed to come?'

Nina hadn't counted on that. She wasn't nervous about talking to a bunch of strangers but knowing Mum and Dad and Jack were among the audience would be something else. But how could she tell them no? 'Yes, family's invited.'

'Not me, sis.' Jack grinned. 'Unless you want me to pull faces at you and make you laugh.'

He pulled one now and she poked her tongue at him. Juvenile yes, but it was the only way to respond to his infantile humour.

'Anyway,' she said, 'it's not at my school, it's at John Curtin High School in Fremantle at six thirty on Thursday and I have to wear full school uniform and be there half an hour early.'

'What do you have to talk about?' Mum stood up and started clearing away the dinner dishes.

'There's a choice of topics. I'm going to talk about the way we put people in boxes, individually and culturally.'

'Bo-ring.' Jack rolled his eyes and took off to watch TV in the lounge before Mum had a chance to rope him in to help with the wiping up.

Nina fetched a clean tea towel and while Dad washed the dishes and she and Mum dried them, ideas buzzed around the tiny kitchen. By the time Nina retreated to her sleep-out bedroom at the back of the house, her speech was already taking shape in her mind. The words tumbled over each other as she scribbled them down, then neatly rewrote them before tucking up in bed with a glow of satisfaction. Mr B would be pleased that she'd made such a great start.

Time seemed to be on a speed dash for the next two days as she worked on her speech and presentation skills under the supervision of her teacher. With his encouragement, the words soon became indelibly etched in her mind and she went to sleep each night filled with visions of herself in the spotlight, accepting first prize in the national final.

On the night of the heat, Nina was ready well ahead of time but because Dad was late home from work they didn't arrive until fifteen minutes early instead of the requested half an hour. Mr B was pacing outside the doors of the school theatre and looked relieved when he saw them.

'There you are!'

Of course. She wouldn't miss this opportunity for all the tea in China.

'How are you feeling?' he asked as he ushered her indoors.

'Fine.' The little flutter in her tummy was excitement, not nerves.

'Contestants are in the front rows and you're mid-way through the program. I'll be at the back of the room with the other teachers.'

'Thanks,' she said and made her way to the front of the auditorium, where she was surprised to see Patricia and Luke sitting in the second row. What were they doing here?

Patricia whispered, 'My dad's one of the judges.'

'And I'm here with my cousin.' Luke jerked his thumb in the direction of the youth sitting in front of him.

'Are you nervous?' asked Patricia.

'No.' Nina settled into her place at the end of the row.

'Why would you be?' Luke grinned. 'You'll walk away with this.'

'Thanks for the vote of confidence.'

By the time she'd heard the contestants who preceded her, however, Nina wasn't quite so sure. Without exception, their presentations were practiced and polished. Her turn seemed to come around far too quickly and she concentrated on walking tall for her approach to the stage. The tummy flutter had gone but her hands were shaking. They'd not done that before. She clasped them together in front of her as she faced the audience, took a deep breath and began to speak.

The words flowed freely. She'd rehearsed them well. But suddenly, without warning, they were gone. Her mind was a blank. She stopped mid-sentence and after what seemed an eternity of silence, turned to the judges.

'I'm sorry. I can't go on.'

Face aflame with embarrassment she returned to her seat on jelly legs. It was all she could do not to burst into tears. If only she could will herself ant size and scurry into hiding among the sea of chair legs. It served her right. Fancy thinking she could hold her own against these kids with their rich parents and their private school educations. She wasn't in their league. Never would be.

Nina blinked back a threatening tear and sat soldier tall in her seat. One thing was sure. It had taught her a lesson: overconfidence leads to a fall. Thank goodness Jack had stayed at his mate's place. She'd never have heard the end of it.

Patricia leaned forward. 'What happened?' she whispered as the judges conferred.

Nina shrugged. 'I don't know.'

'Did you forget your speech?'

'No.'

'Then why? You were doing great. Everyone was listening ...'

'I think it was that—suddenly realising I was standing up there in front of a room full of people I mostly didn't know, and they were all listening to me. A bit like a rabbit in the headlights. I just—froze.'

Luke, when he caught her attention, mouthed a sympathetic, 'It's okay.'

But she didn't feel like it was. She'd let everybody down, made a total fool of herself. She desperately wanted to go home where it was always safe, but instead had to sit there willing the speeches to be over so she could make a quick exit.

At the close of the program when the winners had been announced and escape seemed imminent, the judges bent their heads together in whispered discussion.

'Nina, would you like to try again?' asked the man Patricia had pointed out earlier as her father.

Nina stood. Why not? She had nothing to lose now. The contest was over.

Perhaps that was why it had been so easy the second time, she thought afterwards when she joined everyone for supper with applause still ringing in her ears: no judgment.

'You did great,' Patricia said. 'Dad thought so. He reckons you've got potential as a public speaker.'

'If they want someone who's going to just stand up on stage and stare around the room like an idiot. I still can't believe I did that.' Nina twisted the handkerchief in the pocket of her school blazer.

'It was your first time in front of an audience like this, plus you were being judged. You got nervous. It could happen to anyone.'

'Not to her or the others.' Nina stared across at the winner, surrounded by family and friends and emanating the satisfaction of success. Dad always said it was the inside you that mattered most, not where you lived, what school you went to and how much money you had. Maybe sometimes those things did make a difference.

'Anyway, you were amazing the way you got up and had another go.'

'Yeah. I couldn't have done that,' admitted Luke. 'That took guts.'

Mr B nodded. 'It did indeed, though I wouldn't have put it quite like that.'

Mum appeared beside them with her cup of tea and a biscuit. She slipped her free hand into Nina's and gave it a comforting squeeze. 'My clever, brave girl,' she said softly.

Across the room, Patricia's dad wound up his conversation with the winner's parents and headed towards them. 'I was impressed with the way you returned to the stage and had another go, Nina. That took a lot of courage and you did a great job of it. Unfortunately, we couldn't take that second attempt into account for the judging. However, I would like to offer you a couple of tips for the future.' He raised his bushy eyebrows questioningly.

Nina nodded. It was the polite thing to do, even though he'd be wasting his breath. Her public speaking days were over. Never again would she put herself at risk of failing like that. And forget those ridiculous ideas about being an actress, or a TV and radio presenter. She clearly didn't have what it took.

Mr Matthews was speaking. She'd best pay attention, she owed him that for going to the trouble of offering advice even if taking it was not in her plans.

'You have an expressive voice but you need to use your body more. Don't stand still. Gesture and movement will keep your listeners engaged. For that matter, rather than seeing yourself as addressing the entire audience, imagine you're speaking directly to one person.'

'That's good advice,' Mr B said. 'Keep it in mind.'

'Thank you,' Nina murmured, though given a choice she'd prefer to forget this evening completely.

Nina ran her fingers along the bookshelf in the spare room till she found the title she was looking for. The small, slim hardback novel in its plastic-encased wraparound paper cover looked out of place among the new release paperbacks. It was decidedly dated. Nina removed it from the shelf and turned it over in both hands. It even carried the smell of age and its discoloured page borders told their own tale. She'd not looked at it in years except for the rare occasions when they'd moved house or shifted the imposing jarrah bookcase from one room to another. It hadn't demanded more than cursory attention even when whisking the feather duster across the books lined so neatly on the third shelf.

Now she handled it with the respect it deserved by Mrs Aeneas Gunn. She opened the flyleaf and smiled at the inscription written in a careful, still childish hand: *Youth Speaks for Australia 1965.*

'I thought you were ready,' said Luke.

She tucked the book into her satchel and smiled at him. 'I am now, darling.'

'What's that you've got, Nan?' asked Ellie.

'A book I was given when I was about your age. It reminded me of something I thought I could tie into my speech. I'll tell you all about it on the way to the venue.'

An hour-and-a-half later, Nina stood and smiled at the sea of faces in the crowded auditorium. Her hands were already doing their familiar uncontrollable dance. It was one reason she never read from notes. It would give her away. She steadied them on the podium before taking a deep, calming breath. These weren't children and they would judge her as harshly as she judged herself. Some would ask why she was there where they should be—and who could blame them? It was the roll of the dice. The lucky number draw. And as long as fortune was in her corner on this special occasion, her voice would hold out and at least some of those who'd given up their evening would consider it time well spent.

Nina allowed her gaze to skim the nearest rows. Yes, there they were, right there in the centre. Luke, their daughter Em and her daughter Ellie: her small support team. Luke giving her the thumbs up, Em beaming her sunshine smile of reassurance and Ellie leaning forward in her seat expectantly.

Nina cleared her throat, checked the small microphone on her shirt and stepped out from behind the rostrum. 'It's a pleasure to be here and to have you all join me for this special celebration,' she began, then paused for a few moments before resuming.

'Half a century ago, a fifteen-year-old schoolgirl stood before an audience to compete in a public speaking contest. Although she was a complete novice at public speaking and had only entered at the eleventh hour, she was confident. Until—a few minutes into her twenty-minute presentation—she froze. The words were gone. She couldn't find them.

'It felt like failure of the first magnitude and as she huddled back in her front row seat among the other competitors trying to look invisible, she wondered how she would ever live down such public embarrassment.

'After the final competitor had left the stage, the judges conferred and one of them asked the girl if she'd like to have another go. To her surprise, she heard herself saying, 'yes,' then stood and walked back on stage. This time, although the words she'd practiced in the lead up to the competition were lost, she found new ones. They spilled out spontaneously from somewhere she hadn't realised she could access and addressed the topic in the way her original speech had not. The applause when she finished speaking was indeed the clichéd music to her ears, but the thrill of that didn't begin to measure up to the glow she felt at knowing she'd risked failure again yet done it anyway.

Nina gazed around the room, allowing her attention to linger on the three, special people in the front row before continuing with a smile.

'Of course you will have guessed that girl was me. And if anyone that night had told me I'd lose count of the number of occasions I addressed an audience in the years to come, I'd never have believed them.

'In fairy tales, the newborn baby is gifted with qualities such as beauty, wisdom, intelligence and talent. I choose to believe my gift was resilience. No-one's path through life is smooth and trouble free. We all falter and fall at some stage. If we have the capacity to pick ourselves up and carry on, it makes an incredible difference to our experience of life.

'I don't like to think in terms of success and failure, which are merely creations of the mind. They don't exist in reality. Yet we classify our every experience and attach expectation to all we do. If we can manage to abandon all ideas of success and failure and do what we love doing without hope or fear, then there is only living—and that, I have found, is the greatest adventure of all.

'Sometimes when a dream comes true, it can take us in unexpected directions and one of the joys of being a children's author for me has been the many wonderful opportunities I've been given to share my passion for books and writing with people of all ages—and, I hope, inspire them to write their own stories.

'I didn't expect public speaking to be part of my life as a writer and I certainly never expected to win this award for my contribution to children's literature. I feel both honoured and humbled to be considered worthy. All I can say is thank you.'

Nina bowed her head slightly in conclusion and returned to her seat among the other authors and VIPs on the podium, mentally adding a silent thank you to the public one. The judges who invited her to have another attempt that long-ago speech night could never have known the lesson she'd learn that it was okay to 'try and try again.'

To Be or Not to Be

KAREN WEAVER

'Hey Casey, did you see this opportunity?'

Fiona is a perfect boss. In fact, she was more of a friend than a boss. She harboured her own scars and healing and yet gave her life to helping others heal on their journey. She is a messenger who plants seeds of opportunity in the mind-garden of others. When she said those words to me, I already had a full life. I was working part-time as an administrator, studying for a University diploma in Humanities, and was a single mum to an eight-year-old boy. My long-distance relationship had also moved to the next stage of getting serious. But something from the flyer called to me and so, as I always did when that happened, I took-action.

I never realised that, even back then I channelled a Power of Knowing, one so strong that it aligned magical moments to fruition.

I sent the submission email and never thought about it again until one week later when I was called for an interview in Dublin, Ireland. Again, I *knew* I had to go. If this was meant to be, I would have to commit to each step until I reached a block and then it would be time to reassess.

My sister came with me that day. We always loved venturing together on the wild adventures life took me on. We were always very close. I was the wild risk taker of the family and she the supportive sister cheering me on from the sidelines, ready to pick up the pieces if something went wrong. We all need someone like that in our lives.

We always loved visiting the city. It was so much more vibrant than the small town we came from. It had a feeling of greatness, that big things were in motion. I had always felt destined for more than small-town life, wondering why I couldn't be content with the status-quo where life would be so much easier. But the reality was I couldn't, no matter how hard I tried. Contentment was something I avoided. It wasn't in my DNA. Life was for living in each and every moment, and if something new felt aligned I usually went with it.

We arrive at the traditional 17th Century building crafted with old stone carved features that could be expected from an Irish period construction of the early 18th Century. When we enter, we are surprised by the very modern interior, including a glass elevator.

Following *This Way* signs, we arrive in a hallway where candidates from all backgrounds sit quietly in a line waiting to be called in. We spot two seats and inhabit them straight away, the trials of walking the streets in our favourite six-inch heels having taken their toll and we needed to revive circulation to our toes. Silence thickens the air creating an invisible wall to noise. We silently and obediently wait to be called.

The interview room has three sash windows that beam in light from the bustling streets outside. Being four floors up, it is the Dublin skyline that dominates the view on the hot, Irish twenty-two-degree day.

'Hello Casey, take a seat.' A friendly man in his fifties pops up from the chair and shakes my hand.

'Hello and thank you,' I reply, occupying the designated seat.

'I'm Adrian, and these lovely ladies are the course co-ordinators, Monika and Susan.' A dark-haired, dark brown-eyed woman extends her hand towards me and I quickly return it. She smiles. Wearing all black, her clothes are baggy and she has large boobs with a waistline to match. She looks harsh. The other lady has a friendly, more vibrant appearance. There is a magical essence to her.

'Now Casey, you have applied for a scholarship to our year-long drama training program. Can you tell us why this program is a right fit for you?' Her German accent fuses softly with an Irish twang.

Phew! I can understand her.

Sitting up confidently, I reply, 'Well I believe that this program will work hand-in-hand with the Humanities diploma I am currently studying part-time for with the University of Ulster.'

'Two intense courses at one time?'

'My course overlaps for a short period, but I don't see that being a problem.'

Monika takes notes and Adrian takes over.

'Okay ... tell us about you. What is life like for you right now?'

'I love where I am in life. I am a mum, I work part-time in a mental health day care centre and I study my diploma through evening classes.'

'Do you see fitting in twelve intensive weekends spread across a year being a problem to fit into your busy schedule?'

'I am blessed with a wonderful support network and am fine with the commitment otherwise I wouldn't be here today.'

Notes taken again and Susan takes over.

'Casey our program is designed to train facilitators to go out and create peace-building programs throughout Ireland. What are your plans to support this?'

'I believe that this ties in nicely with my Humanities diploma. I love working with people and plan to incorporate the new skills I learn into outreach programs.'

'Lovely.' Susan smiles.

Monika looks up from her paper. 'Casey it has been nice to meet you, we will be in touch.'

A month passes. I have already moved on from the awkward interview with the three random characters I met that day.

Hello Casey, we are delighted to offer you a place on the Cross-border drama facilitator outreach program of 2004-05.

'Oh wow, Fiona. Look at this!'

'Congratulations! That's wonderful news, Casey. Well done to you.'

'Oh crap! The first month starts this weekend. I will have to organise a sitter for Jake and let Dan know I will be away this weekend.'

Dan is my tall, dark and handsome. Things are getting serious between us. He works away all week and comes home on weekends. Hopefully one weekend away every month won't break us. He seemed to support the idea when I mentioned it to him. I can't imagine him talking me out of it, I am already there in my heart and mind. I probably should have thought further on the affects this course might have on our relationship. But it is something I have been called to, so I have to trust that if it is to be, it will be.

'I'll drive you'. Dan has taken it upon himself to make sure I am not going to be abducted by strangers.

'I'll be fine, Dan.'

'I'm bringing you. Okay?' He swoops me into his arms and my knees turn to jelly as always.

'Well now that you put it like that, how can I say no?'

The venue for month one is an hour away from our home. We didn't say much on the trip. We have a deeply connected, passionate relationship, but I know he silently struggles when I go off on my adventures.

The venue is a small conference centre in a little town not far from the beaches I used to visit as a child. I've always loved the beach. The water soothes and inspires me beyond belief.

It's dark when we arrive. The warm glow from the new, yet old-styled building and vibrant energy from the noise inside confirm we found the right location.

'I won't come in.'

'Okay.' I stretch over and give him a kiss. 'I am going to miss you.'

He hugs me tight and then let's me go. 'See you Sunday, babe.' He zooms off in his sports car.

I take a moment to shift my mindset away from the weekend I could have had and walk into the unknown.

'Are you Casey?' A bubbly lady with red lippy and blond, curly hair sticks a pin on my lapel.

'Yes.' I smile.

'Great—follow me.'

We enter a room full of twenty people of all ages, sounding as if they represent each of the Irish counties.

'Hi everyone, this is Casey.'

'Hi Casey.' A chorus of accents greet me.

'Hi.' I grab the nearest seat beside a young, friendly-looking woman who reminds me of a China doll.

A clink of a glass catches our attention. 'Welcome everyone.' It's Monika. Her presence seems in total contrast to the energy she had at the interview.

'We are delighted to welcome you to this program. We know that you are the best candidates for the job. Our peace-building drama facilitator program is one of the most important courses we deliver. It has the most impact on the community.'

We all obediently sit for fifteen minutes.

'Now that you have heard from us, I would like to invite you to get to know each other. Introduce yourselves and share some fun facts. We are all going to get to know each other very well by the end of the year.'

'Hi, I'm Sarah. Nice to meet you Casey.'

'You too, Sarah.'

'Hi, I'm Angela.'

'Hi Angela.' Angela is a woman in her late forties with fiery, red hair and an air of confidence. After ten minutes of talking, I sense she is usually the one speaking.

'We are going to take you to your rooms. Most months you will have a room of your own, but this month and due to limited amount of rooms you will have to share. We have allocated the rooms as best we can. Come over to me and I will give you your room number.'

I am delighted to discover that the two ladies I was chatting with are in my room. There is also another, much quieter lady who lifts her head up from her book just long enough to say hi. She has long, brown hair and wears black, gothic-style clothes. Her energy is calm and she introduces herself as Louise.

'Monika mentioned that they were going to the pub across the road. Anyone fancy it?' Sarah shares.

'I do,' Angela pipes up.

'Yes please.' I usually went out every weekend so this was always going to be a goer for me.

'Great! Wait till I get my lippy on.' Sarah's hair and make-up are perfection.

The pub is small and cosy and there's a band playing. It's kind of loud, but we grab ourselves a drink and find that Monika and the rest of the trainers have room enough for us at their table.

It's always a strange feeling to meet new people, but connecting with their energy, I gauge the essence of each individual I meet and sense that these guys are good people. We have a few drinks and are reminded by Monika that we have a 7 am start for our extensive training. Feeling like naughty school kids, we reluctantly pull ourselves up and go back to the accommodation.

Our eyes are a little glassy the next morning when we meet at the continental breakfast, but we are ready to embrace our training.

Our first tutor is Paul. His appearance reminds me of Einstein and he seems knowledgeable beyond belief. We do some getting-to-know-you exercises, which tease each of us out of our comfort zones. Everyone seems to have an openness about them. We each stand up and shared our stories. My blushing begins to take over, but no one reacts, unlike some situations I've found myself in over the years, so it quickly subsides. At the end of the weekend and after three huge sessions and more food than I can think about, I find myself feeling so energised with knowledge, but tired beyond belief.

Dan comes to pick me up at 3 pm on Sunday.

'Well, how was it?'

'It was wonderful. I learned so much.'

'That's great.'

'Fancy going for a walk along a beach?'

'Sure. I know one close by.'

We walk hand-in-hand along the beach, rekindling our hearts after two days of distance. That night I lie in his arms and feel total love seep into my soul. He is gone when I wake in the morning. I missed him leaving, but know and admire how dedicated to his work he is. My phone flashes.

See ya Friday babe. xxx

On the second month we are located in a beautiful hotel in a vibrant Irish town. We each have our own room and it is my first ever experience eating tiramisu. It is euphoric. Again, the classes are intensive, but it is the late nights socialising that really drain my batteries.

One of the guys on the course comes from Belfast. A typical skin-head, slim build stereotype, but I sense he's had a tough life—a victim of circumstance.

During an exercise where we walked around the room and stopped when a sound ceased and instructed to look deeply into the eyes of the person beside us, I discovered I find it hard for people to look deeply into my soul. I felt so uncomfortable doing the exercise, even having to close my eyes at some points. This has led me to explore myself further.

The third month is really interesting. We are in Belfast, a location featuring twice on our agenda. Belfast is a pretty divided city, with walls built to separate communities. It is currently peace time, but the rattles of those who are silenced but not reformed can still be felt. It forms the essence of why we were doing the course in the first place, so it is important that we experience and learn from it, further fuelling my passion to make a real difference.

As the months pass, and staying in many different locations, my brain is bursting with so much knowledge, exciting and filling me with purpose and direction. I was a girl who hated learning at school, but absorbing things I feel connected to makes an amazing difference. When the elements of adventure and discovering new places are added to the mix, it forms a magical combination for my adventurous soul. It is as if I've found my tribe, and I feel like the luckiest person in the world.

Dan, however, is struggling with it all and my reassurances are no longer enough. It is month four, and he's had enough. I have some serious thinking to do.

'You come home wrecked. There's no point in me being here.'

'I know it's tough, babe, but it's important that I do this course. We can make it.'

'I'm just saying that I have heard what goes on in drama classes, and you guys are off doing goodness knows what.'

I've never seen him like this before, so stressed.

'You can trust me, Dan.'

'It's not you I don't trust, Casey.'

'How about you come and meet everyone next month when we are closer to home? They would love to meet you.'

'I don't know.'

'Also, I won't be staying at the venue next month. There are two months when we are there and I can drive there each day.'

He seems to relax.

'Okay.' He pulls me close. 'I just miss you. You are my rock, my everything after a week of working away. I miss you.'

'I miss you too, babe, I really do.'

Month five comes, and as promised, I refrain from staying with the group, even though I will miss connecting with my new-found tribe. I know the importance of there being a break for the sake of my relationship. The usual Friday night briefing happens and I meet Dan and my sister in the bar afterwards. As always, the drama group are all there for the night's get-together. I introduce Dan, but the reception from the group is not what I was hoping for. Dan and my sister go and sit somewhere else in the bar and I feel torn between the two parties.

Maybe this wasn't such a good idea.

I say my goodbyes to the group and we leave. We go to a local club, but the dynamics have shifted due to my sister being with us, and Dan feels the need to slag off the group. I feel disappointed, but am wise enough to know that the root of it stems from jealousy and fear on his part. I resolve to enjoy the night because I know Dan needs it from me right now.

But that night I can't sleep and lay there wondering if Dan and I will make it through this rough patch. I know I have to keep going with the course—I was called to it—otherwise I will be compromising my destiny. I realise I don't have that certainty with my relationship, even though there was is so much desire and will to make it work. In that moment, I decide to trust that if it is supposed to be, it will be.

Month six and we are allocated cute cottages. I am lucky enough to get a cottage with the three ladies I stayed with in the first month. It is cool to know that we will hang out together again, but it is cold and the walk back down to the main building is interesting to navigate.

This weekend is my biggest yet, filled with a lot of self-discovery. The group has the opportunity to put together an improvised play based on a social issue we feel needs a voice. Three plays will be chosen and we will perform them in a theatre during month eleven. This blows my mind. I choose to put together a play on the stigma surrounding mental health as I am working in the industry. It isn't chosen, but Sarah's play Lipstick, Powder and Politics is and I am asked to be in it. This is going to be fun. We also had Alan, who has directed plays before, so is a real asset to the group. The play was scripted and we needed to memorise it for the next month. Only problem was … I have a poor memory. There is no way I can memorise a play, is there?

It was in this month that something shifts inside of me and I have a huge realisation.

On the Saturday night, we go down to the complex bar and have a few drinks. I decide to keep it low-key this month as I don't want to be going home as tired as in other months. Sarah, Angela and I giggle our way back to our cottage and Alan follows. I sense he has a thing for me, but it is never going to be an option, so choose just to be me and stay aware of it. The conversation ventures to self-belief, and as Angela is a psychologist in her day job, she challenges us to do an activity. We are all given a piece of paper and told to write twenty things starting with *I Want*. When we had twenty, she guides us to delete two, then four until we are down to just two. It is so tough to choose between my last two sentences, but both of them are really strongly connected to my son. I have to eliminate one.

Angela asks us what our remaining one is. Alan reads his and Angela gives her advice. Sarah reads hers too, then so does Louise. Then she asks, 'What have you got Casey?'

'It was really tough to choose between the last two, but I decided to go with: *I want to be happy, because when I am happy all of those who love me will be happy too.*'

Everyone stares at me. I think I have said something wrong.

'Wow! Never, ever have I ever heard such a powerful answer.'

'Really, why?'

'You truly know the benefits that self-love has on the people around you. Most people focus on external things to fulfil their wants and desires, but you know that you have the power in your control and choose to use it to benefit those around you.'

'Oh … okay. Well, that's cool then.'

We all giggle and finish off our night ready for another intensive day of training.

The next few months focus on the performance. I am so nervous because I don't want to let the team down. I learn and learn and learn my lines when I am home. I get Dan on board, but know that he is really not interested so save it for when he is away during the week. I spend that time getting all of my assignments done. The eleventh hour has always been my friend.

I know that Dan is hanging out for the course to end, and we make the most of the weekends in between.

On the day of the play I have a family engagement, and then it is time to rush off to prepare for the performance. Dan and I stop off for lunch, but it feels really disconnected. I don't like this feeling, knowing our hearts have sung in harmony for so long.

'Thanks for coming. It must have been hard to get away from work.'

'Yes, it always is, but it's important to you.'

'Yes, it is. I hope you like it.'

'You'll be great.'

The small talk is painful. He drops me off at the venue and agrees to be back for the 3 pm performance. I hope that there isn't a replay of my graduation day when he disappeared for hours on end. I choose to focus on doing my best and feel grateful that my family are coming along, excited and proud. I am the first person in our family to ever perform a play.

I go to the allocated room where I have the opportunity to rehearse and get into costume. My skirt is really short, as my character requires it to be. I look for my shoes and they are not there. Disaster! But as they say, *the show must go on.* Then I realise that my sister could be downstairs and she is sure to be wearing six-inch stilettos. I go on the hunt and she doesn't disappoint. *Bridget Jones moment avoided.*

The nerves are all-consuming but exciting at the same time. It is a crazy feeling. The first play is over and it is our turn. I step out into the spotlight. We can't see the crowd, they are in the darkness behind the spotlights. I give it my best performance—I don't want to let anyone down, including myself. My character has a lot of funny lines and it is a relief to hear the crowd laughing when they are supposed to.

When it is over, we receive a standing ovation. The feeling is euphoric—I could really get used to this. It is so much fun. I spy my mum and dad, my son and my sister. They are smiling and I can see pride in their eyes, making me cry happy tears. I then spot Dan sitting beside them—the missing piece to make this moment perfect. I captured the essence of that moment in my heart where it will stay forever.

The final month comes along, and it is time to be tested on what we know already. We have to present our completed folders, are questioned in front of a panel, and have to facilitate our own class. I am comfortable with what I produced.

One month to the day from when we performed the play, and it has been getting rave reviews in the theatre community. Our Lipstick, Powder and Politics has struck a chord.

So much went on this weekend, and we were back in Belfast to finish off the course. I begin to ponder if I will ever see these people again. They have been such a huge part of my year. It is a solemn feeling, like I'm not ready to let go of this adventure just yet, but as all good things must come to an end, I choose to feel grateful for the year we'd had and the significance it will have in my life in the future.

When I come home from the weekend Dan is in a happy state. It seems like a weight lifted off his shoulders for me to have finished with the course, and we have survived it ... or had we? I need to evaluate over the next week where I am at with it in my heart and mind. Is he happy for me to have achieved what I have, or is he happy for himself because it is now over? It comes back to the essence of *If I am happy then those around me will be happy too*. Does my happiness make him happy? I know his happiness makes me happy, but not if I have to sacrifice my own. It all comes down to choice. I am grateful I still have the power to choose, so it rests on me figuring out what feels aligned for me right now.

The next week I receive a phone call from Sarah. 'Casey, how are you?'

'Hi Sarah, I am good. How are you?'

'I have something exciting to share with you.'

'Ooh … tell me more.'

'I have been approached to take Lipstick, Powder and Politics on tour, and if I get the grant, I am going to do it. Would you be able to commit? It wouldn't be the same without you.'

'Wow! That is fabulous news—how exciting. I would love to. Will you send me through some details?'

'That is amazing, Casey. You are the first person I am sharing it with so I will get onto everyone else and let you know.'

'Great Sarah and congratulations.'

'Thanks Casey. I will chat soon.'

A few weeks pass, and other things begin to happen. I get called to go to London for a photoshoot. I get another call to appear on a TV show. It all begins happening and then …

I feel strange and something dawns on me. I haven't had my period for a few months. I was always irregular, but not this bad. I share this with Dan and he says it might explain the reason why I had eaten the strange meal of garlic bread, tuna and beans for dinner the night before. I rush down to the chemist. Within ten minutes I am back at our house and am waiting the three agonising minutes for the test to answer my fate. Dan takes charge and I know the answer by the look on his face. I have never ever seen him so happy. It is as if he has won the lottery, but I don't know how I feel about it and it puts to bed any chance of going on tour. I do feel excited though—new life is an amazing blessing.

Over the next few weeks I see another side to Dan. It's as if everything has now slotted into place for him, and I also feel that way. I find myself slipping into mum-mode pretty fast. Dan gives up working away in favour of being close to me and supporting me through the pregnancy. It feels really good to have moved to this next stage. I put things on hold for the tour and TV appearances, but then another door opens—I am offered a job teaching drama through a college outreach program. When one door closes, another opens, and I soon discover my love of teaching.

I have come to realise that relationships go through evolutions and it can be very unsettling, but if you keep connected by the essence of what brought you together then you can make it through the rough seas into calmer waters again. For now, Dan and I can embrace the magic of new life—this has gelled us for eternity. The Universe has spoken to let us know we are meant to be, this is divine timing and our tank of love is full again.

That year was a big year, one that could have had a completely different outcome had I not chosen to trust in the *to be or not to be* process. I am glad I let things be.

Contributors

Monique Mulligan

A former newspaper and magazine editor, journalist, publisher, and children's curriculum writer, Monique has had a varied career in writing. In 2015, she turned to fiction writing; since then she has had stories published in Serenity Press anthologies Rocky Romance, A Bouquet of Love and Destination Romance, as well as two picture books—My Silly Mum (2016) and Fergus the Farting Dragon (2017)—and romance novelette Under Her Spell (2017). She has also written two contemporary fiction novels and is working on finding a home for them.

Connect with Monique at www.moniquemulligan.com

Meagan Dux

Meagan Dux can often be found drinking way too much coffee while typing faster than she can think. She wrote her first novel, The Rise of Delilah, in three months before writing the follow-up novel, The Miracle of Delilah, all while juggling a full-time university degree, a severe ankle injury and a life with depression and anxiety. Meagan enjoys writing Young Adult and New Adults novels, but would like to write in as many genres as she can. Meagan is currently working hard to finish her third book, a New Adult novel focused on mental illness – something Meagan holds close to her heart. When not working on her novels, Meagan spends her days listening to way too many Coldplay, Dean Lewis, The Script and Imagine Dragons songs, reading and enjoying time with her family, their three dogs and a 22-year-old cat called Jess.

Connect with Meagan at www.meagandux.com

Veronica Gypsy

Veronica Gypsy is a recent wishful writer that has played with words ever since she can remember. She recently completed a life-awakening writing course with the incredible Joanne Fedler and has been working alongside the divine Karen McDermott with writing and magazine projects. She resides in Perth however, has a distinct Latin background of Argentine and Italian influence from her family's bloodlines. This full mix runs through her veins vividly in her passions. Veronica's loves include music and dancing, where her soul vibrates from the tunes of a Salsas beat, smooth Swing to RnB soulfulness. She wraps herself around Mother Nature's beauty as often as she can, walking in the sun, breathing in the salty air and being grounded by the ocean all helping her delve into a wild and wonderful meditative imagination, which slowly finds its way in her stories.

With an engaged passion for influencing and inspiring change in people, Veronica is a heartfelt Results Coach, helping people reach their full life potential, doing what they love which all align, with her gratitude filled mindful and spiritual ways. Veronica also spends her time devouring books to the point of being transported to eras of the past enveloping her mind, and absorbing the essence of strong female characters. Her writing seems to enrich itself with women's soul-searching journeys, including this short story called Freedom. All her stories are filled with intimate emotions and lessons of unique female personalities. She is currently delving into two women's lives, one of finding her unknown existence and one of waking her wildness. Her vivid mind's images unfold on paper any chances she gets.

Sonia Bellhouse

Sonia Bellhouse lives in Australia after spending her formative years in England. Her passion for writing was inspired by Enid Blyton's comment, 'One day you might write a book.' Sonia completed a BA in English as a mature student. Published in multiple magazines, both in Australia and the UK, Sonia has won two major awards in short fiction contests.

A lifelong reader, Sonia shares her love of books and her interest in writing on her blog. Her journey to publication is included in the anthology Writing the Dream published by Serenity Press. A long-time member of Armadale Writers' Group, she organises events and speakers for them. When she's not reading or writing, she's busy ignoring the ironing pile in favour of spending time with her cats.

Sonia had a novella due to be published shortly and is also working on several projects.

Connect with Sonia at www.soniabellhouse.blog

P.L. Harris

P.L. Harris writes contemporary romance, romantic suspense, and young/new adult with a twist of mystery and intrigue. She also enjoys writing cosy mysteries for those that like to play amateur detective from the comfort of their own homes. Her books are rich in storyline and location with characters that stay with you long after you turn the last page. She is a proud member of Romance Writers of Australia and America, Making Magic Happen Academy, and has a Certificate in Romance Writing.

P.L. has published stories with Serenity Press, Blue Swan Publishing, Evernight Publishing, and now publishes the majority of her books with Gumnut Press. P.L. is currently working on the fourth book in The Cupcake Capers Cozy Mystery Series—Mistletoe and Murder. She lives in the northern suburbs of Perth, Western Australia, with her Bichon Frise, Bella.

Connect with P.L. at www.plharris.com.au

Priya Chidambaranathan

Priya Chidambaranathan is an emerging writer who lives in Perth with her husband and two children aged seven and two. She started writing fiction relatively recently although she has been a life-long reader. She is very interested in reading diverse voices and hearing stories from other cultures, especially those written by women. She turned to writing after moving to Australia and experiencing the perils of migration and motherhood and most of her writing tends to centre around these themes. She currently works as a financial analyst and has had many different roles over the years including freelance journalist and IT programmer.

Priya has previously had a story published as part of the collection Stories from Perth and is part of the Mentoring project for early and emerging writers of Indian Ocean heritage, run by the Centre for Stories, Perth. This is her second story to be published.

Amanda Viviers

Amanda Viviers can often be found with a pen in her hand, food spilled down her blouse, and a fresh story in her heart. She is an author, public speaker and radio presenter, with a BA double major in English and Comparative Literature and History. She studied Musical Theatre at WAAPA, birthing her deep love of creativity. She is the author of seven books, the most recent being Pause: New Year Division Daybook. She is a presenter on radio across New Zealand and Australia and is the co-founder of kinwomen, a network created to inspire women to start conversations that matter. Driven by a passion for social justice, she loves supporting projects for children in developing countries. Wife of Charl and mum of Maximus and Liberty, she lives a creative life helping people find their voice.

Connect with Amanda at www.amandavivers.com

Lisa A. Wolstenholme

Lisa is a mum, wife and writer currently working for the Katharine Susannah Prichard (KSP) Writers' Centre in Greenmount, Western Australia as the Executive Officer of their self-publishing service, Wild Weeds Press. She is also the KSP Board Secretary, has facilitated a writing group at the centre and hosted several publishing-related workshops.

Lisa is drawn to penning stories about life and loss, with a dash of love sometimes thrown in for good measure. She has a 12,000-word story, When Love Breaks Down, published by Serenity Press as part of their 'Destination Romance' anthology. Her women's fiction novel, The Sunrise Girl, is currently doing the rounds with Literary Agents across the globe.

When not writing or loitering around KSP, Lisa enjoys reading, travelling, music and wine.

Connect with Lisa at www.lisawolstenholme.com

Kelly Van Nelson

Kelly Van Nelson was born in Newcastle-upon-Tyne and lived in London, Edinburgh, and Cape Town, before immigrating to Australia with her family. Her writing successes include poetry and short stories published in the UK (Short Story Society, United Press, Between These Shores Books), USA (Fiction War Magazine, Wolvesburrow Productions), and Australia (KSP Writefree Women's Group, Karen McDermott Publisher). Her first novel, The Pinstripe Prisoner, placed third in the Yeovil Literary Prize, shortlisted in the PENfro first chapter competition, and longlisted in the Exeter Novel Prize. She is represented by The Newman Agency.

Kelly is also on the Executive Board for the world's largest providers of HR, staffing, and technology solutions. In short, she is a juggler, who likes to embrace the unknown, think positively, and live life to its fullest.

Connect with Kelly at www.kellyvannelson.com

Lia Eliades

She sits on the edge of the Indian Ocean, farmed on the edge of the Australian Outback, created an idyllic life on the island of Bali, and once called Bangkok her home, but in her heart, she will always be a native New Yorker with a creative soul whose journeying led to a life of travel, travails, writing, reflection and revelry. Her work is informed by her life and the wonderful people she has met along the way, who helped to nurture her voice.

Published works in Australia include Outback I Am—Year of the Outback, Australian Broadcasting Corporation, in print and CD. Letter to Phaon, Kail, The Writers Passage—Horst Kornberger, Hindsight Anthology—A Matter of Luck by Warnbro Writers Group. Sign

Language, She Swims, Expiation, Out of the Blue—Rockingham Writers' Centre Anthology.

Jean Frost

Jean is not your typical writer who was born to write, not as a small child could she be found curled up with a good book. It wasn't until her husband fell sick, and with the pressures of nursing him while maintaining a full-time job, that she sought refuge in books. Mainly YA urban fantasy and all things horror. To her surprise, it wasn't long before she was hooked and eagerly devoured everything she could get her hands on, but it wasn't enough. She wanted to write her own novel. Now, while she wrestles with plot-twists and characters who sometimes want to do their own thing, she sharpens her skills writing short stories. Published in the Reflections 2014 and Matter of Luck 2017 anthologies by the Warnbro Writers Group, and Ripples 2017 and Out of the Blue 2018 by the Rockingham Writer Centre.

Tabetha Rogers Beggs

Tabetha has a passion for storytelling, drawing on real life experiences and characters to furnish her tales. In 2017 her work When the Children Came was awarded third prize in a national competition and went on to be published locally. Other published works include Love is in the Air by Red Witch Press, Queenie's New Clothes by Wild Weeds Press and, more recently, her short story, The Woman in the Travel Goods Shop was published internationally by Strange Days Books in Greece.

Tabetha is the Chairwoman of writingWA, the former Chair of the KSP Writers' Centre and a devoted advocate for the arts in WA. She is currently midway through writing two novels and considering self-publishing her collection of short-stories once she's finished renovating her house in the hills. Tabetha is the CEO of the Kalamunda Chamber of Commerce and a single mum of two very sweet and patient children.

Connect with Tabetha at www.tabethawrites.com

Jean Jenkins

Originally from the UK, and after a lengthy career spanning teaching and politics, Jean and her husband Brian retired to Safety Bay. With children and grandchildren mostly grown, Jean started writing her memoirs and, in the process, discovered that she finds writing fiction far more rewarding. The memoirs lie in a drawer awaiting editing. Jean has written more than twenty short stories, experimenting across many genres. Her first attempt at a romance, 'The Next Stage', will be published by Serenity Press in December this year in the anthology Destination Romance. Jean is currently working on her first novel.

Teena Raffa-Mulligan

Teena Raffa-Mulligan is a reader, writer and daydream believer who is convinced there is magic in every day if we choose to find it. Teena writes across genres from picture books to romance, and shares her passion for books and writing by presenting workshops to encourage people of all ages to write their own stories.

Connect with Teena at www.teenaraffamulligan.com

Karen Weaver

Karen Mc Dermott (Weaver) is an award-winning publisher, multi-genre author, keynote speaker, an advanced Law of Attraction practitioner and mum of six healthy children. Inspiring others is her passion, and her journey is filled with success, love and a few mountains to climb. She believes that everyone has a story to share and in the power of writing to heal. Gratitude has been a big part of her life and she has created her dream life through the Law of Loving intention.

Karen lives life to the fullest and pursues her heart-centred passion ALWAYS! In doing so, she believes that she is true to her life purpose. Through establishing the Making Magic Happen Academy she hopes to inspire others to do the same. An author of novels, non-fiction books, children's books and life-enhancing journals, Karen believes wholeheartedly in the power of the written word. Founder of Serenity Press, a traditional publishing press making waves in Australia, is where Karen has gained most of her recognition. Especially as she was the winner of the prestigious 2016 Ausmumpreneur Network Excellence Award and third place in the 2017 Ausmumpreneur Global Award.

Connect with Karen at www.karenmcdermott.com